Until The Guillotine:

A Tale of Two Royals

Until The Guillotine:

A Tale of Two Royals

A novel by:

J.C. SUTTON

For Diane – I understand you're a voracious reader – do hope you'll enjoy this one!

All best,

Jeanne Sutton

WordsWorth Publications 10/6/22

Until The Guillotine: *A Tale of Two Royals*

WordsWorth Publications
P.O. Box 84
West Creek, NJ 08092

www.wordsworthpublications.com

FIRST EDITION

ISBN: 1-7330749-3-3

Cover design by Dawn Frances Simon
Book design by Jeffrey Kuhlman
Author photograph by Ashley Smith

Dedication

For Jennifer Claire, Jessica Kimber,
and Amy Christine

Also by J.C. Sutton

Beau & Eros (2019)
Blood Sisters (2001)

"There is nothing new, except what has been forgotten."
Marie Antoinette, 1755-1793

"It is now sixteen or seventeen years since I saw the Queen of France, then the Dauphiness, at Versailles ... glittering like the morning star, full of life, and splendour, and joy ... little did I dream that I should have lived to see such disasters fallen upon her."
Edmund Burke, 1729-1797
Reflections on the Revolution in France,1790

Dear Reader,

Feel free to skip this, but the genre is historical fiction. It feels right to offer what would be a few footnotes in a more scholarly, historically accurate work. That said, never underestimate the power of memoirs written by non-writers, moved, for any number of reasons, to record the people, places and things they observed and experienced, in the course of a day, a week, or a life.

The English translation of the memoirs that inspired *UNTIL THE GUILLOTINE: A Tale of Two Royals* was published by the St. Dunstan Society in Ohio, in 1901. In 1984, a fragile copy found its way into my hands.

Turning pages coming undone with age, I discovered an insider's view, buried in thickets of flowery 19th century language. Two surprising and intriguing women emerged from the mists of a history that essentially vilified one and ignored the other. I saw them reflected in an intimate new light.

Louisa, Princess of Lamballe , and Marie Antoinette, future Queen of France, met as fellow teenagers navigating the labyrinthine rapids of Court life at Versailles. Their true friendship endured to the brutal end. Neither lived into her forties.

The memoir was presented as the work of Catherine Hyde, self-described as having been pre-Revolutionary secretary and post-Revolutionary courier to the Princess and the Queen. At this writing, I am at work on a companion novel centered on her survivor's story.

Marie Antoinette was the first, and decidedly not the last, "celebrity royal." Her transition from a wildly popular girl determined to have fun, to a criticized and then despised symbol of an age of excess she didn't start and wouldn't finish is a cautionary tale worth telling.

Italian born Louisa, Princess Lamballe, was married off at 15 to a French prince of the blood. She was betrayed into widowhood at 17, by a brother-in-law whose advances she'd spurned.

The two met in May of 1770, as the future Queen was also being married off, to the 16-year-old grandson next in line to King Louis the Fifteenth's throne.

Their friendship blossomed and strengthened through the eight years before the then-Queen bore the first of her four children. The flouting of convention Marie Antoinette became infamous for extended to her devotion to them. The Princess was also devoted. She kept the oath she swore when her Queen and friend made her Superintendent of her Household, to the end of her life.

As author of three novels (and two ghost-written non-fictions) I relished the authenticity my research confirmed. And welcomed the challenge of conveying these women's humanity, along with their history.

J.C. Sutton, Tuckerton, NJ, November 2021

~ Chapter One ~

A late spring chill held back the usual show of leaf and flower along both banks of the Rhone River. The morning's fog was gone, along with the crowds behind the restraining ropes at the quay. No one was there to watch the brilliant sun begin forcing the buds open; the Royal flotilla was beyond the horizon now.

"Custom, you say? Custom? I know nothing of it." The Austrian Archduchess Josephe Jeanne Marie Antonia, called Tonia all her life, shut her lips on the tongue she longed to stick out at the semi-circle of women in full Court dress who all but surrounded her. The youngest, and, it was said, fairest of Empress Marie-Therese's eleven daughters, settled for narrowing her blue eyes.

The Aubusson carpets on the floor under their slippers, and the Lyons silk panels on the walls behind them, couldn't transform the river barge, anchored in the middle of the Rhone. The men chosen to participate in this pre-nuptial ceremony waited on the barge moored to this one, ready to disembark and board.

Tonia hadn't been warned about what the turtle-faced old woman so clearly in charge was repeating: "Your foreign clothing must be removed and replaced with French garments." Her foot twitched with the urge to stamp at the growly old hag, who was gesturing to a gilded clothes-press flanked by ladies-in-waiting.

How could her mother the Empress, with her *morality* police all over Austria, hunting down and humiliating women who showed too much bosom, have failed to so much as mention this far more humiliating custom of stripping the betrothed naked before perfect strangers? None of Tonia's daily lessons through the whole past year covered this.

Ignoring my age, insulting my modesty. Like her tongue, earlier, Tonia controlled her anger, as the women rustled closer, all ages, all sizes, all in full Court finery, all smelling like her mother's chambers

— that same musty mix of cologne and candle-smoke and corsets — eyes bulging, fixed. *Like the carp in Mother's ponds.* Tonia stifled her laughter; she'd been trained to do so, long before this marriage awaiting her was arranged and announced.

She searched their fish-faces for signs of what they might respond to. Up until now, asking a favor of someone like her tutor Gittel, sincerely and agreeably, was the solution to math and other problems. Charming compliments paid to her mother's chief cook, Andre, brought lobster soufflés to her breakfast table. Friendly persuasion convinced Rudi, the head groomsman, to let her ride astride, instead of sidesaddle. And gallop.

I must gallop through this. "Take hold of the reins." Tonia stifled a giggle at the thought. Her dear Papa liked saying that. And telling her he loved her, just the way she was. Everyone else said they loved her, but ... always a but. Papa didn't rein in what others labeled over-indulged, under-educated, stubborn-minded. He saw her free spirit; thought her fearless; applauded her gift for mimicry; encouraged her to speak her mind.

"Never fear who you are." How many times had Tonia heard him say that? *Why did you have to die?* How many times had she asked herself that question? After five years, still no answer.

What do I say now? Her answer formed with surprising speed: *I have come to wed the Dauphin destined to be your King.* Her sudden smile was full and warm. *And I will be your Queen.* The petulant thrust of her Hapsburg jawline disappeared, replaced by a fairy-princess with blushing cheeks, rosy lips, and clear blue eyes. Readied, for over a year, to stand firm on this gently rocking barge.

A year ago, her mother the Empress moved Tonia from the nursery apartments she loved decorating, onto a cot at the foot of the Imperial bed. She was snatched from dancing and singing and playacting, all of which she also loved. She was forbidden to ride astride, kept from rough games, and then *any* games. Cooped up indoors season after season, Tonia turned thirteen, then fourteen, as she tried to master everything expected of her.

The language lessons went the best, since she'd always liked speaking French. The French Court protocols were the worst. The labyrinthine layers of etiquette dictating every aspect of daily life in King Louis the Fifteenth's glittering Court bored her. Bored her beyond belief.

None of it had prepared Tonia for this first contingent of courtiers, crowded around her on this ill-disguised barge, anchored halfway between the shore of the Austrian homeland she would never see again, and the shore of the country she would call home. Forever.

Her fixed, fairy-princess smile widened as a solution to the problem of how to get around this un-welcome custom and still behave correctly presented itself. Looking directly at the turtle-face pushed so close to hers, Tonia spoke in perfect French, lacking any hint of a guttural Austrian accent.

"Please forgive me," she began. "I do not mean to distress anyone, and hope I have not done so. But surely you can respect my modesty — " she paused just long enough to ensure their absolute attention " — if not my wishes."

The crowd stood dumbfounded as the old woman, half a head shorter and twice as big around, took a step backward. "With all respect to our esteemed new Dauphiness," her head bowed low, but her voice was raised, "this is our custom."

"Madame Noailles," Tonia made sure the onlookers heard her use the formidable Mistress of Ceremonies' name. They hadn't been officially introduced, but thanks to her mother the Empress, Tonia knew exactly who the squat old hag had to be. The carp-faced crowd lapped it up, straining to see and hear everything.

"Does the King approve of this custom?" Tonia's tone was civility itself as she added "Does it meet with the approval of my — " her throat almost closed on her next word " — husband?"

"I am sure you understand," the Mistress of Ceremonies' tone was at once placating and patronizing, "that you must retain nothing belonging to a foreign court."

"I do understand." Tonia leaned close enough to the old woman to smell her corsets — corsets she vowed that instant she'd never wear. "And so I will submit," she continued, "to the removal of my outer garments. Provided it is accomplished out of the sight of prying eyes." Her lilting French reached all ears. "I trust you will be pleased to learn that my body linen and stockings were made in France.

Knowing that, I believe you will let me retain them." Her Austrian Hapsburg chin thrust up and out; her smile stayed sweetness itself.

In less than half an hour, Marie Antoinette, Dauphiness of France, clad in full ceremonial dress, approached the central table symbolizing the Austrian-French frontier. There was a moment, a moment only, when her right knee, then her left, wobbled. *Am I going to faint?* She hadn't done that, ever.

This marital merger was a last best hope for ending the chronic conflict between both countries. The Empress Maria Theresa was famed for arranging the most advantageous marriages for all her children. "Let other nations make war," she liked to say. "You, happy Austria, marry." Like her thirteen siblings, the doted-on baby of her large family was born and raised to take her turn.

Pleased with her handling of the clothing exchange, Tonia smiled and nodded her way through the arrival of the men, the reading of the marriage contract, and the several speeches before the men withdrew, with only the Austrian ambassador to the Court of France allowed to remain. Count Mercy of Argenteau was a favorite of her mother's, but Tonia had only met him a few times and so didn't know him. Yet.

The ceremony's last act called for her to circle the table three times, ending up on the French side. The Austrian doors were closed. The French doors were opened. Artillery thundered and church bells pealed as the Dauphiness Marie Antoinette emerged with her spine straight, her smile in place, and her beloved Papa's voice sounding in her high-held head: "*You'll never step in the same river twice, littlest, dearest one. Enjoy it all the time, every time.*"

Dear dead Papa. He'd have loved hearing the band on the barge that was coming for her. Its members rose in unison, striking up a chorus of welcome and praise as she came on board, where Strasbourg's mayor stood knee-deep in children bearing armloads of flowers.

I will have to be myself, Tonia thought, and had to stifle a giggle.

The passage took a matter of minutes. Debarking, she glimpsed a banner ahead, suspended over the road she'd soon travel. Its message honored her in boldly lettered verse: Dauphine, toute ta gras, encante ta race … "*Dauphiness, thy every grace, adds enchantment to thy race …*"

The mayor began droning in dreadful German about the honor she was doing this beauteous country and its wondrous people. She put one rosy fingertip up before her lips, signaling for silence.

"If you please, dear sir," she said, clearly enough to be heard at the rear of the large crowd, in a voice that carried high and sweet, "address me only in French. From this day forward, it is the only language I will understand."

The pandemonium that broke out as she finished continued, in one form or another, all the way to Versailles.

~ *Chapter Two* ~

If one of the horses lost its shoe, or a footman his grip, it would take the carriage out of the procession, before it could carry Louisa, Princess of Lamballe, widow of Stanislaus, Prince of Penthievre, any closer to the Great Chateau of Versailles, where she had never been and had no wish to go. Not even for this grand occasion of a Royal wedding.

I cannot do this. I cannot. Louisa's left thumb found its way to the corner of her mouth. At seventeen, it was an infantile habit, but one she had yet to break. Loosening the edge of the nail, where the buffing powder taste wasn't as strong, she stole a glance at the opposite seat, where the lady-in-waiting assigned to her was peeling pink paper from a bon-bon.

If the sweet sticks in her throat the carriage will stop, Louisa thought, as her teeth closed on the pried-up nail corner. Her tongue worried the bitten crescent until she could ready herself to make conversation.

"Where are you from?" Louisa settled her hands back in her lap, wishing she'd worn gloves instead of fingerless mitts.

"Paris, your Highness," the girl leaned forward, eager to break the silence. "My family serves the Duke of Chartres there."

Chartres! Louisa tasted bile, forced it back as the girl chattered on: "My father is Major-Domo of Monsieur the Duke's Paris townhouse. My mother is Superintendent of laundresses, and at the new year both my brothers were named equerries to the Duke's stables." Her tongue darted out, caught a sweet crumb, darted back. "My older sister came to Versailles three years ago. I followed last year, assigned to accompany esteemed visitors. My sister completes her culinary training next month."

"Your family is indeed fortunate." Louisa spoke quietly, but her mind was screaming: *Chartres! My brother-in-law. My nemesis.*

The carriage rolled on. There was no way to halt what was set in motion, no going back to the countryside where she lived her very private life with her late husband's father, the Duke of Penthievre. Better known as "Papa Time", for his storied collection of timepieces, he was said to be the second richest man in all France. Since her widowing, Louisa hadn't ventured from his estates at Rambouillet, where she'd been sent at fifteen to wed Papa Time's son, Stanislaus.

As a Princess born into Italy's ancient House of Savoy, Louisa was given a wider education than many girls, in everything but the ways of the world. The good match — and good life — in France, ended within weeks of their first anniversary, with her husband's unexpectedly sudden sickness and death.

A death her brother-in-law, the Duke of Chartres, set in motion.

In the two years since, Louisa stayed close to the father-in-law who loved her, but who lived in ignorance of the real cause of his son's early death and Louisa's untimely widowing.

The sweet-natured old man with his pumpkin-round face and pouter pigeon chest and monk's fringe of white hair was a true eccentric, loved by all who knew and served him.

As gregarious as she was shy, Papa Time was delighted with the invitation to the Royal Nuptials. He was eager to travel to Versailles for them, eager to "show you off, dear daughter." His presence would have spared her much of this contact with the larger world. Would have helped ease her dread at being in the presence of the man who'd married Stanislaus' older sister: the Duke of Chartres.

If only Papa Time hadn't taken that fever! From the bed in his room adorned with dozens of his most prized clocks, he'd insisted Louisa be the one to go. "You will so fittingly represent Penthievre, and Lamballe," he'd said, his round face reddening, "provided you take no mourning gowns. Lay them aside."

Louisa did let go of the color black, but the dark cloud of guilt she carried weighed more than her grief. Guilt had threatened to swallow her at his deathbed, after Stanislaus whispered his horrible secret in her ear. About the revenge his brother-in-law took. Revenge she was responsible for. She lived with the knowledge that Stanislaus might still be alive if not for her. He might be pursuing the family businesses, away from Rambouillet. Dallying with other women, as men of his birth and station did. *Men like Chartres.*

Stanislaus had seldom come to her as a husband. The few nights he had resulted in no quickening of her womb with his legitimate heir. The death Chartres was responsible for killed something in Louisa, too. Mourning became her; let her keep guilt and secret safe.

Does she or her kin see through Chartres, to his evil soul? Louisa tried to breathe deeply, "in before out," the way her nurse Serafina showed her, the summer she turned seven. It came easier then; now her stomach wouldn't stop quivering, as they passed fountains bristling with gigantic statues of gods and sea-monsters, spewing great plumes of spray. Spatters swirled inside as a gust lifted the window netting. The lady-in-waiting cried out as she reached for a handkerchief to blot her silk skirt.

Louisa felt the pin-pricks on her face and wished there were enough to hide the tears she needed to cry, but couldn't. Not for hours.

The girl rummaged in a pocket for another bon-bon, offered it with a proud smile. "White chocolate truffles. My sister's specialty."

"No, thank you," Louisa's tongue worried the softening fragment of her bitten nail, "but I'm sure they're delicious." *If only Papa Time were here!* "Do you see your parents often?"

"Hardly ever, your Highness." The girl swallowed the last of her sweet. "But they will journey here for the nuptial festivities. Banqueting, dancing, fire-works! The Ruggieri brothers are doing them, they're the very best in the world — better than the Chinese, even! A grand finale that hasn't happened in years! The entire Great Chateau will be illuminated, and my *parents* will be here to see it."

"With the Duke of Chartres' party," Louisa murmured, hearing her nurse Serafina's voice — *"Feel your tummy rise and fall, dear Princess, feel that, feel only that."* Louisa obeyed, until she could focus again, on what the garrulous girl was saying:

"Her birthday's in November — *'l'Autrichenne'* — the Austrian Archduchess who's marrying our Dauphin. Born under the sign of the Scorpion." The girl leaned closer. "It's the astrological sign for a passionate nature. Headstrong. Given to indulging her appetites." Giggling, she pulled another bonbon from her pocket: "The Archduchess' name changes here in France. *Marie Antoinette* sounds pretty, don't you think?" She didn't wait for an answer. "She's pretty too. Very.

Beautiful, even, if what they say about her complexion is true." The girl touched her own face, free of smallpox pits and well made-up, its girlish eruptions smoothly covered. "Peaches and cream is what they say, and all her own. Natural — not a bit enhanced — the real thing."

"She sounds lovely."

"A breath of fresh air — that's what our new Dauphiness is supposed to be. *Austrian*-scented air, of course. Enemy air. Royal marriages often involve enemies, don't they?"

"Indeed." *But the enemy wasn't my husband.*

The procession of carriages left the narrower *allees*, merging two, then three abreast as they approached the cobbled courtyards surrounding the Great Chateau of Versailles. Accustomed as she was to great houses and greater gardens, Louisa's thumb went back into her mouth as the parade of carriages halted before its immensity.

The sun had set long before the servants finally allowed Louisa her privacy. Standing in the center of her bedroom, the suite's innermost, she stretched her arms above her head, tilting it back, conscious of the weight of the thick braid that fell to her knees behind her. It was the color of dark honey, unusual for an Italian. So were her light brown eyes. Taller, at five-foot-nine, than most women, and many men, Louisa was more slender than buxom. She preferred listening to talking, and remaining in the background to being a center of attention. The skin at the corner of her thumb was tender where she'd bitten it. Exposed.

~ Chapter Three ~

The following day brought brilliant sunshine, and the same talkative girl to share the carriage that left Versailles' Great Park promptly at seven, for the long journey north. The privileged many of the Royal Court of His Majesty Louis the Fifteenth were gathering at the forest of Compeigne for the first meeting of the Dauphiness-to-be and her family-to-be.

Louisa welcomed the lady-in-waiting's familiar face and lively chatter; learned her name was Babette; listened closely to her explanations of how the day would unfold. She expected the welter of noise and confusion surrounding their arrival, but the glade where they would wait was an unexpected pleasure. It reminded Louisa of a painting by Monsieur Boucher that hung at Rambouillet. Shining satin ropes attached to velvet cushions hung from the manicured branches of proud old trees. Emerald moss carpeted the ground, more beautifully than the rug beneath the guests' chairs.

Bright shafts of sunlight struck the double circle of tent-pavilions ringing the glade. The roofs were linen canvas, the walls fine white gauze, and the center poles were topped with gold *fleur-de-lis,* the stylized lily that symbolized centuries of Bourbon rule over France.

Louisa declined the Major-Domo's invitation to occupy the inner-circle tent reserved for the house of Orleans. She sipped at her syllabub in the outer ring's Penthievre pavilion, glad she'd chosen gloves over mitts to keep from nail-biting, careful to keep her gaze from the banners bearing the Orleans' coat-of-arms waving before the tent where her brother-in-law, strong branch of the Orleans family tree, was holding court.

Penthievre was Papa Time's dukedom, one of many rewards that had come to him as a freely acknowledged bastard of the Sun King, Louis the Fourteenth. His mother was an official mistress, a position that carried no shame for a French noble. Papa Time's son, Stanislaus, born to him and his long-departed wife, was Prince of Lamballe, making Louisa a princess twice over, by birth and by marriage.

Papa Time's daughter was Duchess of Chartres in the Royal house of Orleans. She'd loathed the snail pace of life at Rambouillet. Louisa had met her only once, at the wedding. She'd been keen to return to Paris and the Palais Royale. Her husband, the Duke of Chartres, was first in line to outright ownership of the Orleans-owned sprawl of lavish living quarters, shops and entertainments. Her advanced state of pregnancy with what might be a son had kept her from the glade today.

The gauze tent sides sucked in and out, suddenly, amidst shrieks of laughter. A wiry little towhead appeared at the opened flaps, a tail of boys whipping behind him.

"The Count of Artois and his — entourage," Babette giggled, finishing her second syllabub.

The boy stuck his head in the tent, pulling a face as he stuck out his tongue. "Now you see us, now you don't!" he whooped, yanking the tent flaps shut.

"He is the younger brother of the groom, yes?" Louisa asked, more to distract herself than from any genuine interest.

"Yes. Artois is thirteen. And the few times I've seen his brother the bridegroom, he looked older than sixteen."

"What makes you say that?"

"Well," Babette paused, clearly trying to think of the best way to put it, "Well, he's so, so, um, dull, your Highness. Not book-dull; in fact, I hear he's very well-read in Latin and Greek. But he takes no interest in Court life."

"What are his interests?"

"His favorite is common *carpentry work*, if you can imagine that." Babette's curled lip showed what she thought of Royals at manual labor. "And metalsmithing — not jewelry, but *practical* things. Gates, locks, grill works."

"I see," Louisa murmured.

"And you should see, well, you *will* see, how plainly he dresses. Breeches and vests that look bought ready-sewn from some *tailor*. No satins, no brocades, no silk stockings, not even a *heel* to his brown leather shoes. If it weren't for the retinue required when he goes out,"

Babette sniffed, "you really couldn't tell him from the man in the street. That's the effect they say he's after." She broke off to pluck a third syllabub from a circulating server. "His only other interest is hunting, the smallest vole to the largest boar. And my sister can vouch for his fondness for food."

"Is Monsieur the Dauphin here today?" Louisa leaned forward, gesturing to the tent beside the King's; the one with linen, not gauze walls. "Is that his?"

"Yes indeed, your Highness. So he can see and not be seen. Bad luck, you know, for bride and groom to set eyes on each other before the wedding day."

Drum rolls sounded on either side of His Majesty's pavilion as Louis the Fifteenth emerged to *bravos* and applause. At sixty years, fifty of them lived as King, his shoulders remained broad and his stomach flat. From the silvery gleam of his double-tailed, tight-curled periwig, to the dazzling diamond buckles on his shoes, Louis looked every inch the heir to the throne of the Sun King, and a splendid ruler in his own right.

The illusion vanished with his first words: "All I wish to know is, has she got *breasts*?" His tone was petulant; his voice a reedy squeak.

"Oh, indeed she has," his closest courtier assured him. "Like two ripe peaches," another chimed in, followed by yet another: "White peaches, your Majesty, with that blush of tint upon them."

His Majesty's ringed fingers reached out, crudely, as if he fondled them.

The glade reverberated with the sound of distant trumpets and *hautboys*, drawing closer. Babette jumped up; the swings were abandoned; the crowd roared as the King was escorted to his greeting position, in the precise center of the glade.

A collective gasp rose at the first sight of Marie Antoinette's coach, emerging from beneath the canopy of trees. It appeared to be made entirely of glass, with blue velvet upholstery and bouquets of yellow and white gold roses along its rooftop. The gilded hooves of six pure white horses flashed as they pranced across the turf in effortless unison.

Marie Antoinette alighted from her glass coach to spontaneous cheers. Resplendent in full Court dress, with satin *paniers* wider than a doorway, and a ten-foot train, she still appeared to float along the scarlet carpet as it was ceremoniously unrolled. Sunlight struck fire from the diamonds twined through her ash blonde curls as she closed the distance. Reaching him, she dropped a perfect curtsy, to howls of acclaim, as he held out both his hands to receive the sprite before him.

At just that moment, the Duke of Chartres moved into Louisa's line of sight. He was across the glade, but for how long? *You must face him sooner or later,* she told herself, as fiercely as she could, but nothing could stop the convulsive motion of her heart as he appeared to be moving toward her.

Others thought him vigorous, even handsome. From the first moment she'd laid eyes on him, on her wedding day, Louisa had recoiled from his fleshy cheeks and thick lips, from the oily black eyes under brows so high-arched they gave him a look of permanent surprise.

The forces of memory shot to the surface, like steam from a hot spring through cracks in rock, all the more powerful from long entrapment; Louisa was gone from the glade, gone back to a grape arbor, gasping for breath in an atmosphere thick with his lust and her fear —

"Your Highness? Your Highness?" Babette was at her elbow.

"What? What is it?" Louisa shook her head clear.

"The receiving line, your Highness. We should go."

"Of course." Louisa gathered her skirts to stand, grateful for the billowing folds of silk that hid her shaking hands.

One by one, those up ahead had their moment with the Dauphiness. Most drifted back with dazed looks. When Babette's turn came, the Dauphiness' attendant lifted a lace-edged cloth to ready the Royal cheek for the next salute. Louisa saw that the perfect skin wasn't rouged at all; it was rubbed raw, from countless kisses. Breaching all etiquette as she made her bow, Louisa kissed the air.

For a moment, as she rose to move on, Louisa looked directly into eyes as blue, bright and clear as the sky over Turin. She was completely unprepared for the intensity of her feeling for this enchanting child. Younger, but only by three years. A slight shudder — the French called it a *'frisson'* — passed through her. Louisa fought to control her sense that something was about to happen. Or already had.

~ Chapter Four ~

Louisa decided to use the time until they came for her to make her first use of Papa Time's parting gift. She left the lap desk in its gilded stand; lifting its ornately carved lid, she admired the green baize interior with its ascending rows of writing implements, each cradled in the hollow designed for it.

Taking the cork stopper from the ink bottle and a quill from among several, she fingered the catch on the tray that held parchments cut to letter size. Sliding out the top sheet, she cradled her left hand above it, and began the first of the letters she'd promised to send:

The 16th day of May, in the year of Our Lord 1770

My dearest and much-missed Papa Time,

I am unaccustomed to writing, but I intend to keep my word to give you the details of all you are missing.

I have been awake for an hour or more, have knelt to prayers, breakfasted, and been dressed. The wedding procession begins at one, and so there is ample time for this practice …

An hour later, Louisa's left hand and forearm ached, but her nails remained unbitten. It was her heart that ached that night, as she opened the desk and continued.

… Versailles' Royal Chapel reminded me of nothing so much as a jewelry box, with the bridal couple fittingly dressed, the Dauphin in a cloth-of-gold suit trimmed with diamonds, the Dauphiness in white brocade, roped in pearls and ablaze with diamonds.

She didn't add that nothing could disguise the bridegroom's bulk, or that his Bourbon features — large nose, rounded chin, prominent eyes drooping at the corners — were an ill fit on his otherwise sixteen-year-old face.

> *... The Archbishop of Rheims, where the Dauphin will one day be crowned, said the Nuptial Mass. Cardinal Rohan offered the nuptial blessings. A silver canopy was held over their heads as we prayed the Our Father. The Vicar of Paris's Cathedral of Notre Dame bore the marriage contract for the couple to sign. He was followed by the King and all his blood relations ...*

... including her brother-in-law, Louis Philippe Joseph d'Orleans, Duke of Chartres.

Seeing him had brought Louisa to tears.

"Inhale," the stout, unsmiling woman who'd appeared beside her had commanded, thrusting a flask of hartshorn under Louisa's nostrils. "You do not wish to earn attention." Her tone was as sharp as the fumes.

> *... Outside the Chapel, he wedding party first received the entire Royal Household, followed by the priests, stewards, valets, surgeons, doctors, fencing, music and dancing masters, before the lackeys and the kitchen brigades — cooks, butlers, wine bearers, scullery maids — had their chance.*
>
> *Five thousand in all, dear Papa, and the Dauphiness offered her hand and spoke directly to each of them.*
>
> *The wedding supper was held at Versailles' new Opera House ...*

The grand building was so barely completed velvet drapes had to be drawn over huge heaps of stone and lumber outside. Inside, the smell of paint and gilders' chemicals had been sickeningly strong.

... I was given your place at the central table set in the area the stage and orchestra will occupy.

Louisa didn't write of her relief at seeing Papa Time's daughter and her husband in an upper tier of the Court boxes lining the Opera House walls.

... A sudden storm descended as the last of the soups were being taken away. The thunder was strong enough to rattle the service plates, with many making the sign of the cross against the ill omen. I declined to attend the blessing of the nuptial bed.

Thunder still vibrated the bedroom floor of Louisa's suite, but lightning didn't penetrate the drawn curtains the way it had in the Opera House, where the blinding white-light bolts sucked the color from everything.

Papa Time's daughter arrived the following afternoon for that night's public feasting and fireworks display. She was mercifully unaccompanied by her husband, who sent regrets — something to do with his gout.

Murmured greetings to her sister-in-law accomplished, Louisa retreated to a window-seat with a view of a crowd said to number two hundred thousand, dancing to the music of street bands, feasting at open air buffets, toasting the newlyweds with wine from fountains spouting champagne.

Louisa didn't miss Babette, who was sick, unsurprisingly, with indigestion. Her replacement was so eager to make herself known to as many of those in attendance as she could. Louisa left her to it, content to observe the human river of nobles and clergy and commoners flowing below, until the fireworks began.

Enormous astronomical wheels took shape against the black velvet sky. In their centers, fireworks formed, somehow, into the leaping dolphins featured on the bridal pair's coat of arms. Frenzied roars greeted the display, as cascades of rockets exploded into blazing waterfalls, bright suns, and huge pyramids of shimmering fire.

The grand finale filled the entire sky with explosions of light and sound. Just as the last of them faded to the night's blackness, the immense outlines of Versailles' Great Chateau appeared, picked out in points of flame from the lanterns attached there, every one of which had been lighted in unison.

The fantastic effect of the Grand Illumination flowed out and into the gardens of Versailles in great rhythmic waves of flickering light, until every pool, basin, and canal gave back images of dancing fire. Enchanted by the incredible sight, Louisa didn't notice the Royal party's approach, hearing them only as they passed.

"What do you *mean* I can go no closer?"

Louisa knew at once who had spoken. The Dauphiness' voice was clear, musical, far more pleasant than her words. And surely it was the Dauphin who answered, sounding older than his years: "We'll see more fireworks, and better ones, when we are presented to the city of Paris."

Louisa had already heard that close inspection of the nuptial night sheets failed to reveal any sign the marriage was consummated.

"Not a drop of blood, not a speck, not a hint of a stain," one chamber-maid had chortled to another. "And not at all unusual," the other had clucked, "given her age and his awkwardness."

It took Louisa a long time to fall asleep. When she did, she dreamed she was being married, in a gown of coarse sacking crusted with dirt at the hem. At the moment Stanislaus was to place the ring on her finger, she was sucked away, down some misty corridor, flying, her arms spread like wings, before she was inside, alone, in a dim hallway lined with doors, leaping dolphins carved into each. The doors all opened on a rocky path through a darkened cave. The path evaporated; she stood against a wall in a huge room, wearing the Dauphiness Marie Antoinette's wedding gown. The soaring space was lit by thousands of candles, suspended and burning in the air.

Versailles' first Gentleman on Duty, resplendent in his scarlet and gold livery, appeared beside her.

"*The King's meat,*" he bawled out, raising his silver baton.

Four men floated into the room, untouched by the blazing candles, holding a silver platter as big as a bed aloft. Her brother-in-law sat cross-legged in its center, waving a flask of hartshorn under the nose of the harlot lying beside him, wearing nothing but the black matted tangle of her hair. He wore the bladder of an unborn lamb, wrapped around the blue-veined column of his erection.

~ Chapter Five ~

The 12th day of August in the year of our Lord 1770

Dearest Papa,

I am eager to return to Rambouillet, to remain with you. My visit last month was far too brief.

Louisa took the blotting bar from its niche to press it against the wet ink.

Papa Time had been as firm with her as he'd ever been, the morning she'd left.

"Oh, no, my dear. You must return to Court." His fingers moved restlessly among the watch-chains crisscrossing the vest she'd only just finished embroidering for him. "Take up your life again. Be young again, dear child."

"Can that happen at Versailles?"

"I cannot say, but it cannot happen here."

He meant the routine they'd established at Rambouillet, where Louisa rose at dawn to pray, before being dressed in severe black, her mass of bright hair coiled under dark veiling. She would hear Mass and barely touch her breakfast before going to Stanislaus' bed-chamber. She'd find his father there, holding one or more of his watches, staring at the space where the bed once stood. The bed where his son so seldom claimed his conjugal right. The bed where he'd drawn his last breath. A thing of beauty, that bed, with its ebony corner posts topped by ivory cherubs with wings of gold. Papa Time ordered it all burned, and the melted gold, blackened ivory, and charred wood buried, when her widowhood was less than a week old.

Louisa would take a bit of meaningless needlework from the *chateleine* at her waist. Threading any color onto a needle, she would push it absentmindedly to and fro in a scrap of linen, while Papa Time pretended to read from a volume of *Lives of the Saints.*

"No, not here," he'd repeated. Louisa recognized Rambouillet wasn't the whole of her life, but she hadn't shared the thought with him. And hadn't anticipated the spritely image of Marie Antoinette, dancing through her mind's eye.

"You must think, sometimes," Papa Time had told her, "I have left the real world so far behind I couldn't possibly know — what time it is!" He'd cackled at his own feeble joke. "I will miss you sorely, and grieve for your absence, but you must take up the tick and tock of your own life now. Like it or not."

"I like it not."

"Don't be so certain."

But I am certain, Louisa thought, closing the lid of the lap desk as a flurry of knocks sounded from the other side of the highly carved doors. The Major-Domo assigned to her apartments entered, followed by his wife, who held the day's copy of the *Almanach de Versailles,* the newspaper delivered to every member of the Court. Her hands were trembling.

"Accident! Tragedy! Terrible misfortune!" the Major-Domo announced, urging her forward.

"First that dreadful storm on their wedding day, and now this." His wife was close to tears as she unfolded the thick paper.

A MARRIAGE MADE IN HELL? The headline was blazoned across its front page: "You are aware, your Highness, that yesterday was to have been the Dauphin and Dauphiness' first appearance in the city of Paris?"

Louisa nodded.

The Major-Domo took the paper from his wife and lifted his *pince-nez* to his left eye: *"A huge fair was set up along the boulevards leading to the Place Louis the Fifteenth,"* he read, *"where the happy couple were to have been presented. Several new private hotels remain under construction there, leaving many unfilled trenches. Wide planks were placed for foot crossings. Food and wine were given to one and all. The nuptial couple were due at dusk, to witness the brilliant fireworks of the Ruggieri Brothers. The grand finale was to be the Ruggieris' magnificent construction of the Temple of Marriage. The edifice was to spout fire from its leaping dolphin parapets."*

He paused to clear his throat. The edges of the paper began to shake. *"The tragedy ensued when a rocket ignited the dolphins' fire, attracting a great new tide of onlookers. The planks over the ditches dislodged, toppling victims who were trampled to death in the melee. A survivor told of walking out over piles of corpses."* He cleared his throat again: *"The number of dead is estimated at one hundred thirty-two."*

"Dear God," Louisa breathed.

"The bodies filled eleven carts, which have been taken to the Cemetery of the Madeleine, in the Fauborg Saint-Honore. They will remain laid out on the grass there until they can be identified."

"The Royal couple? Were they harmed?" Louisa's question was sudden, urgent.

"No," the Major-Domo's wife reassured her. "But the Dauphiness was much affected. She was seen weeping, in that wonderful glass coach of hers. First tears anyone has seen her shed."

"I must go to her." Louisa didn't realize she was speaking her thought. "I must."

Protocols followed, the Dauphiness Marie Antoinette received the Princess of Lamballe within hours. The pearly glow of Dauphiness' complexion was gone, replaced by a ghastly paleness, stark white against the black of her high-necked dress.

"I have come to pay my condolences, your Highness. I wish to express my sympathy on this sad occasion."

"So kind of you, Princess. I appreciate your concern."The Dauphiness leaned forward, peering more closely. "I recall you! You spared me your salute in the forest of Compeigne, yes?"

"Yes," Louisa said, astounded that the kiss she never gave was remembered.

"I wanted to thank you then, but etiquette forbade. May I do so now?"

"Yes, of course."

The Dauphiness reached out with both hands, taking Louisa's, holding them longer than etiquette permitted: "Do you wish to hear of what I witnessed?"

"Yes, of course," Louisa repeated, surprised by the intimacy of the touch.

Room servants withdrew. The Dauphiness gestured to a divan known as a *confidante,* for the S shape that allowed two to sit face-to-face.

Once settled, Marie Antoinette's startlingly blue eyes caught and held Louisa's soft brown ones. "It seemed I waited forever for the coach to leave," she began, as frankly as if she spoke to a friend. "There was so much delay here, and we were so late starting out. It must have happened when we were crossing the *Pont de Sevres,* almost there."

She paused. Louisa felt sure she was back at the scene.

"The sky filled with blinding white light," she went on, "and there was a deafening sound. I thought the fireworks had begun. I became upset because I was so looking forward to seeing them close up. But when we reached the middle of the bridge, I knew it wasn't fireworks." She fell silent, her blue gaze gone black. "Screaming and howling, terror and pain."

"How awful for you," Louisa ventured.

"I begged, actually *begged,* to give some assistance, but we remained halted where we were. '*It is not allowed*'." Her lilting voice became a bitter imitation of whoever had spoken to her.

"I read of your generosity in this morning's *Almanach de Versailles,*" Louisa said.

"They ferret out every snippet of information, don't they? I wished to remain *anonymous.* The funds were given from my *private* allowance."

"I'm sure the families of the victims are most grateful for your contribution."

"What good is gold to the dead? More than a hundred of them! No amount of money can compensate the survivors' grief." The Dauphiness shook her head. "Oh, the tongues that wagged over the ominous storm on our wedding day. What will they make of this?"

"I have no idea." Louisa hesitated. "But I can offer you my thoughts."

"Yes, please!"

"I think evil omens and dire predictions and all such superstitions are foolishness. *Foolishness.*"

The lady-in-waiting's appearance in the opened doorway was an unspoken signal to end their conversation.

"You are staying on at Versailles, Princess?" the Dauphiness asked as Louisa rose.

"Yes," she answered, recalling Papa Time's fingers working in his watch-chains. "I am."

"Good. Then I will be sure to see you again."

They did see each other, over the next days and weeks: at prayers in the chapels; in Versailles' splendid gardens; along the crowded corridors of its Great Chateau. They greeted each other on these occasions, and spoke briefly.

Papa Time never managed a Court visit, but wrote in response to Louisa's letters that it appeared her cordial relations with the Dauphiness Marie Antoinette were benefitting both of them: *"She has more need of you than I,"* he'd ended his last letter, adding a sketch of a clock in place of a signature.

The Dauphiness sent a note on the 7th of September, asking Louisa to dine that evening "*to celebrate your eighteenth*" she'd added, in her own hand, below the formal calligraphy.

~ *Chapter Six* ~

It took Louisa almost an hour to settle on a gray figured brocade with point-lace flounces at the bodice and sleeves. It showed the Penthievre pearls, unworn since her wedding, to advantage. She had her hair dressed up and loosely bound with deep pink velvet roses.

Marie Antoinette wore off-white silk, sprigged all over with tiny hand-painted bouquets of forget-me-nots that echoed exactly the color of her eyes. Matching satin bows gathered the sleeves in at the elbow; another circled the whiteness of her throat. Her ashen blonde hair was gathered high and rolled into curls on one side of her neck. Three creamy white ostrich feathers waved from the crown of her head.

The simple, delicious meal began with thin, succulent slices of iced melon, followed by a rosy-pink soufflé of lobster, crisp-roasted duck surrounded by artichokes, and a salad dressed only with lemon juice.

"I rarely take wine or spirits," the Dauphiness sipped from her goblet of mineral water, "but you are welcome to anything you like."

"This is fine. I need nothing else."

"Not even dessert? Chocolate croissants?"

"I haven't heard of those."

"No reason why you should," she smiled. "They were invented in my homeland!"

"Austria?"

"Of all places, yes, years ago, in honor of some successful siege against the Turks. The name *croissant* comes from Turkish for 'crescent'"

"I am most interested in tasting them."

"And I am most interested in learning more about you."

Louisa's throat closed. *Does she know?*

"I was given a note in advance of this visit. I have it right here," she was reaching into a pocket, "but it only says — " she squinted at the paper-"*The Princess of Lamballe is a dutiful daughter of the house of Savoy, foremost in all Italy. Not given to flightiness or frippery, silent amidst gossip, makes scant conversation, but a quick mind."*

She slid the paper under her plate. "I also know you have a lovely dimple, but only in your left cheek. And only when you smile. I know your blonde hair is characteristic of your northern Italian family. I also know you are the untimely widow of Stanislaus de Bourbon Penthievre, Prince of Lamballe."

Louisa managed a nod. *And what else do you know?*

"These facts are all I need to know."

The two teenagers looked at each other. *Are you reading my mind?* Louisa wondered.

"I say what is on my mind always, but prying into another's? Never. And I *never* trust anything I hear second hand. My father taught me that." Marie Antoinette raised her goblet. "Like my water, I prefer my facts to come from the source."

You did *read my mind,* Louisa thought, murmuring only "So kind of you."

"Perhaps. But it's the way I go about my life. I may seem young," her well-defined chin thrust forward, "but I'm old enough to know you should never attempt to be who you aren't. So. Let's hear — what do you know of *me*?"

"Little. Nothing, really. Except for gossip."

"Nothing from the source?" The Dauphiness teased.

"Not as yet."

"So. What are you thinking right now?"

Louisa was too startled to do anything but reply: "I am eighteen in September. You won't be fifteen until November. You seem older, somehow."

"I'll take that as a compliment, if you don't mind!" Her laughter was silver bells. "Far too many see only a spoiled and willful child when they look at me."

"Well, I see someone who is — very much her own person. That's not childish."

More laughter pealed. "I'm no fool when it comes to knowing who I am and what I want, and I don't intend to let any happiness pass me by. My father gave me that gift. A real Lorrainer, he was, and they know how to enjoy life. Which is *exactly* what I intend to do."

She rose from the table, gesturing to Louisa to join her. Together, they crossed the room, to a chaise-lounge long enough to put their feet up without the soles of their kidskin slippers touching.

"The dinner was wonderful," Louisa broke the comfortable silence. "I've enjoyed myself so much."

"Better than *grand couvert*, yes?"

Louisa had yet to attend any of the public meals required of senior members of the Court.

"How I *loathe* having to put on full Court dress for them!" The Dauphiness pulled a face — "those *paniers*! I feel like a mule with saddle bags, plodding along to yet another enormous, unappetizing meal I must eat in full view of an equally enormous and unappetizing crowd." Her ostrich feather ornaments danced. "Stuffed pig, ruffed grouse, giant carp! Chewing and swallowing while gawping strangers hang over the balconies, watching the animal menagerie at feeding time." Her impromptu imitation, all snuffling, grunting, and eye rolling, made Louisa burst into laughter.

"But *grand couvert* is the custom," Marie Antoinette continued, when she could keep a straight face, "*c'est pay-ci*, in this country. Of Versailles. A custom I will put an end to when I am Queen." The frivolous tone was gone, but not for long. "Speaking of custom, tell me Princess, have you met the Mistress of Ceremonies, Madame Noailles?"

"I have," Louisa replied, recalling the old woman's beady eyes, and the stinging sharpness of the hartshorn she'd thrust at her in the chapel, when the funny, clever, enchanting girl sitting at the opposite end of the chaise lounge was being married.

Marie Antoinette's laughter escaped the hands she'd clapped over her mouth. "I must tell you what happened this morning. I'd had *enough* of her turtle-face in mine, attending me everywhere I go. Which is why, when I woke today, I went to the water-closet. Alone!"

It was Louisa's turn to hold her laughter.

"It took less than a minute for word to reach Madame Noailles, and only two more before she and her minions were pounding on the water closet doors. I was the only one in there, so I had to admit them myself! Can you imagine?"

"I can."

"Her cheeks turned royal purple, though she managed to hold her tongue. Even after I informed her that henceforth, when nature calls, I will answer in private."

"But Court etiquette demands — "

" — the opposite. Well, '*No more,*' I informed 'Madame Etiquette'."

"Who?"

"Madame Noailles, of course! Ideal nickname, don't you think? Came to me on the spot — well, on that other throne. The one in the water closet."

Louisa laughed again.

"Oh Princess, if you'd seen the look on her face! His Majesty the King wasn't amused when he heard about it, I can tell you. But he's forgiven me, I think."

"Who *wouldn't* forgive you?"

"Madame Etiquette, that's who."

They erupted into such open laughter they missed the first taps at the door, followed by the announcement of the Dauphin Louis Auguste's arrival.

In the intimacy of the night-cozy room, Louisa was much more conscious of Louis Auguste's ponderousness. Broad as his shoulders and chest were, below the waist he was even broader. *Like a pear,* Louisa thought, guiltily, *but he has a good strong profile, and a nice mouth.*

"Greetings, husband," the Dauphiness called out. "We were just discussing my Mistress of Ceremonies' devotion to — " she caught Louisa's eye, " — my duties!"

He lowered his bulky frame onto the chair brought by his room servant, as another appeared with a small table bearing a dish of what looked like chocolate croissants under a mound of whipped cream. He set to immediately, grunting slightly as he ate, unaware of the noise he made, oblivious to the two women still seated on the chaise lounge.

They lowered their feet to the floor, looking first at him, then at each other, as they took some kind of measure before making a leap neither had made before. A bond forged, and strengthened, as they watched Monsieur the Dauphin, his face screwed up like a baby's, his tongue tunneling like a mole beneath his cheek as he sucked something out from between his teeth. With the last bite gone, he wet a finger and swept it along the plate's surface. Catching the last sugary morsels, he swallowed them, along with the sauternes in his wineglass. Heaving his chair back, he brushed at the crumbs on his vest. "I'm going off to sleep now," he said, pleasantly. "Enjoy yourselves."

"Is it any wonder," his bride murmured, as they watched the gilt-paneled doors close on the sight of his prominent rear end, "that we are the butt of so many jokes?"

Louisa failed to stifle her gasp.

"Do I give offense, Princess?" her dinner companion asked.

"No. None at all. I was caught off guard by your — openness."

"Does openness meet with your approval, Princess?"

"It does, yes." Louisa paused before adding "I lack your gift for it."

The Dauphiness leaned closer. "You possess other gifts, you know."

"I do?"

"The gift of understanding without judgement."

Louisa felt herself blush. "You honor me."

"And this evening? You gave me the gift of — escape, from pomp and protocols. Have I returned the favor?"

"Yes. Oh yes."

"I sense the need for more good times," the Dauphiness paused. "We need to loosen that huge lump of sorrow stuck at your center. Laugh it loose." She suited action to her words. "I will see you soon, Princess. And often."

Louisa woke the following morning to the sight of a bedside tray bearing a crystal goblet of juice, freshly squeezed from the trees of Versailles's famed *Orangerie*, and a napkin cradling a croissant still curling steam, split open and topped with a rosette of melting butter. The Meissen chocolate service was decorated with the Bourbon *fleur-de-lis* and the twined initials "*MA*". Beside it was the exquisite fan carved from a single piece of ivory Marie Antoinette had carried the night before.

There was no note with the birthday gift. And no need for one.

~ Chapter Seven ~

The Dauphiness Marie Antoinette was as good as her word. Before the week was out, she'd sent for Louisa twice, making sure she stayed, "until I see that dimple."

"It must only happen when I smile," Louisa told her. "since I never noticed it before."

"Exactly!"

The third time she was summoned, Louisa couldn't miss the distinct absence of smiles. Entering the dressing chamber, she found the Dauphiness stamping her foot at the tire-woman who held a corset in trembling hands.

"My mother the Empress writes I must keep wearing them, Princess." She stamped again. "I absolutely refuse! The corset stays are *knives* in my sides. *Horses* have a better time of it." Another stamp. "*Their* harness pieces are padded."

Louisa caught her eye. "It appears you've come up in the world."

"How so?" The temper tempest was blowing over.

"At my birthday dinner, condemning your Court dress, you were a mule, not a horse."

The Dauphiness dissolved into laughter as the tire-woman made her hasty exit with the spurned harness piece. When Louisa turned to follow, Marie Antoinette held up a hand. "I insist you stay. It's time you met the other important men in my life, aside from his Majesty and my husband."

They were barely seated when the Austrian ambassador, Count Mercy of Argenteau, and the Swedish-born diplomat Baron Besenval, were announced.

"Mercy's known my mother and all my family since long before I was born. And the Baron's been in the diplomatic service even longer."

Louisa thought the tall, broad-shouldered Mercy handsome; mature, but far from aged. Impeccably attired, poised and polished, his bow was perfect, his smile just warm enough, his murmured greetings enthusiastic without being forward.

No one could call the Baron handsome. With his bulbous nose, jutting jaw, and bottom teeth resting outside his top ones, the short, bow-legged Swede resembled a spritely gnome. Stoop-shouldered, carrying a cane he clearly needed, his bright brown eyes missed nothing. His delight in seeing the Dauphiness was undisguised.

She was delighted too. "With all those diplomatic years, the Baron Besenval knows everything about everyone."

"And I tell all," the old man winked at them both.

"Which is why you are my 'Grandfather Gossip'."

"Though I've not sired a child, let alone a grandchild."

"Lucky for you," Marie Antoinette teased, "since you've never managed to grow up."

"And how do *you* manage," the old man grinned fondly," to remain such a budding rose in this hothouse of spent blooms?"

"Flattery will get you — "

" — Anywhere and everywhere," the Baron interrupted, "my oh so dear child!"

"Grandchild," she corrected him with a laugh.

In the short time they stayed, Louisa came to appreciate the Baron's gaiety of spirit, and his knack, equal to the Dauphiness' own, for droll imitations, comical faces, and joking banter. Best of all, his affection was clearly for her personality, not her position.

Ambassador Mercy, whose every comment was correct and sincere, was harder to fathom. Louisa had heard how closely he kept his focus on the Dauphiness. Observing him, she not only believed it, but couldn't help wondering what he did with what he discovered.

Summoned to Madame the Dauphiness the following morning, Louisa found her working furiously on a letter. "Will you see if you can make out what I've written?" she asked, handing over a wrinkled, blotted sheet of parchment.

"*I beg my very dear mother to forgive me,*" Louisa read, "*if my letter is dirty, but I have had to write it on two successive days while I was at my toilette because I had no other free time.*"

"Nothing will improve its appearance, but could you help me

make it sound the way it should? My mother the Empress awaits her answer. You are well-educated. You read, and what's more, you write, yes?"

"Yes. Of course I will do what I can."

In what soon became a welcome routine, Louisa listened while Marie Antoinette read the near-daily letter from her formidable mother. They discussed replies while Louisa took notes. The notes went with her to her rooms, where she did her best to incorporate them into the version the Empress' daughter would recopy, adding bits here and there, before she wax-sealed it with the leaping pair of dolphins beneath a *fleur-de-lis.*

Their mutual efforts weren't always successful.

"How *dare* she?!" Marie Antoinette flung the words at Louisa the moment she appeared. "I'm a married woman now, and I will be Queen of France one day. She has no right!'

"Who?" Louisa already knew the answer.

"My mother the Empress! I sent her my portrait, you know, the one in my hairdo 'a la Minerva', with the ten feathers — "

" — the one that all Paris and beyond is copying."

"Yes, that hairdo. She sent the portrait *back* — can you believe it? With this note!" She pulled open the drawer of her *escritoire*, tossing its contents every which way. "Here you are," she said, passing Louisa a handful of parchment torn into remarkably tiny pieces. "I know you can't read it — but she wrote "*This is a likeness of some painted-up, low-born actress, not my daughter, the Dauphiness of France.*"

Louisa had heard the voice before: it was the mother's voice, imperious and disgusted, coming from the daughter's mouth. *You are a born mimic*, she thought, but only said "You are not low-born."

"That's not the point and you know it." She was smiling; her temper-storm had blown over. She told Grandfather Gossip all about it, the way she told him about her efforts to carry on what Grandfather had dubbed the "corset wars". They continued over the protests of the *collet montes*, the "straight-laces."The Court's aristocratic women, led by the turtle-faced Madame Etiquette, found nothing amusing in the impertinent upstart's nickname for them.

Bitter cold set in and continued, with new snow falling mercilessly on top of old, from Christmas Day of 1776, well past Twelfth Night.

Later in January of the new year, Madame the Dauphiness discovered a cache of old sleighs among the hundreds of carriages and other equipages in a remote stable building. She immediately ordered them refurbished according to her specifications. Before the week was out, Louisa was hurrying to take her place under an ermine lap robe in one of the dozen sleighs drawn up before the Great Chateau's Hundred Steps.

Brass bells jingled from the small, shaggy ponies' head-pieces as they set off, ranging farther from the confines of Versailles each time. They went as far as the *Champs Elysee* in Paris to deliver blankets and other relief supplies to the poor there.

Marie Antoinette insisted her charity be kept anonymous, but the Parisian gazettes and the *Almanach de Versailles* were soon printing the truth and singing her praises.

The snow melted, but not before a last run the Dauphiness celebrated with an impromptu snowball fight, "boys against the girls." Cheering crowds gathered before it was over, but the "performance" drew mixed reviews from the Empress Marie Therese in the letter that arrived only a day later.

"She kisses me on the one cheek, and slaps me on the other," she grumbled, handing over the creased page.

"No one dares argue your popularity with your subjects," Louisa read, *"but how dare you pit women against men in such vulgar manner?"* She thought it uncanny that the Empress always seemed to know exactly what to praise or scold her youngest daughter for, but didn't share the thought. "She is at least faithful about communicating with you,"

"Your mother doesn't?"

"My mother entered heaven when I was eleven."

"I didn't know. I'm so sorry."

"There is much we don't know," Louisa murmured.

"Not yet. But we will. Were you close?"

"Not really. She was much taken with — prayer."

"If only my mother the Empress was. Oh, she makes a great

show, always has, but the way she goes about it seems driven more by politics than religion."

"And you are driven by neither?" Louisa's question brought a rueful smile.

"My mother the Empress may be right when she accuses me of placing personal enjoyment over both."

~ Chapter Eight ~

The days, and the weeks, melted away as winter gave way to spring.

Marie Antoinette began to "indulge my riding habit," she joked to Louisa. She'd forgiven the Princess for not joining in, agreed that seeing a groom trampled to death when she was only six, could put anyone off horses. The Dauphiness reveled in her freedom to ride astride instead of side-saddle. It distressed more than her mother, but no one dared go against King Louis the Fifteenth. He gave his permission after witnessing her effortless demonstration of accomplished *equestrienne* skill.

Other permissions were longer in coming.

"I can go! I can go! His Majesty says so!" Marie Antoinette was so excited Louisa could hear her in the outer hall.

"Go where?" she asked, as the salon doors were opened.

"To the Opera Ball! In Paris! In costume!" The welcome guest skipped across the Aubusson carpet's bouquets of budding and blooming roses. Real roses stood in vases on the side tables, perfuming the close, warm air. "You'd think he'd have allowed me a masked ball long before this."

Louisa's forehead wrinkled. "No member of the Royal family has gone masked anywhere open to the general public," she said, "let alone in Paris."

"So far as I'm concerned, Princess, I already wear a mask portraying the Dauphiness of France, at every meal and Mass and ceremony. What a relief wearing a *real* mask will be."

Despite the Dauphiness' urgings to have a costume made, Louisa went to the Opera Ball as 'Rapunzel', with her hair brushed into a sweep of honey-gold waves that rippled to her knees. The only clue to her fairy tale character was the pearl-trimmed comb she carried.

Marie Antoinette came costumed as 'Fatima', according to legend the last wife of the infamous Bluebeard. Her peach satin overdress was cut like a man's frock coat, to cover a bust-line that now measured a full forty inches. A scandalously short tulle underskirt showed off her slender feet in spangled slippers, their up-curled toes tipped with tiny silver bells. Black curls from her wig escaped a blue satin turban fastened with a sapphire so large it looked like a paste imitation. Her skin had been tinted to the olive tones of the Orient, and her brows and lashes blackened, but not even the close-fitted domino mask disguised the distinctive blue eyes.

The Dauphin made a brief appearance, swathed in harlequin-patterned satin as the clown 'Pierrot'. Ambassador Mercy, who made an early departure, wore his Roman senator's toga and laurel wreath well. Baron Besenval — Grandfather Gossip — was a most comical Juliet, from his high-coned headdress to the papier-mâché balcony he clutched to his over-padded bosom. He was too bothered by rheumatism to join in the dancing, and so left sooner than he generally did. It was the Dauphin's younger brother, the Count of Artois, who stayed and stayed.

The Count had his spurt of growth not long after the wedding, giving him a mature appearance for his fourteen years. He insisted his 'Bluebeard' costume was a coincidence, but Louisa wasn't the only one who took notice of how often he and 'Fatima' danced together.

The hour grew late, and the crowd so reduced the fire-men no longer replaced the candles in the chandeliers. Only a few remained on alert, their sponges ready to extinguish falling sparks. The musicians with a taste for drink were slumped over their instruments. The air reeked of sweated wine and soured perfume. Only Artois and Antoinette remained on the dance floor, practicing a new waltz step without music, absorbed in its complex sequence of dips and glides, pauses and turns.

"One, two, three — One, two, three — get the rhythm!" She was laughing, her head thrown back, a cloud of tulle floating out around her, to the tinkling accompaniment of her slipper bells.

A courtier hurried up to them, bringing the waltz to an abrupt conclusion. The man was unfamiliar to Louisa.

"Say you'll go! Say you'll go!" The Dauphiness was running towards her.

Where?" Louisa asked.

"To the Palais Royale. We've had an invitation from the Duke of Chartres to join his party." She giggled. "His after-the-party party."

"His Majesty's permission was given only for attendance at the Opera Ball," Louisa managed to murmur, through the lump of panic all but closing her throat. "I doubt he would extend his permission, especially at this late hour."

"Early hour, Princess. It's nearly one in the morning."

The lump enlarged. "I must decline."

"Why?"

"I — I cannot say."

"Something bad?" The mask was long discarded, but the honey-gold makeup masked Marie Antoinette's milky complexion. Her eyes held Louisa's.

"Yes. Something bad." Louisa couldn't look at her.

"Very well. I will also decline."

"Not on my account, please." Louisa kept her head down.

"Really, it's all right. I can live without going to the devil." The joking reference was to the Duke's costume, but Louisa flinched at the sudden stab of memory. Had she only imagined it was the tip of a pitchfork parting her hair from behind? *I didn't imagine the whisper*: "Rapunzel, Rapunzel, you've let down your hair." When she'd forced herself to turn around, whoever it was had vanished.

"I know he is kin to you by marriage," the Dauphiness was still talking, "but frankly I find him more than a little obnoxious. Let Artois go on. I'd rather return to Versailles and — make chocolate. And dine on omelets. Yes?"

"Yes."

~ *Chapter Nine* ~

It was past two when they reached Versailles, and another half hour before Louisa presented herself at the Dauphiness' private suite. Marie Antoinette wore an undress gown in her favorite shade of blue, the one the whole country had taken to calling "French blue." Her shining blonde hair was freshly washed and dried, her slender arms bare of bracelets, her graceful fingers free of rings.

"Observe," she laughingly announced, "how adept I've become." Turning her attention to the tray of chocolate implements on the stand beside her chair, she beat whites of egg until the foam was gone; melted squares of unsweetened chocolate over a small brazier; folded it into the egg whites, and poured the result into the silver chocolate pot, adding warmed water, milk, and a pinch of sugar.

"I love the aroma," she inhaled deeply as she handed Louisa's cup to her for the final step. They dipped their silver chocolate sticks, rapidly, until the dangling rings created a frothy foam.

"The omelets will be along shortly, Princess. Thank you again for coming."

"My pleasure."

They frothed and sipped, going over the night's events.

"Do you suppose there'll be gossip over my not dressing as 'Pierette' to the Dauphin's 'Pierrot'?" Marie Antoinette asked.

"I doubt it," Louisa answered. "Artois' marriage is declared, after all."

"I think the King is concerned," her companion spoke slowly, "that Artois' marriage will bear fruit before ours." She hesitated. "May I tell you something?"

"Certainly."

"Something you will never tell?" Her scrubbed face came nearer. "I know you won't," she added, before Louisa could reply. "His Majesty and one of his doctors came to my study yesterday. They took care that no one else knew of their visit." She took a sip from her chocolate cup, looked over its rim. "They came to give us the facts of life. In case we weren't clear on what we're supposed to be doing." Another sip. Another look. "It presses on me. Some nights when he — tries and fails — I think the failure is also mine. Most nights, I am certain it is all his."

"It cannot be you."

"How can I know that?"

It was Louisa's turn to sip. "He — he may not — know desire yet."

"They were saying that a year ago. That he hadn't developed enough to feel any desire. Well. I can tell you he *feels* it." Her gaze was cool and direct.

Louisa returned it unflinchingly.

A soft series of scratches at the door announced the omelets.

They both welcomed the distraction of the food.

"I can't believe I'm confiding so much in you," Marie Antoinette spoke first. "Is it really safe?"

On impulse, Louisa set her cup down and crossed her hands over her heart. "Yes." They held each other's gaze for a long moment, before Louisa said "You live among so many liars and flatterers. It is my duty — and my intent — and my pleasure — to offer my honesty. Always."

"Do you swear it?"

"I do."

"On a blood oath?"

"A what?"

"Don't look so stricken!" Antoinette's laughter pealed. "A blood oath, done exactly the way we did in the nurseries at Schonbrunn." She set her chocolate cup aside, reached beneath her chair and drew up an embroidery work-bag. "Here!" She pulled out a tangled heap of silks, shaking it until a gleaming steel needle dropped down, swinging on the end of a bright blue thread.

Louisa's hands uncrossed.

"It's so simple, Princess. I prick my finger first, and then you prick yours, before we mingle our blood, to signal we will never lie to each other, or about each other, because we are friends to the end."

"Yes, yes, but I'm afraid that — I'm afraid."

"Of being friends to the end?"

"No, not that. It shames me to admit it, but — the needle."

"No need for shame, the fear is common, my — friend to the end?"

"I am that."

"And I am yours. And this isn't a bleeding lancet, just a little embroidery sharp. Here." Before Louisa could move, Marie Antoinette had grasped her fingertip, pricked it, withdrawn the needle, and was pricking her own. Her blood spot touched Louisa's before their fingers separated.

"There, that's done," she said, as Louisa pressed a handkerchief to the painless wound, blotting up the small stain of their blood. "Now we are truly sisters. I can tell you everything without a care you might carry tales. I never believed you would, or did, but now I can be absolutely certain."

"You can."

"And I can know the sweet, sweet relief of relying on you to be honest with me at all times."

"You can."

"You are so easy to talk to."

"I enjoy listening."

"Lucky for me! But come now, time to share confidences!" Antoinette refilled her cup from the chocolate pot. "Will you … tell me your very worst fault? The one thing you'd change if you could? For me, it's holding my tongue. It's gotten me into more trouble: 'Tonia, you are so impertinent!' 'Tonia, when will you learn to hold your tongue?'" She stopped imitating. "What are you grinning about?"

"I was imagining how it would look if you held your tongue for real."

Her blood sister did just that, crossing her eyes to such comical effect Louisa laughed until tears came.

"I've told you mine," her blood sister was wiping her eyes, too, "now you tell me yours. Worst fault, if you please?"

"My nails," Louisa replied immediately. "I must stop biting them. It looks so vile."

"Ah, that's easy enough. I'll kiss them and make them better." She did, setting off a tingling thrill, from the tips of Louisa's fingers to what felt like the center of her heart.

"Dear Louisa!" Louisa heard her name spoken for the first time, as Marie Antoinette reached out her hand. Louisa took it, forging another link in their intimacy.

" 'Tonia' is the name I grew up with, the name my father always called me. And my mother. And sisters. Will you call me 'Tonia' too?"

"Tonia." Louisa tried it out. "Tonia. My blood sister — "

"Louisa — my blood sister."

They made no more chocolate, but talked until dawn.

~ Chapter Ten ~

The 13th day of June in the year of Our Lord 1772

Dearest Papa Time,

I am sorry to be so tardy with this letter, but my days are much occupied, and so I have fewer hours to devote to my own messages. I thank you again for your thoughtful gift, and hope it makes you smile to learn I have long since worn out the swan feather quills you provided.

Louisa tilted her head back, easing the weight of her undone hair. Night braiding did away with the weight, but she didn't want anyone to braid her hair unless it could be Tonia. Which of course it couldn't.

Growing up, I did not see my father often, but I am grateful he wanted his daughters to learn to write a fair hand, to read for pleasure as well as enlightenment, and to write letters.

There is so much to explore here, …"

Louisa hesitated before making the private name public.

… in Tonia's company. I explained in my last letter her wonderful acceptance and easy informality is the reason I address her so. It no longer sounds strange to my ear, especially when we are off on the spontaneous excursions she announces when we are otherwise occupied with the many things she finds boring.

Yesterday, for an instance, we set off for a far garden before we had half read through the menu lists and seating plans presented for her approval. I agreed, as I often do, and our lengthy walk to the wild-kept acres was rewarded by the unexpected sight of a bed of ripe wild strawberries. We stained our gloves picking them ourselves, and our fingers as we ate them without waiting upon bowls of cream.

After dinner, dear Tonia has re-discovered the billiards she played as a child. Her eye is so accurate at play, and her hand so steady, but can you believe I am her close competition? She is amused by the flatteries her guests aim at her, in their fierce competition for her attention. I am not as amused …

Most mornings, though, as Tonia's dressing neared completion, Louisa brought the correspondence folio, thankful for the skills she'd been encouraged to master. She kept her concentration on the task at hand, knowing Tonia's span of attention was short, aware that excursions like yesterday's wild strawberries were imminent. Nights, at billiards, Louisa enjoyed calculating her shot, controlling the force of her stroke, and then retreating to observe, quiet and un-noticed.

Tonia was neither, but her observations were just as keen. Louisa loved the looks they exchanged, swift, side-eyed glances that asked "*Did you see that? Did you hear that?*" louder than any words.

The suave Austrian Ambassador Mercy was a regular player, first to arrive, and to take his leave. The impish "Grandfather Gossip," Baron Besenval, was another regular. He sometimes arrived with Horace Walpole, son of England's former Prime Minister, popular as a writer and publisher. He often brought the Irish writer and legislator Edmund Burke. Of late there was also his Swedish protégé.

Hans Axel Fersen was a Count, scion of an old and respected family thought to have originated in Scotland. It explained why his looks, although handsome in the extreme, were opposite a Swede's typical blondeness. From their first meeting, the Count made no attempt to hide his intense admiration for Louisa's blood sister. Tonia, as always, ignored the wagging tongues and wagging fingers, making no secret of her enjoyment of his company, along with Grandfather Gossip's.

As serious and self-effacing as he was direct and absent of artifice, Fersen soon stood out from the rest of her "platonic champions". Tonia laughed off the sneering Court label for every idle male who swanned around her. She ignored the swirl of rumors and gossip about his life as a soldier, husband, and keeper of mistresses. Much of it was true, but Fersen was her platonic friend and staunch ally. Nothing more.

She also ignored the constant stream of stories in the popular gazettes. They fed an insatiable public appetite for every juicy detail. Her fashions were copied far beyond the borders of fashion-conscious France. Her favored amusements and lavish entertainments were everywhere imitated. Her subjects couldn't get enough of their bewitching Dauphiness. It was as close as they could come to the Court's glittering life.

Inside the Court, the *collet montes,* straight-laces, grew ever more critical of the impertinent Austrian upstart. She snubbed them so freely, but had yet to give France the heir she was imported to provide.

On November 2nd, 1773, a large Royal party attended the Opera in Paris, in celebration of the Dauphiness' eighteenth birthday. A military guard had to be called out to keep order in the streets. When word came that Marie Antoinette had entered the cavernous building, the massed crowd in the pit, and their betters in the tiers of boxes above them, all rose, spontaneously and in unison. The upswelling of sound intensified as the party ascended the private staircase to the Royal box, where the floorboards vibrated with the cheers.

It frightened Louisa, but Tonia loved it. Her husband stood, impassive, as his radiant wife stood on tiptoes, leaning out ever farther, waving in all directions.

At month's end, Marie Antoinette sent for Christoph Gluck, her childhood music master, who'd found success as composer, director and conductor. His most recent opera, *Iphigenia*, was a popular sensation.

"It's playing to acclaim everywhere but here," she told Louisa at their morning correspondence meeting, "as well it should be. The people of France must be treated to his breath of fresh air. There *will* be a French production. I will see to it."

Madame the Dauphiness was as good as her word. It set new tongues wagging, over her disrespect for the grand traditions of French opera. Ignoring the critics, as usual, she poured funds into the project. Royal protocols, however, couldn't be set aside. Approved public appearances did not extend to visiting the foreign commoner she insisted on addressing as Herr Gluck instead of Monsieur. By day, he was allowed to work on the first French production. By night, Tonia was allowed to hold musical evenings within the Great Chateau.

Louisa couldn't help but notice Herr Gluck never asked his former pupil to play the harp, or harpsichord. She understood why, though, having heard her blood sister's less than expert renditions of even simple melodies. After the third of these evenings, Tonia asked her help in circumventing the prohibition on watching the maestro at work.

"You will be my eyes and ears."

"And report back on what you can't see for yourself?"

"Exactly. I know you're shy of crowds, but you have such a — self-effacing way about you." The Royal shoulders shrugged. "You won't attract overmuch attention."

"I suppose I should take that as a compliment?"

"Our opposites attract, don't they?"

"They do," Louisa agreed.

"Ah, there's that smile dimple."

Louisa bit her nails for the first time in months as she made her first foray beyond Palace borders that wasn't to Rambouillet. Tonia was right about her not attracting notice; her destination, a cavernous rehearsal hall on the outskirts of Paris where Gluck was conducting unheard-of auditions for "*Iphigenia*", had attracted throngs of noblewomen. With casting completed, the raucous rehearsals got underway. And Tonia got it right when she started calling Louisa her "self-effacing spy."

The critics loathed the result they saw and heard, but the opening night acclaim for the Royal rule-breaker who'd brought the opera to France was even more thunderous than the birthday ovation she'd been given.

Tonia achieved her majority at eighteen, but the restraints of mature behavior hadn't followed. She continued to indulge her gift for mimicry, of the bow-legged roll of a hapless courtier's gait, or the exaggerated swish of some straight-laced lady's coiffure. She took care to stay behind their backs, but didn't care who might be watching, aghast, behind which fan, or what hand.

On the eve of Christmas, Louisa helped supervise the arrangement of evergreens above the fireplace in Tonia's innermost reception room.

"Most of the year I think there is nothing more beautiful than work like this,"Tonia traced the alabaster mantel's rose garlands with the pink polished tip of one nail. "But at Christmas, I'm reminded they're only stone."

It was nearing midnight when Louis Auguste, Dauphin of France, woke with a start in the unaccustomed surroundings of his wife's bed. For some time now, they'd slept in their respective suites of rooms. Once a month, and always on the nights before Christmas and the new year, Louis Auguste made the determined effort to do his duty.

He searched beneath the pillows for the vial of salve, a special concoction urged on him by the Royal physicians. Finding it, he rubbed some on the uncooperative worm of his manhood, breathing heavily through his mouth until the salve delivered its pain-deadening effect. Even then, the skin covering the blind eye at its tip still hurt. A hurt made worse when worm became club, as it always did, at the sight of her. And worse still after he touched her shoulder, and she rolled onto her back.

Tonia arranged herself beneath him, without so much as a gauze night robe covering her milky, perfumed skin. Her white blonde pubic hair barely showed between her gracefully parted legs, as her unkissed lips parted in a welcoming smile, and the rosy nipples of her rounded breasts rose to greet him.

Louis Auguste gritted his teeth and followed the doctors' instructions. Supporting himself above her on bent elbows and splayed palms, he inserted his erect penis as far as he could into her vagina, before he froze, groaning with pain, not pleasure.

Tonia did her best to keep the smile on her lips and the warmth in her gaze; to encourage this fat, dull, clumsy, kindly, hurting boy to ejaculate through intercourse. Once again, she wished with all her heart there was some other way to go about it. Some other method of getting his seed into her womb. Some other means of insuring that the pear-shaped organ she and her mother and all France depended on would ripen finally, and bear fruit. Male fruit.

~ Chapter Eleven ~

The 15th day of April in the year of Our Lord 1774

Dearest Papa Time,

This spring has brought days on end of dampness and rain. Most of the Court is afflicted with some illness or complaint, my dear sister and myself included.

Light and simultaneous colds allow us to send regrets to all others, leaving us free to share the few gossip tidbits that reach us, since Grandfather has to keep away.

We drink near constant cups of rosewater heated with lemon, clove and vanilla. We also enjoy the unexpected benefit of more sleep hours than we are generally granted.

The 20th day of April in the year of Our Lord 1774

Dear Papa,

Our regimen has resulted in speedy healing, but that is not the case with his Majesty the King. He has had to remain at Trianon, in the house of his mistress Madame DuBarry, where he arrived with a touch of fever a week ago. There seemed no cause for worry at first, but now it appears he might suffer from influenza.

The 13th day of April in the year of Our Lord 1774

Papa dearest,

I write in haste, so as not to miss this morning's courier. I have learned His Majesty King Louis the Fifteenth was brought back to the Great Chateau just before dawn, amid rumors he suffers from smallpox.

Tonia and I and much of the Court have been inoculated against it, but the King was suspicious of its efficacy, and so he never was.

The first day of May, in the year of Our Lord 1774

Oh Papa,

For the first time in anyone's memory, there will be no festivities to mark May Day. The King's condition worsens. We are all in a state of held breath.

Daybreak on the tenth day of May found the 18-year-old Dauphiness Marie Antoinette already at her kneeler, and the 20-year-old Dauphin Louis Auguste at his, both of them staring across the courtyard to the black-draped windows of the King's sick-room.

Never before had Tonia's entire being been so concentrated on something outside herself. Everything had absorbed itself into the flicker of the single candle, burning before the black drape.

Stay, stay, stay, she commanded the flame, silently, with every breath she took. *While it burns, he lives.* Her consciousness compressed to the size of that tiny, wavering point of light, as Louis Auguste perspired beside her.

The flame vanished so suddenly her field of vision registered the ghostly after-image, dancing against the dark. A voiceless murmur rose, swelling to a crescendo, as the Court closed in on the quarters where they'd kept their vigil.

His Majesty Louis the Sixteenth knelt still as a stone while the crowd filled the doorway and began squeezing through. Queen Consort Marie Antoinette clutched at her husband's hand: "Protect us, Lord," she was heard to nearly scream. "We are too young to rule."

The following afternoon brought the first waves in what soon became a river of solemn faces, flowing by hour after hour, as each lady of the Court, and each female representative of the aristocratic nobility, presented her personal condolence.

Louisa stood quietly in what had become an eddy of the river, her gaze fixed on her blood sister's chalk-pale face, stark against the black moiré gown hastily dyed from its original blue, its animation extinguished by numbing fatigue. Despite the toll the shock had taken, she managed a formal clasp of sympathy for every woman's hand, along with a few murmured words for each.

The drapes had been drawn against a shaft of late day sun when a lady-in-waiting Louisa knew to be as foolish as she was young appeared in a doorway barely wider than the paniers of her Court dress. *Not her*, she thought, *not now.* Louisa stared as the girl gained Tonia's attention, with a signal meant to summon the Queen Consort to wade closer, through the human river.

Tonia saw, but didn't move. Louisa was letting out her held breath when the girl tilted the mass of her skirts back, revealing a more petite lady-in-waiting. The silk swished down, but not before Tonia saw, along with most of the room. All her breeding, all her training, all her better instincts failed to keep the Queen Consort from erupting in laughter. Her composure returned almost immediately, but not before dozens of hands rose up in front of mouths opened in O's of shock.

They will not excuse her this time, Louisa thought. *But it did her good.* The pallid flatness of her complexion had warmed, and she held her demurely coifed head a fraction higher.

~ *Chapter Twelve* ~

Tonia hadn't turned the hour glass in the small salon where they had finally retired, but Louisa was well aware it was past midnight. Their omelets waited, warm beneath porcelain cloches, while they shared the last of the decanted brandy they rarely drank.

"My father died ten years ago this summer. August. Beastly hot." Tonia's child-blue eyes lost their focus. "He was walking away, across the lawn, to the courtyard where his carriage waited, when he turned and spread out his arms. I was the first one there." She lifted the cloche, set it down again.

"They waited until the next day to tell me. His heart. He'd never shown a sign of it. I like to think it burst from its bigness."

Louisa lifted the cloche from her omelet, and Tonia followed suit.

"He could make my mother — my *mother* — laugh. Like *no* one else. But he never found fun at others' expense — do you know what I mean?"

"I do," Louisa answered, "and I envy you. My mother was always at her prayers, and — I rarely saw my father. Yours sounds wonderful."

"He *was* wonderful. They say he over-indulged me, and I suppose that's true. When I insisted on riding astride, for instance, he replaced my sidesaddle with a blue leather one that was *so* pretty. Mother objected, said he was spoiling me."

"Well, did he?"

"Of course," Tonia giggled. "He said that's what papas are for; to spoil their children silly."

They ate and drank in a silence Louisa finally broke. "When did you realize you would be living a life like this?"

"Early on. I grew up watching my mother auction us off, one after another, to the highest bidder. Their offers were different, but the outcome was the same." Tonia reached across the table. "You're the exception."

"Exception to what?"

"To the sorry rule that everyone leaves me."

"I never will." Louisa reached back.

Tonia was the first to turn her attention back to her omelet. "No more on the subject now. Choose another." She struck an exaggerated pose, Hapsburg chin upthrust. "I command you — as your Queen."

"Forgive me, your most excellent Majesty, but shouldn't that be 'Queen Consort'?"

Tonia laughed. "Not until after the coronation. A year, at the least."

"You could be so great with child by then you won't be able to travel to Rheims for the ceremony."

Sudden silence bloomed. "Do you want children?" Tonia whispered into it, finally. "I've never heard you speak of them. Or of your husband. Of his — end." Her grip on Louisa's hands tightened. "Will you make an exception tonight?"

Louisa swallowed hard before she nodded. "Stanislaus left for an extended tour of his properties in late summer. He didn't return until the first hard freeze." She swallowed again. "Are you sure you want me to go on?"

"If you can."

"He brought his sickness with him."

"His fatal sickness?"

Louisa hardly heard the question. "His symptoms worsened all through Advent. He sank into a coma, two days after the Feast of the Epiphany." Louisa's inner eye saw herself, suddenly, moving through the fog of incense that didn't mask the smell of death. Saw herself moving past the physicians and priests, gathered like ravens at the bedside. "His face was puffed up," she went on, when she could, "like risen dough. His eyes were closed, but the lids twitched. I bent close, called his name." She was back in that stifling room again, his feeble breath brushing her ear: "*He gave me — drinks. He gave me — girl. She gave me — death. Shame. On. Me.*"

I was the cause. The shame is mine, Louisa thought, but could only say "He took his revenge on the wrong person."

"I don't understand," Tonia said. "Who do you mean?"

"Surely you might have guessed, on the night of the Opera Ball."

"The Opera Ball? It was Chartres!" Tonia struck her forehead with the heel of one hand. "Dummkopf! For not suspecting, then, or since. Dummkopf!"

She never uses German. The thought almost made Louisa smile.

"Chartres! Of course! You declined his invitation so vehemently, I wondered what the story was."

How much can I tell you?

"You've held back for so long. I understand your reluctance, but — please. Can you tell me now?"

" — Six weeks after the wedding, my husband traveled to Paris on family business, while his older sister and her husband remained at Rambouillet. My brother-in-law's behavior towards me had already made me uneasy."

"Of course it would. He is a notorious rake. But how could you have known?"

"I didn't know, but he learned my maid was abed with a headache, and so I would be walking alone that day. He followed me. He — he made advances."

"Serious advances?"

"Yes."

"Did he — lay hands?"

"He would have. I — I stopped him."

The silence lasted a minute or more before Tonia prodded, gently: "And?"

"They went hunting together when my husband returned, and the Duke gave him a gift. A living gift. Knowing full well — "

" — knowing what?"

"That the harlot was infected. That she would pass a rare and virulent form of pox to Stanislaus. He succumbed to it. A week after what would have been our first anniversary."

"Oh, no," Tonia spoke through tears. "I heard Chartres was a monster. I had no idea how monstrous. Sister, dearest sister, I'll have him arrested, banished, tortured even. Anything! You have only to ask."

Louisa held her own tears back. "All I ask is these confidences remain between us."

"It was your secret. Now it is mine. But he *must* be punished for what he did."

"That cannot happen."

Tonia's tears gave way to anger. "He took your husband's life as surely as if he did it with some horrible weapon — to get his sick, twisted revenge. I'll show him *revenge*."

"Tonia, sister, revenge won't bring Stanislaus back to life."

"What about his making you a widow at seventeen?"

"I've made my peace with that."

"What about children? Don't you want children? A husband can easily be found for you."

"I have no reason to marry again, because I never intend to have children."

"What? Why?"

"The same vile virus that took Stanislaus might somehow have infected me. Anything that infects me is something I might pass to my offspring."

"You can't be sure of that."

"That may be so, but I cannot be certain. The mere possibility is a risk too great to take." Louisa paused for breath. "And so, my sister, I will not become a mother."

"You will not set your decision aside?"

"Not for anything. Not for anyone."

"Not even me," Tonia whispered. "Oh, Louisa, I've given you less credit than I should. For having such incredible strength. I am in awe of it. And of the courage you've shown, in sharing your awful secret. I see you in such a different light." She looked down at their plates; her smile dazzled as she looked up. "And I also see our omelets have congealed. Should we order again, or would you rather enjoy dessert? Safe in the knowledge your secret is safe with me?"

"Dessert," Louisa replied, feeling a door open somewhere inside her, into a room not opened before. The room where her sister lived.

~ Chapter Thirteen ~

Week after week, the crowds in the hallways between the Princess of Lamballe's suite and the wing holding Her Majesty's swelled. Their grumbling grew louder when the door guards escorted her past, leaving them to wait in vain for admittance.

The last week in June brought the year's first serious heat. It did nothing to diminish the crowds. but they were rewarded with an actual sighting of — yes, it was Marie Antoinette herself, flanked by her guards, greeting the Princess with everything except the embrace protocol forbade in public.

"Sit! Sit close!" Tonia instructed the guards to remain in the outer reception room, closing the door behind them herself. "I have such good news for you!"

Louisa hadn't seen her sister so excited in a positive way since the candle of Louis the Fifteenth's life was snuffed out and the burden of rule descended on her.

"I have succeeded in renewing a position that's been dormant for at least fifty years." Her smile was triumphant. "With His Majesty's consent, I have nominated you as Superintendent of my Household."

"Me?"

"Yes, you. Who else would I choose?"

Louisa hadn't any answer, and so asked a question: "My duties?"

"Much the same, believe it or not. Assist with correspondence and record-keeping." She raised two fingers. "Resolve small problems before they enlarge. Offer good advice," she made a thumbs-up fist, "while remaining my blood sister."

Louisa was so surprised she said the first thing that came to her: "But what of Madame Noailles?"

"Madame Etiquette? What *of* her?"

"She is your Mistress of Ceremonies. She holds first place in your

Household. Does the Superintendent take a place before hers?"

"As a matter of fact, it does. *You* do. I mean you *will.* Don't confuse me."

Louisa set aside the correspondence folio she'd held onto. "You do me great honor, but flouting such established order? There'll be such opposition."

"True, but what can the old turtle do about it? Snap me to death for my impertinence?"

Louisa had to smile at that.

"I have revived the Office of Superintendent of the Queen's Household," Tonia repeated the title with relish, "and I am nominating you."

"As your obedient subject, I accept your nomination," Louisa spoke slowly. "As your blood sister, I wish with all my heart to go on as we have."

"Of course we will. Don't be silly."

"Small chance of that," Louisa's retort brought the gift of Tonia's laughter.

The oath was administered on a hot, cloudy afternoon in August of 1774:

"I, Maria-Theresa-Louisa of Savoy-Carignan, Princess of Lamballe, swear my loyalty to the House of Bourbon, to the throne of France, and to Madame Josephe Jeanne Marie Antonia, Queen Consort to his Majesty Louis the Sixteenth.

I vow to serve her as Superintendent of her Household with every energy at my command. I further vow to carry out all that is requested or desired of me, to the greater glory of my God, my monarch, and my Queen."

Afterward, at the small reception in her apartments, Tonia caught Louisa's eye as glasses were raised for a toast: "To the second oath you've sworn on my behalf." They both smiled at the shared memory of a gleaming steel needle dangling from a bright blue thread.

Madame Etiquette arrived minutes later, in full regalia, flanked by half the ladies of the Court, to tender her formal letter of resignation.

Everyone present knew the protest to be public show. The new Queen played her part in it, as she refused to accept the letter, but her next pronouncement was totally unexpected: "I refused the 'Girdle of the Queen,' the customary gift of 200,000 *francs*, from the people of Paris. I have sent it instead to the priests of Paris, for distribution to the poor there."

The people of Paris, for whom five francs a day was a fair wage, flocked to Versailles in wildly enthusiastic droves. Their countrymen poured in alongside, as King Louis the Sixteenth, his Queen Consort, and the Superintendent of her Household braced for a sea change, each in their own way.

His Majesty increased the hours he already spent hunting. Her Majesty established a "Minister of Fashion". And the newly-sworn Superintendent of Her Majesty's Household prayed she would be equal to her new tasks.

~ Chapter Fourteen ~

Tonia had discovered Rose Bertin early on. She'd achieved early success in Paris for her sought-after millinery designs, followed by the *haute couture* gowns that had made her Paris *atelier* a magnet. The plump, pretty, apple-cheeked gendarme's daughter from Picardy was also determinedly single. Mademoiselle Bertin was as proud of her country origins as she was of being in business for herself. True to her nature, Bertin was also refreshingly free with opinions on the whole of society that Tonia shared, and Louisa also admired.

Six days out of seven, the "Minister of Fashion" arrived just after sunrise, followed by a troupe of her girls, each carrying a huge oblong box. Their contents turned Tonia's dressing-chambers into a garden as they made selections for the day and the week, discussing and settling on new designs, giving names like "Sweet Modesty" to Bertin's sketches. The finished gowns were widely published and instantly copied.

A few hours later, generally later than promised, Monsieur Leonard Autie and his entourage made their grand entrance, with the bearer of the folding stairs he used to arrange the top of the towering *coiffures* she favored for public appearances. The sharp-eyed man about town who'd come up in the world from his humble origins as a country barber enjoyed looking down his long nose at any hairstyle he hadn't created.

He and Bertin shared undeniable talent, but Louisa couldn't share Tonia's enthusiasm for her "Knight of the Comb." Unlike the unflappable Bertin, Leonard was a self-described "bundle of nerves and vapors," who delighted in making mountainous fusses over mostly imagined slights.

Bertin made a request on her first Palace visit after the mourning period ended: "I wish — and since Monsieur Leonard might not have gathered up the courage to approach you on the matter — I petition you on our behalf, to continue serving our patrons other than your most esteemed self."

Word of Bertin's visit, and the reason for it, reached Madame Noailles, who appeared with her retinue shortly after Bertin took her leave.

"I protest this impossible alteration — if you will pardon my pun — in the established order," the older woman made a mockingly deep bow.

"Your pun is pardoned," Tonia's tone was pleasantly neutral. "May I ask what has caused you such distress?"

Noailles was ready with an answer. "When such underlings are elevated to your august level, it becomes the *only* level at which their skill can be practiced."

"Who says this?"

"It is a matter of custom, your Majesty. Tradition. The *right* way."

"Is there some written law requiring these artists to serve only me?" Tonia's forehead wrinkled in obvious confusion. "A law forbidding them to benefit from our association? Forcing them to accept no payment for their services to others?"

"I don't believe so," Noailles muttered.

"It seems to me, then," Tonia's smile tightened as her back went ramrod stiff, "that Mademoiselle Bertin and Monsieur Leonard seek a measure of personal freedom. Since nothing but the doing of things in the 'right way' opposes them, I see no reason to deny their request — Madame Etiquette."

Dead silence dropped on the chamber as the two adversaries took each other's measure. Noailles glared at Bertin's couture lists, spread about on the tables, marked with pins and Tonia's comments, then at Tonia herself, cool and correct, with only the ice in her blue eyes giving any hint of her true feelings.

"Will that be all?" the old woman inquired, stiffly, finally.

"Not quite. I have also decided to eliminate the tradition that decrees I must be followed everywhere within the Great Chateau by at least two women in full Court dress. From now on, only a single Valet of the Chamber will accompany me."

Noailles' exit was swift in coming. So was loud criticism, from many who had held their gossiping tongues until now.

Tonia was indifferent to the chorus of criticism.

Louisa wasn't. "People are making arrangements to leave," she said, from her chair on the opposite side of the double desk strewn with half a dozen folios. "They're saying they will never set foot in your Court again!"

"Their feet are probably covered with corns anyway. Shall we go for a walk in the gardens before we develop corns ourselves, from sitting so idle?"

They set out in sun-warmed air, with a cool breeze tugging at their skirts. Ten minutes passed; twenty; the breeze grew warmer. At the outskirts of Trianon's 45-acre preserve, Louisa turned back, but Tonia tugged her elbow, waving the pair of footmen following them to take the lead.

They moved through glades of fine old trees, past a natural-looking, wind-ruffled pond, through the ranks of topiary walling off the small house the late King gave his mistress, Madame DuBarry. It was unoccupied since she'd retired to her country estate.

"Last night," Tonia clapped her hands, "I asked my husband if I can have all of *Petite Trianon* for my own." She hugged herself. "Oh, Louisa, he said yes! If I'm to spend the rest of my life stepping to the tunes of others, I want a place of my own. Where I can step to my own."

"Where you can be happy." Tears threatened, but Louisa held them back.

"Happy as I once was. *More* so. And better. *Much* better."

~ *Chapter Fifteen* ~

Trianon wasn't the only project Tonia had more and better plans for.

"The King's Passage!" The long, linen-wrapped tube Tonia thrust at her blood sister contained detailed plans for a corridor, concealed behind walls, that would connect the Royal bedrooms.

"Privacy," Louisa nodded. "Imagine that."

"It will eliminate all need for public exposure at" — Tonia tapped a circle on the plan where multiple hallways converged — "the *Oeil de Boeuf,* the Bull's Eye. He visits seldom, but when he does? They take aim at him from all sides, while his retinue struggles to get him through."

The King's Passage looked like a tunnel to Louisa, all odd angles and sharp turnings through the labyrinth of the Great Chateau.

The project was completed with such surprising speed that Tonia called on her Superintendent of Buildings, a position established long before Louisa's Household title, to alter her apartments for added privacy.

She threw herself into the re-design and decorating with the same unerring eye she brought to her gowns and her coiffures. The results were a dazzle of bleached wood and gilded carving, beautifully lit by crystal-prismed chandeliers, closed off from the rest of the wing with padded doors.

The critics of her flouted customs voiced their indignance at this latest insult. From the commoners denied easy access to their Majesties via the Bull's Eye, to the courtiers cut off from eavesdropping, the chorus of complaint grew louder.

On a blustery early March day in 1775, Ambassador Mercy and Baron Besenval waited in one of the newly redecorated reception salons. Mercy pulled his watch from his vest-pocket at five-minute intervals while he read his dispatches. Grandfather Gossip contented himself with the contents of his snuffbox and the official daily news filling the *Almanach de Versailles.*

The Superintendent of her Majesty's Household had made some progress with her Majesty's habitual disregard for punctuality. Louisa, Princess of Lamballe, was, however, paying a first visit to her father-in-law since being named to her new post.

The high-ceilinged antechamber where the two men waited boasted graceful new furniture upholstered in bright blue and yellow, set against white-on-white *Chinoiserie* wallpaper. Even those who complained bitterly of the ways Marie Antoinette flouted tradition had to admit she was amazing at discovering and inspiring the cabinetmakers, *ebenistes*, sculptors, and other artists who had achieved triumph after triumph, in room after room.

Both men knew she'd gone out with her brother-in-law, the Count of Artois, in a sleek two-wheeled carriage called a *cabriolet.* The Baron wondered if the Ambassador knew Artois liked to drive his cabriolet standing up? Or that his sister-in-law did the same when she took the reins? *But what is she to do, while she waits to fulfill the only obligation that really matters?* He felt as protective of her as a real grandfather, as ready to amuse and indulge her, as eager for a true consummation of a marriage nearing its fourth anniversary as she surely was. *If her morals were as loose as this Court's,* he wished, not for the first time, *she'd have taken a lover while she waits.* Such a pity Axel Fersen insisted on remaining her platonic champion. He was off on another overseas posting. *Pity he's so serious about his soldiering. And so faithful to wife and mistress.* He turned another *Almanach* page.

"She isn't riding, at least." Mercy broke the silence.

"The young must have their fun, yes?" Besenval shrugged. "Artois' wife has no interest in the out-of-doors, so he amuses himself by amusing his sister-in-law. Where is the harm?"

"The harm," Mercy's reply was sour and immediate, "is that she hasn't the least notion appearances are all that really matter in this country. *C'est pay ci,*" he repeated, in French, as Tonia burst into the room, breathless and beautiful in a Bertin creation striped in black and the vivid shade already called "cabriolet yellow" by a public clamoring for copies.

Both men rose, bowed, and remained standing through her animated excuses for her lateness.

"You should have heard the people shouting and cheering when they recognized us. The clucking tongues can't catch up when you move that fast." Her smile widened. "When we passed a statue of good king Henri the Fourth I saw a placard on the ground there. Guess what it said?"

"It said '*Resurrexit*' ?" Grandfather Gossip volunteered.

" 'Risen again' — yes! His subjects are so happy to have my husband on the throne they compare him to that ancient saint. They *love* us, I tell you. The people love us!"

"Love and respect, your Majesty," Mercy was unable to keep the tartness from his tone, "are two different things."

"I know. I know." Her tone was melted butter. "But I never *am* going to step in the same river twice, am I? Thank God I was brought up with the *freedom* -" the butter hardened-"to be exactly who I am. No more, but no less either."

"Who can argue with that?" Besenval blew her a kiss.

"So long as I fulfill my obligations, how does *anyone* dare think they have a right to put me in a cage?" Her glance went around the airy room. "No matter how beautifully it may be gilded?"

"You *are* loved," Besenval crooned.

"True enough," she agreed, reaching up to remove her hat, a rakish concoction of black velvet and yellow feathers. "But these are contrary people all the same. So contrary my mother ought to take that fact into account before she sends off my daily scolding." She shot Mercy a sharp look, tossed her hat to a waiting room-servant, and motioned both men to re-seat themselves.

"Surely you appreciate your mother's desire to shield you from unwarranted criticism," Mercy spoke slowly, carefully. "Beyond that, you can surely understand her genuine concern for your *future*."

"If you're about to remind me that I mustn't endanger myself by riding astride when 'General Krottendorf' is on the march, you can spare me."

Mercy the man flushed with embarrassment at her use of the code mother and daughter used for menstrual periods; Mercy the diplomat responded with, "Were you perhaps thinking of reassuring your mother when next you write?"

"Yes, I am." Tonia's smile blazed full out. "Forgive me for being so disagreeable. Now, gentleman, if you'll just let me know what you need from me, I'll be delighted to oblige."

Besenval spoke right up: "I need nothing but another smile, and your word you'll make an appearance at my masque tonight. Refreshments at cards to follow."

"I'll come, provided there's no *lasquanet.*" The card game was dear to the old Court's heart, and bored the new Queen Consort to tears.

"You needn't stay," Besenval assured her. "The promise of your appearance, however brief, will fill every seat. And the substantial admission charges go to charity."

"Which charity?"

"Plural, your Majesty. Charities." The Baron fussed in a pocket, held up a paper, squinted through his lorgnette, let it flutter to the floor. "I cannot find the dratted list, but it was widows. Or orphans — "

" — or who knows who? For you, Grandfather, I'll try, though I cannot promise. Without the Superintendent of my Household here, I've yet to look at today's list of obligations. Were you on it?"

"I haven't a clue, dear heart, but I'm certain Monsieur the Ambassador must be." The Baron tucked his *lorgnette* away. "Carry on, but mind you — no carrying on!"

The sweet, light peals of Marie Antoinette's laughter followed him out the door.

~ *Chapter Sixteen* ~

Louisa's time at Rambouillet passed peacefully, even pleasantly, though she couldn't make herself use the garden path to the grape arbor. She didn't pause as she passed the bedroom Papa Time still kept like a shrine. And when the ten days of her visit were over, she was more than ready to return to Versailles.

For Tonia, it was an occasion for celebration. Fatigued as Louisa was by her twenty-mile journey, she put in an appearance and performed her guest of honor duties at the *grand fete* held in her Majesty's newly-enlarged card-room.

Louisa had said her good-nights, and was in the process of leaving, when she noticed the petite stranger primping at a new foyer mirror. The convex surface distorted the young woman's reflection, but her cap of tight, glossy curls framed a clearly pretty face, heart-shaped and dimpled, with long-lashed eyes the color of violets, a pert, turned-up nose, and lips curved as a Cupid's bow. The newcomer was so absorbed in her image, dainty hands patting here and there, and Louisa so absorbed in watching her, neither noticed her Majesty's approach on the arm of Grandfather Gossip.

"Princess!" The old man greeted her. "You are *most* welcome home. And your charming friend?" He nodded to the woman at the mirror.

"We are not together," the petite stranger replied. Louisa felt ungainly as a giraffe as the little *gamine* ducked her curly head and dropped her curtsy: "Allow me to introduce myself. The Countess Jules of Polignac." Her voice was surprisingly robust and resonant. She stood again, brown eyes bright, Cupid's bow lips parting to show a perfect row of very white teeth. "I cannot tell you, your Majesty, what a thrill it is to be part of this marvelous evening. I have never been so honored, or so excited."

To Louisa, the Countess Jules' expression seemed clever, avid, sharp — *a fox's mask,* she thought, suddenly, miserably.

"Such a pleasure to make your acquaintance, Countess," she heard Tonia say. "Allow me to present Louisa, Princess of Lamballe, who is Superintendent of my Household. And the Baron Besenval, who specializes in knowing everything about everything that goes on."

"Guilty as charged," Grandfather Gossip quipped.

The Countess curtsied again, almost but not quite as deeply, in Louisa's direction. "An honor, Princess. And Baron."

"I have not seen you at Court before, Countess. Why?" Tonia asked.

"I lack the financial means, your Majesty."

"Can you mean it? Can you possibly mean it?"

Countess Jules dropped into another curtsy. "It is a truth I prefer not to hide, your Majesty."

"Oh, Countess," Tonia bent to the bowed, curly head, "such honesty! Such a breath of fresh air in this stuffy place! Come," she reached out, "let's see to it you enjoy your first Court visit. Surely not your last!"

Louisa kept the sudden sting of her tears in check. By the time she reached the privacy of her suite, she'd shamed herself into not shedding them.

The Countess Jules of Polignac and the *coterie* of family and friends she'd brought with her from the provinces all enjoyed what became three days at Court. It was long enough for Louisa to learn that the Countess was in her mid-twenties; married to a Colonel of the Regiment she never saw; and, despite her title, not at all well-off. Nothing unusual in any of that. What was out of the ordinary was Tonia's interest in her.

On the fourth morning, Tonia went to the Royal country estate of Fountainbleau with the entire Polignac party in tow, to watch the sun rise from a vantage point near the forest of Compeigne. The Superintendent of her Household was not among them.

Later that afternoon, when they met to go over correspondence, Tonia was still praising the dawn's early light: "Nothing but fresh air then. Nothing but stuffy old necessity now."

They began with latest "slap and kiss", the name Tonia had given to the letters from her mother the Empress, that unfailing pierced her daughter's armor of indifference.

"*No*, Mama, the King's Passageway hasn't proved an answer to your prayers." Tonia let the letter fall into her lap. "I can't write her that. Not today." She blinked against tears. "It isn't my *fault* I'm married to a man who cannot make me a mother."

"It will happen," Louisa soothed. "You are so young yet."

"Spare me the platitudes. When you were my age you'd been widowed how long? Two years?"

"Yes. I'm sorry."

"I'm sorry, too. But words won't change anything, will they? Enough for today." Tonia stood, making no move to retrieve her mother's letter from the carpet. "Why don't we breathe the fresh air? Walk to *Petite Trianon* perhaps?"

"All right," Louisa agreed, as she picked the letter up and returned it to the folio.

"I can't wait to watch the sun rise in a place of my own," Tonia hugged herself, "but it's taking so long. The expenditures aren't all coming from personal funds, and the new Finance Minister must approve the rest. He descends from a long line of snails." She pulled an appropriate face.

The Countess Jules was increasingly present, invited to come along on excursions, or encountered enroute. *Not accidentally*. Louisa kept such thoughts to herself; tried to appear pleasant, but felt she often failed. That Tonia didn't appear to notice her discomfort made Louisa feel even worse.

The 7th day of June, in the Year of Our Lord 1775

My Dear Papa Time,

You have asked for a full report of his Majesty's coronation.

I was among those invited. Like others, I did not attend, to show support for the financial reforms the new Foreign Minister, Monsieur Turgot, has instituted. Our newly-crowned King, God bless and save him, also gives these reforms his strong support.

He agreed that expenses incurred over a journey of two hundred miles called for a smaller party. This also spared the city of Rheims the burden of needed renovations to the great Cathedral.

I do not envy Monsieur Turgot. I rarely hear his name mentioned without some ridicule of his slogan: "No new taxes, no loans, no bankruptcy." It rings hollow, given the true state of the Royal Treasury.

I am aware that bills incurred for the Royal wedding remain unpaid, even as the coronation costs are added in …

~ Chapter Seventeen ~

In early August, a son was born to Louis Auguste's younger brother, Artois. Tonia followed protocol, attending the birth in the company of a dozen others. When his wife bore him a son after a labor of only two hours, no one dared express the thought they all must have shared: *it is the King who needs the son.*

As they braved the milling crowds in the *Oeil de Boeuf*, the Bull's Eye, a shout went up from a band of Parisian fishwives with no such scruples: "*Give us an heir!*" they shrieked at Her Majesty.

"Awful, awful!" The Countess Jules of Polignac fluttered up beside Tonia and Louisa. "How dare they scream at you?" She clasped her mitted hands. "Why must they hate you so?"

"Because, Countess, I am young and they are not. I am not ugly and they are."

And because you haven't borne a son, Louisa thought, thrusting both hands behind her at the sudden urge to bite her nails.

Six weeks and four letters to her mother the Empress later, Tonia informed Louisa she was considering a Dame of Honor position for the Countess Jules.

"But there are others with stronger claims to this Court position, others named to the list long before — "

"The list, the infamous *list*," Tonia snapped. "Will you let me see it, please?"

She'd taken to wearing a pair of sapphire earrings Louisa thought gaudy. They were a gift of the jeweler Boehmer, the most forward of several talented commoners who asked only that her Majesty wear their creations. The earrings jingled as she held the list up before the fan set with a magnifying glass, since she refused even a lorgnette, let alone spectacles.

"No praiseworthy candidates here." She squinted. "I'm sure dear Julie will agree."

"Dear Julie?" Louisa echoed.

"The Countess Jules' pet name. From her childhood."

Does "dear Julie" call you Tonia? "I have heard the Countess has a lover."

"Surely you know she's barren?" Tonia put the list aside. "Know that she can never bear children? A path she didn't choose."

"I — I hadn't heard," Louisa murmured. *A path I did choose.*

"And you must have heard that her husband the Colonel is posted elsewhere, enjoying his *amours,* in hopes of siring a natural, if not legitimate, son. And surely you've met dear Julie's own *amour,* the Count Vaudreil?"

"Last week, yes, at your quadrille."

"If her husband not only acknowledges, but approves the arrangement, who are we to judge? The honesty, the openness, it's so refreshing!"

How can she fail to see that "dear Julie's" barrenness frees her to flaunt her lover? How does she ignore the ever-increasing number of "dear Julie's" friends and relations? They never decline an invitation or a donation. How sly their smiles are, how upturned their palms.

Tonia picked up the list with a toss of her head that set the earrings to tinkling again. "I suppose I'll have to finish this task, but I must make ready for the horse races. I've been asked to give a trophy to the winning jockey."

"You cannot be there and back by three. Your schedule calls for receiving-" Louisa checked the list " — the English and Spanish ambassadors."

"Let them wait. They should get to know each other better. They can discuss the defeat of the Spanish Armada," Tonia grinned. "Won't you please come too, dear sister? An outing would do you good."

The leaves of the trees in the *Bois de Boulogne* made a blazing late October backdrop around the emerald turf of the central racecourse, where a gazebo covered in vines and flowers had been erected to shade the Royal party. The rest of the spectators made do with umbrellas and parasols.

Louisa stood silently in the small circle she and Tonia and "dear

Julie" and her lover Vaudreil made, oblivious to the crowd pushing and shoving not six feet away.

"You're the only smart one here," the Countess Jules remarked, brightly, when Louisa refused to wager on the race. "Those who do not play, cannot lose."

"Ah, but you never lose your enviable uprightness, Princess," Vaudreil the *amour* drawled lightly, his tone just at the edge of mockery. "How fortunate we are, to have your high-minded presence."

Louisa's forehead burned, but before she could gather her wits to respond, he turned smoothly away.

The horse from lower Normandy came in first. The little English jockey on his back bobbed and grinned and looked for all the world like a monkey in his green and white striped cap, as he made his victory circuit around the grass oval. Tonia herself handed him his trophy, amid thunderous shouting and applause.

The second week of Advent found King Louis the Sixteenth waiting for the Court physicians he'd summoned. When they arrived, he wasted no time raising his frank question: "What can be done about the sad situation of my marital relations?"

An hour passed as they offered alternatives. Each leaned as close as he dared to his Majesty's ear, jealous of the one before him, and the one to come. Halfway through their whispered advice, Louis Auguste realized the alternative urged over and over was the one he hated and feared most: circumcision.

"A simple removal of a superfluous bit of skin," they assured him, would correct his *phimosis*, the constriction of his foreskin that brought agony with every erection.

He'd tried all their salves and followed all their advice without success. He pulled his bulk to the front of his chair. Swinging his large head from side to side, he took them all in.

"I'll do it," he announced. "I'll have it. Off, that is. The foreskin. The sooner the better." He spoke in breathless chunks, as if he'd been running a long way.

The following night was agreed on.

Louis Auguste arrived at the appointed suite of rooms at the appointed time. A linen-draped trestle table, gilt-tasseled ropes dangling down on either side, awaited. Realizing they planned to tie him down brought a great gout of bile from his belly to his mouth. He stumbled backward into the nearest physician, sending the covered tray the man carried crashing to the floor. One look at the evil array of knives and hooks and razor-edges, all tossed together, all gleaming viciously under the intensity of candles surrounding the operating table, was all it took. His Majesty's substantial supper splashed the physicians' silk stockings and contaminated the surgical instruments.

He hadn't told Tonia of his decision, but she heard, almost as it happened, of his failure to carry it out. Grandfather Gossip hastened to her suites at four in the morning, determined to bring the news, so she wouldn't have it from the *Almanach*, so she could prepare herself for the cruel taunts sure to be hurled at her in the Bull's Eye as she went to Mass.

"If she does attend, it will be a miracle," the old man muttered, almost hopping along in his effort to keep up with his footman, wishing he'd waited for the chair-carriers. Once there, he did his best to make light of things. "The original visceral reaction, I guess you could say, right?"

"Not funny, Baron," she retorted. "Not funny at all."

"I know. Shall we send for the Princess? She can always cheer you."

"No, no need. Let her have her rest. We'd planned to meet for Mass."

"You are going to attend, then?"

"With my ears plugged, I assure you. Smiling prettily and waving happily." Her smile wasn't pretty, and her hands were chasing each other in her lap.

"My friend Horace Walpole was right," he said. "If you'd been born a — a milkmaid, you'd still cut a swath with your *joie de vivre.* 'Joy of life.' How apt the description is."

"Yes, well, we only live once, so we must take all we can from the experience. Something my father liked to say."

"Interesting bits for the history books, eh?"

"There's nothing new, is there?" She answered his question with one of her own, adding "except for what has been forgotten."

The first months of 1776 were gray and cold. Ice storms made the roads deadly. Food and fuel shortages made life in France harder than ever for all three of the country's estates: the commoners, from the new-rich *bourgeoisie* to poor peasants; the nobles, wealthy or impoverished; and the clergy, whether over-indulgent or ascetic. All could be heard complaining about the monarchy's response to the shortages. At best it was snail-paced; at worst, non-existent.

The Crown collected its taxes and revenues, while the Crown's subjects waited in vain for some form of benefit from them. England's colonists in the distant Americas were making the same complaints, weren't they?

The talk in the salons and cafes wasn't all political; gazette and eyewitness gossip about Marie Antoinette remained wildly popular. What she did! What she refused to do! The latest hair-do! Where and with whom she was last seen! Always, always, what she wore!

~ Chapter Eighteen ~

Snug in Tonia's inner chambers on a bitter February day, Louisa half-listened as her blood sister attempted a reversal of Grandfather Gossip's assessment of the man who'd made himself the talk of Paris, Versailles, and much of France. "This Anton Mesmer, he's nothing but a handsome charlatan," the old man grumbled, sipping at the chocolate Tonia had made them.

"He's ever so much more," Tonia's cup hit its saucer. "He's an Austrian. A countryman."

"Of that *other* country." The Baron arched the wispy eyebrows he refused to have plucked or made up.

"Mesmer is a genius."

"At what, my dear?"

"Astrology, Grandfather. It inspired his 'animal magnetism' theories."

"Theories you can explain to the skeptical likes of me?"

"Especially to the skeptical likes of you! Mesmer believes in a vital fluid bathing our nervous systems that's subject to the same magnetic forces moving the tides, the stars, and the planets."

The Baron set aside his chocolate cup and held both gnarled, ringed hands out to the ceramic stove. "What think you, Princess, of vital fluid?"

Louisa sat more upright. "I suppose it makes sense."

"You only suppose?" Tonia teased. "He's cured people, you know, of headaches. And other — complaints."

Louisa and the Baron both knew what she meant.

"Mesmer studied to be a priest," Tonia hurried on, "and then a lawyer. He got his medical qualifications late, at thirty-three."

"Like Christ," the Baron joked.

"Don't blaspheme. You can't see or touch the magnetic force because it's ethereal."

"Ethereal, eh?" The Baron grimaced. "Hard to pin down. How very convenient."

"Don't mock, Grandfather. Mesmer was offered more than twenty thousand *livres* for his secret. He wouldn't sell."

"Ah, but he must surely collect from those who attend his sessions."

"No one has mentioned collections," Tonia bristled.

The Baron's eyebrows arched higher. "Don't tell me you're planning to test his theories for yourself?"

"Not *by* myself." Tonia caught Louisa's eye. "My Superintendent will accompany me, of course."

"Just us?" Louisa had to ask.

"Just us."

"The two of you will stick out like a pair of sore thumbs," the Baron grumbled.

"Nonsense. We'll go disguised."

"Disguise all you want, dearest dear. You can't disguise the way you move, or hide the Princess' height." The sisters' six-inch height difference was a long-standing joke.

"So? I'll limp and she'll slump. Will that suit, Grandfather?"

"Enough to fool nobody, but your mind' is clearly made up."

"Clearly."

It rained the April night the blood sisters, accompanied by the Countess Jules of Polignac, who'd succeeded in having herself invited, arrived under oilskin wraps at Mesmer's establishment on the *Boulevard des Invalides.*

"Dear Julie's" chatter came easily; it took longer for Louisa to overcome her discomfort at being so removed from the familiar. The much ballyhooed "music of the spheres" filled the large chamber. Concentrating on it, Louisa traced the source to a human voice, coming from an upper floor gallery masked by the same elaborate draperies spangled with stars, moons, and planets that covered the walls.

"The design is said to match Mesmer's robes," Tonia whispered in Louisa's ear, from her seat between blood sister and dear friend.

Nine others also sat around an enormous oak barrel, filled with a mixture of water and iron filings magnetized by Mesmer himself.

Iron bars bristled from the barrel, each clutched in an ungloved hand. The unseen voice went up and down the scales, tonal and atonal.

"Now what?" The Countess' stage-whisper cut through the music of the spheres.

"Now we hold fast," a woman across the circle replied. "This is my third attendance. The experience grows more powerful," the woman shivered, "and the effect lasts long after Mesmer has completed his uncanny contact."

"Because he Mesmer-izes you." Dear Julie's pert comment brought open laughter from everyone except Louisa.

"I've heard he also puts you in a trance," one of the men remarked. "What's the point of that?"

"To ensure the suggestions he gives you take hold," the woman beside him explained.

"What sort of suggestions?"

"Things you'll do after he brings you from your trance." The woman paused for effect. "Without knowing *why* you're doing them."

"Can he suggest things you wouldn't ordinarily do?" It was Tonia, giving voice to Louisa's concern.

"Oh, no," the woman chuckled, "but he's been known to suggest foolishness."

"Such as?"

"Well, on my last visit he suggested to my friend that she cluck like a chicken every time someone opened a fan."

"And she did?"

"Absolutely. Most amusing."

The music of the spheres broke off as Mesmer appeared, clad in a star-spangled swirl of floor-length cloak, arms aloft, one waving an elaborately twisted wrought iron wand.

Excited murmurs rose as Mesmer began his circuit: lowering his handsome head; raising his wand; laying hands on each believer; using his seductive voice to bring about a trance state. One by one, he whispered what only that person could hear, while the others waited their turn, or regained their awareness.

Louisa didn't think Mesmer succeeded with her. He kept repeating she was growing sleepy, but she wasn't. Or maybe she was: just as he moved on, the whole chamber seemed to ripple momentarily, as if she were seeing it reflected in water.

He completed his circuit, vanishing with a flourish behind his star-spangled draperies. The Royal party went on to an "entertainment" given by a no-longer-distant relative of Countess Jules of Polignac.

The town-house was so new it reeked of paint and gilding chemicals, overlaid with too many competing perfumes. The close air in the overcrowded music room was hard to breathe, and the tenor's recital so awful Louisa found herself wondering if he'd paid for the opportunity to put his wretched excuse for a voice on display before this mostly noble audience. Such bribes happened with dismaying frequency among the Polignac clan.

When the assault on their ears was over, the honored guests repaired to the billiard room where the *buffet elegante* awaited. Anchoring the *hors d'oeuvres* display was a sailing ship with a hull made of force-meat and a deck planked with veal strips. The galley was filled with little birds in a ragout. Skewers of sweetbreads protruded from each side of the ship, alternating with cannons fashioned from foie-gras and bacon. The mast flew a cocks-comb pennant, and the rigging was festooned with sausages. A display of live lobsters, circled by a moat of green-tinted ice, came next.

The tentacles trembled at Louisa. Eyes stared atop waving stalks. The rippling feeling returned to engulf her. She fainted, amid a chorus of shrieks and cries.

Louisa came to seated in an armchair, terrified of the strangers' faces filling her field of vision. Panic overtook her as she clawed at air, at black, at nothing.

"Stop, please!" Tonia's voice cut through the chaos. "Ease yourself. You'll be fine, you're all right. It was only a joke."

Louisa shook her head. Someone offered a dampened handkerchief, murmuring "at least we know it works."

"What works?" Louisa heard herself ask.

"The silly suggestions Mesmer makes," Tonia answered.

"He made a suggestion to me?"

"Yes, and we thought it would be amusing to prove it for ourselves."

"We?"

The Countess' fox-face appeared over Tonia's shoulder. "It *was* funny, you know, she chortled. "Face to face with a lobster and whoops! Down you went."

"I was assured the effect vanishes within hours," Tonia's whisper reached only Louisa's ear. "We'll soon be sharing our lobster soufflés."

Louisa nodded her excuses and fled the room.

Tonia came after her. "Don't go off this way, please. No one meant any harm."

"Harm still happened. I was so frightened I fainted."

Tonia's blue eyes narrowed, along with her smile. "No need to make such an issue, is there? No harm was intended. None. Come on back with me."

"I think not."

"Why not?" There was a petulant edge to Tonia's question.

Louisa couldn't respond at first. "Because I am," she finally began, "not needed."

"Of *course* you are."

"No, I'm not. Not in the way I once was."

"And when was *that*?"

Silence stretched. Neither woman looked at the other. Louisa was the first to break it. "When you still had need of a sister. Not by birth, but — you made me your blood sister because I was your friend. A friend you could confide in. Could *trust* to tell you the truth. Keep your innermost secrets. Support you in all your decisions — "

" — to love me," Tonia broke in, "without question, or condition?"

"Yes. Yes!"

"I once had *just* such a friend." Louisa had to lean in to hear what Tonia said next. "What do you suppose has happened to her?" The words seemed to come from a great distance, suddenly, as something foggy rose in the air, and the room became an impossibly long corridor.

Louisa's next awareness was of Tonia shaking her, clearly agitated and upset. "This isn't Mesmer's work, dear sister, this is mine. I'm sorry, so sorry. What a cruel and stupid thing to say. You know I didn't mean it."

"I know."

The crack was there, though. They knew that, too.

~ Chapter Nineteen ~

Her Majesty did not object to the Superintendent of her Household's request to return to Rambouillet for a visit of unspecified length.

Concern with Papa Time's health wasn't the real reason Louisa, Princess of Lamballe, was leaving Court, but neither woman acknowledged it. They maintained formal relations, avoiding any mention of that distancing night.

Louisa no longer needed to make excuses for refusing invitations to anything involving dear Julie, because those invitations were no longer forthcoming.

A month passed, two, another. At Rambouillet, Louisa kept the first hour after waking not only for prayer, but for breathing, the way she'd learned as a girl from her nurse Serafina. It was better than prayer, sometimes. She heard Mass most mornings, took a spare breakfast, and tended to the Superintendent of Household dispatches that arrived weekly by courier relay from the Royal stables.

Louisa lingered over each of Tonia's large, looping notations in the margins of official petitions. She also wrote informal notes on the papers she used to pin comment to Mademoiselle Bertin's fabric swatches. They said everything and nothing: *"All is well." "Hoping your father-in-law improves." "So busy with everything."*

Louisa did her best to keep her replies casual. After she sent them off, she would walk in the gardens, though never to the grape arbor.

In July of 1776, the Duke of Orleans went to his eternal reward. By sheer coincidence, Papa Time developed another of his frequent, severe catarrhs a day after news of the old Duke's death arrived.

It spared Louisa, who insisted on staying with him, from attending the funeral ceremonies, followed by the installation of the new Duke of Orleans — Papa Time's son-in-law, her nemesis, the Duke of Chartres. As head of the House of Orleans, he inherited additional fortune, along with the Palais Royale in Paris, where the social influence his wife already enjoyed ascended to new heights.

The full harvest moon was rising when Ambassador Mercy surprised Louisa with a visit.

"Have you seen these?" he inquired, without preamble, as he handed her a sheet of fine linen paper. What appeared at first to be hand-tinted borders of curlicued scrollwork swam before her eyes as she realized they were naked, writhing bodies, with recognizable faces: dear Julie, Vaudreil, Artois, Fersen. And — Louisa gasped — *Tonia.*

"The quality of the paper and the high caliber of the artwork indicate this came from the Duke of Chartres — excuse me," Mercy corrected himself, "the 'Duke of *Orleans*'. This is a product of the pornographic press he operates in supposed secrecy, most likely within the Palais Royale, since that is his now. Shocking stuff, but I'm afraid such sordidness has become all the rage." Mercy paused. "He is your brother-in-law, is he not?'

"We are estranged," Louisa thrust the sheet back at him, but not before the verse inside the obscene borders seared itself into her memory:

All of us ask, in whispers:
Is the King able or not?
The sad Queen despairs, la, la, la.
Someone says: he can't get it up.
Another, he can't get it in.
Still another: he's a transverse flute, la, la, la.
But that's not the real trouble
Reports the Royal clitoris:
All that comes out is rain water, la, la, la ...

"Estranged?" Mercy repeated, giving close attention to his lace cuffs. "Then I can hardly ask you to have a word with him, can I? In the interests of the throne to which, as a further elevated Prince of the Blood, he can lay closer claim." His handkerchief materialized, dabbed at his lips. "Times are difficult enough without — stooping — to such disgusting allegations. Not to mention embellishments."

His handkerchief disappeared up one lace-cuffed sleeve. "Had you known Orleans was *capable* of this sort of thing?"

I know he is capable of anything. The thought was so loud in her mind, Louisa was afraid she'd spoken.

"I'm sorry to have troubled you, Princess."

"No trouble," she managed to murmur.

Late afternoon found Louisa in a distant corner of Rambouillet's gardens, on a stone bench in the grapevine-covered gazebo she hadn't entered since the day her brother-in-law stalked her.

"You bribed my tire-woman," she'd blurted out when he appeared, dressed for the boudoir, in velvet slippers and a soft linen shirt, tucked into doeskin breeches.

He'd run his ringed fingers over his flower-sprigged vest. "The handiwork of my dear wife." His eyes were oily black; his voice, an insinuating whisper. "Your sister-in-law."

"I barely know her." Louisa could hardly hear herself.

"But you know your tire-woman," he went on. "The one who won't smile because she is missing so many teeth? The one who thinks we are discussing a gift for my dear wife? Who has reached the stage of her pregnancy where she feels the full vigor of the babe within." One be-ringed hand reached for the fastenings of his breeches. "This is far more vigorous." The laces loosened around his erection as he pulled what looked like a whitish worm from a vest pocket.

"The bladder of an unborn lamb," he'd waved it at her. "Insurance against my seed creating life in your womb." He'd wrapped it around his stiff, bobbing member. "Your marriage has been consummated," he'd gone on, as pleasantly as if they stood in a crowd at a public function, "so there is no threat to your virginity. And no threat of further pursuit. I seldom come to Rambouillet, or Versailles, and I am told you have no interest in the delights of Parisian life. We are distant relations, living separated lives."

She had never forgotten how the greenish light filtered through the large flat leaves, alive with the sound of the bees she'd wished, frantically, would sting them, would stop him. They hadn't, and he'd come nearer the stone bench.

"You remind me of a rabbit, Princess. Stiff with fright. Tangled in traces that need loosening. Loosening," he'd repeated. Reaching out for her cambric underdress, he'd pulled it below her breasts. "How fortunate I am the day-fashion favors such flimsy covering for such beauty," he'd whispered. "Such beauties."

He'd pinched the tips of each nipple, hard enough to cause pain. A purgatory passed, an eternity, until a trickle of moisture rose in her fear-dried mouth. She dared a direct look at his leering face as the trickle became a pool; her cheeks pursed, and she spit in his face.

He'd mottled red; the skin around the left eye he'd failed to close twitched. She'd sensed the war taking place within him, between the monster who wished to break her bones, and the smooth survivor, who knew when to retreat.

The survivor won.

"I forgot, Madame," he'd said, "your Italian roots, in the legendary House of Savoy. Wasn't it Turin where you spent your sheltered childhood? Where they venerate a cloth claimed to be Christ's shroud?" He'd snickered then, tucking himself away as if he'd only finished urinating, before he turned and left.

Louisa returned to the Chateau at dusk. She took her dinner early, in the distracted company of Papa Time, and went to her bed filled with a sadness so heavy no amount of Serafina's breathing exercise lifted it.

~ Chapter Twenty ~

Back at Versailles, Ambassador Mercy arranged to show Tonia the loathsome broadside. To his utter dismay, she shrugged it off.

"At least I'm depicted with men," she giggled. "They have me in love with women, too. The Princess of Lamballe, for example. I have loved her for years. As my *sister,* not my lover. They couple me with 'Dear Julie', the Countess Jules now, too. Ridiculous! She only has eyes for Monsieur Vaudreil. *He* is her lover!"

Mercy sat stunned.

"I know this upsets you, and I apologize," Tonia soothed him, "but what can I do about it? People will think as they choose, and they will write what they please. If I react with outrage, or even dignify them with a response, it will only give them more cause for attack."

"I fear," Mercy said, slowly and deliberately, after a long pause, "that you may be falling victim to your own celebrity."

"And I fear," her mouth smiled, but not her eyes, "that you may be falling victim to foolish fears."

Grandfather Gossip followed Mercy to Rambouillet.

"Have you befriended a certain 'green eyed monster'?" he asked Louisa, gently. "Is that your reason for staying on and on here?"

"My father-in-law," Louisa murmured, embarrassed at her excuse-giving.

"Your father-in-law, with all due respect, appears to be getting on well enough."

"He often suffers from catarrh," Louisa couldn't look at him.

"Versailles would be a happier place with you there. This Countess Jules and her *coterie* — their escapades don't enhance her Majesty's reputation." He grunted with the effort to close his gnarled hands around the knobbed head of his cane. "And even though I brought them together, I fear the attention she pays to my protégé Fersen adds fuel to the gossip fires."

"Count Fersen has no wish for carnal connection because he is her platonic champion. Platonic," Louisa repeated. "Idealized. Free of the physical, but a champion who would lay down his life for her."

"And if Axel Fersen were a cat, he'd lay down eight more. He has had many opportunities to shift from platonic to passionate, but you and I know, Princess, he will never overstep."

"And neither will she." Louisa found her voice.

"You also know she doesn't give a fig or a feather for public opinion. Takes a perverse pleasure in alienating the 'old guard'. They speak nothing but ill. They take care, still, to keep it behind her back, but they despise the way she flouts them, supporting artists and artisans and merchants and charities with no *hint* of noble connections." The tip of his cane rapped the floor. "And now these vile verses circulate everywhere. Even her staunch admirers have been heard wondering if she might be up to something."

"If *she* knows she isn't, that is all that matters."

His shrewd old eyes took her measure. "Tell me something, Princess. I know she can be downright outrageous if a fancy to flirt overtakes her when there's a man about, but does she really fancy women as well?"

"As friends, yes. *Friends.*"

"And as sister," the Baron reached for her hand. "Don't be such a sober-sides. Come now, dimple up."

The flow of official correspondence to and from Rambouillet increased through 1776, so much so Louisa had to agree with Tonia that a position of Household Secretary should be created, to be filled with someone outside of Versailles, chosen, the way Her Majesty so favored, for ability, not rank or influence. This Household Secretary would report to the Great Chateau to assist the Superintendent of her Majesty's Household, currently in residence at her father-in-law's estate.

Louisa had delayed as long as she could. With the year drawing to a close, she consented to a month's stay, to select and train her Household Secretary. "You must make the choice among the final three,"

Tonia had written, "not a one with a hint of a Court connection."

Will we be two sisters, or three? Can I free myself of — Louisa couldn't allow the word jealousy, even in her thoughts — *of my reluctance to share Court life again? For even a month?*

Their only contact that first week at Versailles was at Mass. Tonia was delighted to see her; Louisa was delighted Countess Jules didn't attend. Most of her days were occupied with travel to and from Paris, where she met with each of the final Household Secretary candidates. She visited two earnest, accomplished, overawed girls, one at a milliner's shop, the other at a glovemaker's, before meeting the third, at a music-master's.

Catherine Hyde was respectful but not awestruck. She was refreshingly matter-of-fact about her secretarial abilities, her fluency in English and German, and the remarkable singing voice she'd been blessed with. A voice that brought Louisa to tears as she listened to the simple but moving *rondeau,* chosen without knowing it was one of the Princess's childhood favorites.

"She also performed at His Majesty's Coronation in 1775," the music-master bragged.

Louisa's lengthy conversation with the nun who'd received the child when she was first sent to France revealed the harsher realities of life she'd glimpsed in Catherine's green eyes. She'd been English-born, on the "wrong side of the blanket," with parent or parents able to see to her upbringing and education removed from her birthplace.

The nun, Sister Catherine, admitted her affection for the child might have begun with the coincidence of their same names, but that it had grown stronger year by year. "The other girls were legitimate, most lacked interest in the foreign orphan — "

" — an orphan?" Louisa had asked.

For answer, the nun had produced a fawn-colored kidskin portfolio. "All you might choose to know, including their last will and testament."

The blood sisters came together through the final week, but their time was spent settling the new Household Secretary into the routine they followed for nearly a year.

Catherine Hyde continued to live in Paris, presenting herself at Versailles each Monday, to prepare the correspondence and other items she took to Rambouillet on Wednesday. The "Inglesina" — Tonia's nickname for the tri-lingual Mademoiselle — returned by carriage that evening; Louisa sent the completed items back three Fridays of each month. On the fourth, she brought them herself, met with her Household Secretary, and, at times, Her Majesty, before returning to Rambouillet after Saturday Mass.

Grandfather Gossip made the trek to Rambouillet once each season, grumbling about his rheumatism, to share the tidbits he called "true facts" to the flow of dispatches.

He arrived in August with an invitation requesting the pleasure of Louisa's company at a dinner honoring her Majesty's brother Joseph.

"You really can't refuse her Majesty's invitation." Grandfather Gossip lifted his wispy-bearded chin. "He is Emperor of Austria now."

"He co-rules," Louisa commented.

"And I won't argue that it's the Empress who rules that royal roost, Princess. Be that as it may, aren't you curious to meet one of her Majesty's family members?"

Louisa wasn't. Her curiosity was more than satisfied by the only correspondence she attended to herself. Like "General Krottendorf", the mother-daughter letters marched on, filled with intimate detail and unwanted advice.

"I always say," his chin dropped, "look to family trees for fruitful traits."

~ *Chapter Twenty One* ~

A rainbow of fresh flowers covered the table where the King and Queen Consort, Ambassador Mercy, and the Princess of Lamballe were seated, along with the guest of honor. Countess Jules of Polignac's place had been hastily removed when she was called to a cousin giving premature birth.

Louisa had seen only likenesses of the Emperor Joseph. Shorter than his sister by almost a head, with a more pronounced Hapsburg jawline, he had Tonia's clear sky-blue eyes. Where hers were large and expressive, though, his all but bulged, and his unfortunate blinking habit drew even greater attention to them. His speech was blunt, his manner crudely direct, and he monopolized the conversation.

Tonia wore a new gown of French blue Lyons silk, woven to match her eyes, created for the occasion by Rose Bertin, the commoner dressmaker who'd become Tonia's "Minister of Fashion".

Tonia's makeup was expertly applied, so heavily Louisa wondered if it was meant to match the impact of the new pair of diamond earrings dangling almost to her bared shoulders.

"To my sister, still the youngest and fairest of us all," Emperor Joseph raised his goblet as the *foie gras* was served. He repeated the toast twice before they finished it. "I am much struck by something, dear sister," he announced, as their palate-cleansing champagne *sorbets* were carried away. "When you enter a room, every candle it contains is lighted. When you leave — a minute, an hour, a day later — they are extinguished. And replaced." His blink became even more rapid. "Coming through your salon earlier, I had to dodge three maid-servants, scuttling away with aprons full of candles."

"They resell them," Tonia explained.

"At an exorbitant price," he snapped back, "since they are the Queen's candles."

"It is the custom *c'est pays ci*, in this country." Her shrugged shoulders reached her diamond earrings.

"In France?"

"No, dearest brother. This country of Versailles."

"And what a country it is!" Joseph's eyes bulged further. "These halls, these staircases! Turkish bazaars!" He pinched his nostrils shut. "The sweet smell of the Crown's profits must mask the stench. Does no one here believe in bathing?"

Mercy could be heard, discretely choking, and Tonia went pink-cheeked beneath her makeup. "You always were the worst tease of *all* my brothers. I *have* water closets, you know, and I *use* them. My hair is washed daily, before it's dressed. And I *don't* drench myself in perfumes."

The Emperor let go of his nose. "I know."

"Think for a moment, brother dear. If you tear up a tree by its roots, it dies, doesn't it? I cannot uproot a custom as fixed as the sellers here, or the Crown's candle revenues. I do enough that meets with disapproval as it is." She wiggled her fingers behind her earrings, "Take these; the work of the jeweler Boehmer. Unpleasant person, given to over-pricing, but he is especially good with diamonds." She waved at his plate of food. "Try your dumplings. Truffle-filled, just the way you love them. Or used to."

The pastry course was followed by sole soufflé with lobster sauce, roasted partridge on toast, and grilled rib of Charolais beef with bone marrow.

Watching the Emperor fill his mouth and empty his glass, Louisa barely tasted anything. Mercy also watched, with his mouth set in a line so thin she doubted a knife would fit between his lips. Even Louis Auguste, who rarely paid attention to anything beyond his plate or the servers' platters, noticed.

Just before dessert, the Emperor half-stood, swaying on his feet: "You, dear Tonia," he hiccupped, "have applied more color to one blushing cheek than Rubens used on an entire nude."

"That will do, sir." His Majesty's near whisper could have been a shout.

"What will do?" The Emperor demanded. When he got no answer, he turned his bulging, bloodshot eyes to Mercy.

"Sire," Mercy's handsome features remained a neutral mask, "it was surely not your intent, but you appear to imply that her Majesty is — is — "

" — dissipated," Tonia finished for him. "The word you want is 'dissipated'. Brother dear, how kind of you to want to save me from myself." The jeweler Boehmer's earrings danced. "No need, I assure you. Now where are our snow eggs? My sweet tooth aches for them."

The meringue and custard dessert was brought. Louis Auguste concentrated on his plate, excusing himself the moment he finished.

Tonia, uncharacteristically, rose and went with him.

Louisa pled fatigue, returning alone to apartments so refurbished since her last brief visit she barely recognized them.

The Emperor Joseph came to Tonia's apartments the following night, unexpectedly and unannounced. "What say *you*, Princess?"

Louisa looked up, startled, from the needlework she'd brought.

"Married seven years, three as Queen Consort, and my sister remains childless. What say you?" He repeated.

"May *I* not have some say?" Tonia bristled.

"You may *not*, sister. I asked the Superintendent of your Household for *her* opinion."

"Go on, then," Tonia was clearly annoyed.

"She's quite bright, this sister of mine. Sees through things, and people, quite clearly. It surprises me she doesn't seem to see through these upstart newcomers."

Louisa lifted the cloth on her lap to hide her flush of guilty pleasure at his obvious reference to Countess Jules and her coterie.

"What is *that* supposed to mean?"

"It means your pursuit of their idle excesses leaves you precious little time for his Majesty."

"Are you saying it's all *my* fault?" Spots of color appeared along her cheekbones. "You've been here three *days*. Hardly long enough to get a true picture."

Tonia's brother said no more; he left, as scheduled, the following day. Louisa had also planned to go; Tonia all but begged her to extend her stay, "until my card party, please?"

"Card party?" Louisa repeated. "But gambling at cards is prohibited at Versailles."

"Prohibited, perhaps, but a King may set such a prohibition aside. And so my husband agreed to a single gambling session," she wasn't looking Louisa in the eye, "provided it is confined to your apartments."

"*My* apartments?"

"To avoid the clucking tongues if I'd ordered others readied, the way I did yours." Her smile was deliberately irresistible. "Isn't everyone after me to economize?"

Louisa sat unsmiling, head down, silent.

Late the following morning, however, she held out a sheaf of receipts and acquisitions she hadn't seen until her earlier meeting with Catherine Hyde.

"If I read these right," she said, when Tonia refused to take them, "they show charges for reimbursements *far* in excess of what is approved for payment from your Household accounts." Louisa took a deep breath. "Who is reaping profit where it's not warranted?"

"Why concern yourself?" Tonia's jaw jutted the way it only did when they were alone. "You can't even be bothered to live here anymore." Something left her eyes. "Some blood sister you are."

Some blood sister you are. The ringing in Louisa's ears obscured the immediate apology.

~ Chapter Twenty Two ~

The 15th day of August, feast of the Assumption of the Virgin Mary, in the year of Our Lord 1777

Dear Papa Time,

This will reach you before I return. How I wish I were there already.

You wished to know if the tales of her Majesty's gambling are embellished, and so I send my first-hand descriptions.

At dusk, the bankers arrived from Paris with their portfolios of pre-printed promissory notes.

The games of faro and lasquanet and baccarat and chemin-de-fer went on in my apartments all through that night, past the dawn, through the following day, and after the sun set again …

Louisa set her swan quill down and let her head fall back, glad of the loose wrapper and night braids, after the late, long hours cinched into stiff bodice and tight shoes.

She'd hated seeing the puffed bluish skin beneath Tonia's eyes, their sparkle dulled with fatigue. Hated watching her skip proper meals, to follow the fad the Earl of Sandwich started when he had cold meat between slices of bread served to him at his gaming table, so he could eat without stopping his play.

Tonia had lost interest in billiards, with its good-natured wagering. This betting was serious. Winning required skills with cards she also possessed, so she rarely lost. What upset Louisa most was the look on Tonia's face when she won — mindlessly gleeful as an infant sucking on a sugar-cloth.

Louisa rolled her shoulders and picked up her quill.

... When His Majesty made his first appearance the following afternoon. Her Majesty was ready with an explanation. "Your Majesty lifted the prohibition to allow a single gaming session. You never said how long it had to be...

The quill went down again. When Tonia told him the length was thirty-five hours and counting, silence descended.

"Go on!" Louis Auguste had slapped one huge thigh. "You are all worthless. The whole lot of you." He'd lumbered away laughing, shedding powder from his ill-fitting wig.

There was nothing more to write to Papa Time. Not tonight.

In November of that year Louis Auguste made another attempt to go through with the circumcision the Royal physicians and surgeons urged, and the Royal advisors advised. He took care to arrive blindfolded, after drinking deeply of the relaxation draughts he'd refused before.

The operation went off flawlessly, with the surgeons declaring it a success even as the physicians finished dressing the wound with scraped lint and a linen bandage. Louis Auguste healed with heartening speed.

The knocks were timid, but they still woke Tonia in the middle of the night before Christmas.

"Enter," she called out, softly. The panel concealing the King's Passage creaked and pivoted as her nervous husband, nightshirt billowing unevenly from his half-fastened breeches, stepped heavily across the raised threshold.

He cleared his throat twice before he said "I come to bid you a happy Christmas. And a good-night."

Tonia pushed her feather-bed aside and undid the blue ribbons at the neck of her diaphanous night-robe. Reclining against her satin pillows, the vision of a milk-and-honey Venus, she opened her arms, whispering "a happy Christmas, and a good night to *you*."

On the rare occasions when he'd come to her bed these last long years, she'd been able to shut her eyes against the sting of his salt-clean sweat, but not her ears, against his painful outcries.

Tonight's cry was different, as he pushed his breeches down to reveal an erection, swaying and trembling beneath the sag of his stomach. Shorn of its tight skin-sheath, the reddened tip glistened wetly as he lumbered towards her.

Tonia closed her arms around as much of him as she could. For an eternity of seconds, as he pushed himself into her, he softened and began to slide out.

"No," he wailed. "*Nooo.*"

Tonia's private muscles rolled and rippled around his shrunken manhood, willing him hard, coaxing him back, until, at long last, gasping and thrashing, he ejaculated. "*Yesss!*"

For the first time in her life, Tonia felt a man's passion find release against her secret skin. She reached up, kissed her husband full on his fleshy lips, and burst into tears.

The 8th day of June, in the year of Our Lord 1778

The date at the top of the page was as far as Louisa got in her response, before she sat back, lost in thought of the sea change Tonia's note had made.

It was the first item in the blue leather dispatch box the Household Secretary who'd earned Louisa's increasing trust conveyed weekly, on horseback as of this spring. The earnest girl with the wondrous voice, independent mind, and head-full of red curls, had revealed her yearning to see the world between Paris, Versailles and Rambouillet from the back of a horse instead of through a carriage window. Louisa arranged for a suitable mare from Versailles' stables to be kept near the girl's convent, where she lived in her own rooms. At Rambouillet, her own less grand writing desk stood beside the table made to cradle Louisa's.

She rubbed her finger over the note's wax stamp, the Royal couple's dolphin coat of arms. The second seal, set with her initials "M.A." made an official announcement of Tonia's hasty scrawl:

It has been three months since the march of General Krottendorf!

Tonia hadn't gone on to urge Louisa to return.

Louisa traveled to Versailles at least once each month, spending more of the day with her secretary than her blood sister, and leaving before Mass the following morning. Their shared times were cordial, but not close; neither arranged for privacy.

At Rambouillet, Papa Time was in most ways the kind, abstracted eccentric he'd always been. The one way he wasn't involved recalling who people were. Or why they were there.

On the morning of August 7th, 1778, Marie Antoinette went to her husband's apartments, dropped a perfect curtsy, and said "I have come, Sire, to complain to you about one of your subjects who has been so audacious as to give me a blow on the stomach."

Louis Auguste looked up from the piece of ironwork in the clamps on his table. "You are quickened?"

"I am quickened."

His embrace engulfed her. The same day, with his approval, she donated twelve thousand *livres* to the city of Paris, and another four thousand to the town of Versailles, all to be given to women unable to afford childbirth nurses. Marie Antoinette was stubborn about revealing the donor; the gifts were given "from an anonymous benefactor."

"You never let your charities be known," Louisa remarked, when she saw the record of the transaction on her next visit.

"As long as I have the means to do something, why shouldn't I? And if I prefer to do so without seeking public praise or blame, why not?"

"The Crown has huge debts — "

" — Many dating from before my time. What's one more entry on the debit side of the ledger? I feel so *fortunate* these days. If I choose to share my good fortune by funding nurses for women who wouldn't have them otherwise, where's the harm?"

"I don't recall saying there was any harm."

Silence fell, and lengthened, before Tonia broke it. "I don't recall your saying a single word about the fact I've stopped gambling."

"I *have* noticed, and I'm sorry."

"I hardly even play cards anymore," Tonia went on, increasingly indignant. "Billiards are my only indoor amusement, and I don't wager on the outcome. I sleep required hours, and beyond. I eat only nourishing foods. I walk every evening, out of doors in fair weather, indoors in foul. I look after my health, and my child's, you know?"

"I know."

~ Chapter Twenty Three ~

Tonia continued to be a fashion innovator, co-designing the comfortable, stylish percales made in Mademoiselle Rose Bertin's shop. Loose and lightweight, the pastel dresses couldn't be bought, or even copied, quickly enough to satisfy a demand that went well beyond the borders of France, to England, the continent, even the colonies, embroiled as they were in their war for independence.

Out of doors, Tonia wore the gowns with large, soft, straw hats, alive with trailing ribbons anchoring the light muslin veils protecting against insects. She was, unquestionably, more beautiful than ever before, her skin blushing peachy cream against radiant white. A new peacefulness marked her expression, and a new grace her movements, even five months into her pregnancy.

Her Majesty's unpowdered hair gleamed in the full moonlight as she exchanged gossip with the Baron Besenval, her only walking companion this night. She'd refused a sedan chair; his rheumatism had him accept his. The latest topic was the recent *soiree* held in honor of the American Emissary and Plenipotentiary Benjamin Franklin, and Joseph George Gilbert, Marquise de La Fayette.

"Quite a diverse group attended," the old man reported, "all elbowing for position, all eager to pay respects before both men depart. La Fayette's taking quite a leadership position there. He certainly cut quite a figure in his uniform. And those blue eyes, so unusual for someone with red hair."

"We've not met, Grandfather, but I hear his wife calls him 'a statue in search of a pedestal'."

"His new post might just end his search."

Their laughter followed them down the terrace stairs and out along garden pathways bathed in full moon light of mid-summer.

"Monsieur Franklin had these sent ahead of this visit," she nodded to a pair of graceful trees with branches spread like *paniers* and glossy green leaves setting off fragrant white flowers. "*Franklinias*, they're called. Named for him by his botanist friend John Bartram."

"Bartram should have named the tree for you," the Baron sniffed.

October turned Versailles' still-blooming *franklinias* to a blaze of crimson foliage, as Tonia's time grew nearer. The changes in her body astonished her; once the continuing nausea had subsided, she'd welcomed them all. She was eager for the child to come, ready to become a mother, wanting that title more than she'd ever imagined.

"I cannot understand why she *pressures* me so."

Louisa and her Household Secretary, the Inglesina Catherine Hyde, watched her Majesty lift her mother the Empress's latest letter from the shelf her lap had become. "Advise me about wet nurses and baby names, mother dearest," she squinted as she read further, "but she is insisting I persuade my husband to support her and my brother the co-ruler in yet *another* of their meaningless Austrian conflicts, with — I don't even know who!"

Louisa nodded to Catherine, who recognized the signal to take no notes.

"The French Crown is already supporting enough war. Floating huge loans, to — what are those colonies called?"

"The United States, your Majesty," the Inglesina bowed an answer, "of America."

"I do not interfere in politics, or advise my husband. Except on the subject of these loans. But when I pointed out that the King of France is contributing to the overthrow of the king of England? He shrugged his shoulders and smiled his smile." She folded her mother's letter into a triangle, pinched it up between thumb and forefinger, and aimed it at Louisa. "Give me a polite response to her, please? One I can copy and sign."

In late October an ugly incident took place in the Bull's Eye at Versailles, where the main galleries met and people thronged around the clock.

Minutes before Tonia and Louisa passed through the *oeil de boeuf* with their retinue, a rock was hurled with such force it shattered a mirrored panel, embedding itself in the plaster of the wall. The words and pictures on the parchment wrapped around the rock claimed her brother-in-law Artois fathered the child she carried, and condemned *l'Autrichienne* as a spy for Austrian interests.

Tonia attempted to laugh it off. "Playing spy with this abdomen requiring a wheelbarrow? And that bastard claim? So old it has a beard. People can be such fools."

"People can also be dangerous."

It was impossible to determine if the male voice came from the retinue or the crowd.

~ Chapter Twenty Four ~

The 8th day of December, in the year of Our Lord 1778

Dearest Papa Time,

I send this hastily, by the hand of my Household secretary, who will bring your reply when she returns.

In your last letter, you urged me again to come home once her Majesty's child has been delivered. I have given much thought, and prayer, to your urging, but cannot yet be certain …

Marie Antoinette's labor began just before midnight on December 19th, 1778. Her water broke at eight the next morning. Her blood sister had returned to Versailles the preceding week, with plans to remain until Twelfth Night. Footmen arrived at noon, to escort Louisa to her Majesty's bedroom, where she joined a crowd of nobles, clergy and commoners grown so large some had climbed onto her chairs and side-tables.

Unlike so many others, the custom of giving birth in public proved too entrenched for Tonia to flout. Louisa found it as ridiculous and invasive and obnoxious as Tonia described it. She couldn't see over the mass of heads, but she could hear the infant's faint cry, as the *accoucher* bawled the traditional, "She is happily delivered."

A crush of people from the outer rooms burst the doors open, cheering, just as His Majesty made the announcement: "You have a fine daughter, Madame." Louisa broke through the wall of humanity just as her blood sister smiled, shuddered and fainted.

Her husband snatched a gold candlestick from a side table and pried it under the edge of a shutter nailed to the window sill. Every sound in the room died away, except for the oaths King Louis the

Sixteenth swore when the candlestick bent. Enraged, he hurled it into the crowd. Howling like an animal, he used his bare hands. People shrieked and trampled each other as the great shutter fell into the room.

The window was unlocked. Freezing cold air slashed inside as he threw it open, returning to his wife's side just as a thin, wavering stream of her blood, steaming as it met the frigid air, fell into a golden bowl the surgeon held beneath one high-arched foot.

"Barbarians," someone hissed, close to Louisa's ear. "First they suffocate her, then they butcher her to bring her from her faint!"

More layers of custom and protocol kept Louisa from her blood sister until the following morning. She was admitted to the outer reception room just as the doors opened on the suite where Tonia would spend a fortnight in the company of ladies-in-waiting selected for *postpartum* knowledge and experience.

She passed Dear Julie in the doorway, grateful it was wide enough to keep their skirts from touching.

"The babe is *the* most beautiful," her rival crowed, clearly pleased she'd been there first, "but of course she *would* be,"

Her blood sister's eyes shone clearer blue than Louisa had ever seen. *She is transformed*, she thought.

"Oh, sister," Tonia greeted her, "I had no idea she would be so red, so wrinkled, such a monkey-face!"

And her tongue is as tart as ever.

"But her mouth is a rosebud, her hands are starfish, and I swear she opened her eyes, well, one eye, and smiled. At me. At her mother.""

"Of course she would," Louisa fought tears.

"So tiny, so helpless, so perfect, so — mine! I can understand now, why my mother birthed so many of us."

"The name has yet to be made official," Louisa heard the following morning, "but I have succeeded in my desire to call her Marie Therese Charlotte."

Another desire was being met with greater resistance. "They are insisting on a wet nurse, but I am her mother, and her cries bring my milk. They want to bind my breasts with corsets, and make me drink vile drying-up concoctions."

"Customary," Louisa murmured.

"Do *not* use that word to me. Please. I was made to give birth unnaturally. Couldn't keep them from jamming my bedroom, gawking and gaping when I needed my privacy protected. I want to follow nature's way now. Bring her to me, please," she called to the pair of ladies-in-waiting standing at attention before the curtains she'd had them open with the sunrise.

"I had to meet with possible wet-nurses yesterday afternoon," she went on. "They were sincere, and they were worthy, and yes I will allow them — when *I* decide to."

Despite the bitter weather and the storm of protest over the Queen Consort nursing the Royal daughter, that Christmas at Versailles was the happiest Louisa could remember.

"Even in her sleep, she smiles," Tonia told Louisa, as they stood on either side of the sleeping baby's cradle, taking turns giving it gentle pushes.

"And so alert when she wakes." As if on cue, the infant's squeezed-shut eyes trembled open, and both fists went to her mouth. "And I fancy she thanks me for forbidding to have her swaddled, like some fowl trussed for the oven." Tonia glanced down at the front of her dress. "Not to mention the pleasure she takes from me. So *robust*," she sighed. "Why can't this be Austria? Or even England? They let a woman sit on the throne. France will *never* allow it." Another sigh. "I was married off when I was far too young. You were, too. Wouldn't it be grand to live like Mademoiselle Bertin? With no husband to put in first place?"

"Ah, but Mademoiselle has no children."

"True." Tonia's smile began as pure joy before it disappeared like sun behind cloud. "Sister, dear, I did not mean to gloat."

"I know."

The 5th day of January, in the year of our Lord 1779

My Dear Papa,

Her Majesty has nicknamed her beautiful daughter "Madame Royale". Both of the babe's parents dote on her. Neither cares she is not a son. His Majesty visits each morning, and returns most afternoons as well.

Come spring, her Majesty plans to keep Madame Royale with her, instead of moving her to the Royal nursery on an upper floor. His Majesty has already begun fabricating a set of wrought-iron grilles designed to keep Madame Royale from toddling onto the terrace off her mother's rooms. Her loving mother has twice taken her babe in arms on a nature walk, wrapped in layers of swans-down and ermine against the winter weather …

But for the state of Papa Time's health, Louisa would have extended her stay. His catarrh returned, though, with a vengeance, at the end of January. Her days at Rambouillet became weeks, and then months, as she absorbed herself in his care, relying on her Household Secretary to handle the lightened load of her Superintendent duties.

The routine changed in late May, when Catherine Hyde brought a note Tonia had written herself:

Dear Sister,

I understand your father-in-law's health has improved with the improving weather. The Countess Jules of Polignac and Monsieur Vaudreil have joined a number of family members already in residence at the Duke of Orlean's Palais Royale.

Nothing further was said. Or needed to be. The question of where Louisa belonged was answered.

"Yes indeed, a good plan, a good plan," Papa Time said when she told him she would be returning to Versailles as her primary residence. He lifted a giant hourglass from the table beside him. "The wonderful thing about all manner of time-pieces," he upended it, "is they are forever starting over. Take a lesson from this. Take all good things that come your way; we are not given to know when their time might be up." His attention wavered, then left her for the hourglass. "Dearest dear," he crooned, turning it over and over. He might have been talking to Louisa still, or to the swirling powder-fine sand inside the crystal globes. Louisa realized she was free to go.

The sun had just risen as the Great Chateau came into view, gilding the ranks of its windows and tinting its marble walls a warm honey. *My home,* Louisa thought, wondering for a moment whether Babette, the lady-in-waiting who'd shared that first carriage, was watching this same early sun, from the country acres she'd have retired to. Louisa almost laughed aloud as she realized she no longer even thought of biting a nail.

Settling into her apartments, preparing to be in her blood sister's company for the first time in months, she took guilty pleasure in the knowledge she would not have to face the fox-faced Countess who, more than Papa Time's catarrh, had kept her from her sister.

"She grew bored with the pace of maternal life here, and the Palais Royale offers many alternatives to boredom," Tonia told Louisa, as one of the nursemaids chosen for reasons having nothing to do with rank, took Madame Royale from her mother's arms to put her down for a nap. Marie Therese Charlotte remained robust; so chubby her elbows were dimpled; so happy she chortled far more than she cried.

The offhand mention of the domain of the Duke of Chartres, now Duke of Orleans, stopped Louisa's breath. *Viper. Thief. Took my chance at motherhood.*

They were thoughts, but Tonia read them. "Sister, please, I'm so sorry."

Back in her apartments, Louisa was sorry too. For her cowardice in leaving her blood sister's side. *No longer*, she prayed, *no longer*.

~ *Chapter Twenty Five* ~

The celebration of Madame Royale's six-month birthday in June of 1777 was the occasion for the presentation of a model of Petit Trianon, so amazing it brought gasps from the most jaded in attendance. Created in one inch to a foot scale by a collaborative group of famed factories and decorative artists, the model showed every detail of the former house of pleasure's transformation. It was surrounded by a scale model of the 45 acre grounds.

Tonia lifted the roof off with a flourish, revealing ceilings of pleated silk in the cream, cherry and blue color scheme carried throughout the seven room, two-story house. Miniature Aubusson tapestries with the entwined initials *M.A.* decorated the walls; small Savonnerie carpets covered the brightly varnished floors. She pressed a concealed button: a tiny table, set with perfect replicas of Trianon's own porcelain and cutlery designs, ascended to the second floor dining-room from the kitchens below, through a specially-cut hole in the ceiling.

"If I still wagered," she told her enchanted guests, "I'd bet the 'flying table' becomes Madame Royale's favorite 'peek-a-boo' game."

Her pink-polished fingertips traced winding paths, through naturalized gardens and along glass-lined streams, to an inch-deep lake. A marble-columned "Temple of Love", the height of half an egg, crowned the knoll beside it. Marvelously carved musicians waited inside, holding infinitesimal instruments, ready to play when wound at their waists.

The "Hamlet"was the last planned construction, to be built on the lake's far side. The model showed what the finished cluster of country peasant cottages — thatch-roofed and rough-plastered on the outside, opulent on the inside — would resemble when completed. It too, was perfect in every detail.

Summer ripened into full flush.

In the mornings, Her Majesty, often accompanied by the Princess of Lamballe, walked to Trianon with Madame Royale in her carriage, to watch the workmen busy themselves with the Hamlet.

The cow-shed was the first Hamlet building to be completed. The morning after it was, Tonia seated herself on a sturdy three-legged stool, and patted the flank of the pure white cow tethered to the wall with a braid of blue silk. Pulling firmly, one after the other, at all four teats of the cow's well-washed udder, her Majesty filled the porcelain pail the factory at Sevres had sent. Finishing, she tipped one teat sideways, attempting without much success to squirt drops of the fresh, hot milk directly into Madame Royale's laughing little mouth.

Madame Royale's second birthday parties, planned for months, were abruptly canceled when word of the Empress Maria Theresa's death reached Versailles.

Louis Auguste was notified first. He delayed telling his wife while he summoned the Superintendent of her Majesty's Household and others to accompany him. A retinue of nearly a dozen people finally entered Marie Antoinette's chamber. Protocol forbade anyone to speak before her Majesty did.

"What is it?" she asked, finally.

Ambassador Mercy had been selected to say the actual words. Her face went chalky at them.

"November 29th, you say?"

"Yes, Madame."

"It took eight days for word to reach me? I've been going about my life for *eight days*, not knowing? Her last *letter* just arrived." Fumbling through her pockets, waving off assistance, Tonia found a crumpled sheet of paper, smoothed it out, held it close enough to read: *"I am very glad to hear that you intend to resume your Court state at Versailles. It is far better for your public image, although I know how tedious and empty it is —* " her voice rose, sharpened, "No, my mother, you *don't* know! Didn't know. Now you'll *never* know."

She reached out both hands suddenly, the tips of her fingers near enough to Louisa's arm to count as a touch. Near enough for Louisa to hear her fierce whisper: "She didn't live to see what she wanted out of me — I delivered a daughter but not a son. I *will* bear him. I *will.* But what good will it do now that she's dead?"

Physicians arrived just then with other functionaries, crowding the chamber to the point of discomfort. As Louis Auguste and his party took their leave, Louisa found herself at Ambassador Mercy's side. At any other time, she would never have questioned him so bluntly. This wasn't any other time, and Louisa surprised herself: "You were the Empress's spy, weren't you? Sent to discover and report to her on everything her daughter did — or failed to do."

"I prefer to think of myself as a conduit," Mercy murmured, finally. "Will you inform her Majesty of your — realization?" Louisa glimpsed anxiety in the expression he hastened to mask.

"No."

"My humble thanks," his bow was deeper than protocol required, "your Highness."

~ Chapter Twenty Six ~

Tonia became pregnant again in 1781. That summer's official portrait, in her blue velvet Bertin overdress, holding a single white rose beside one cheek, captured her radiant happiness.

The artist, a Madame Vigee Le Brun, was a recent discovery of Tonia's. Both shared the glee of infuriating the stuffy old "centuries" — Tonia's nickname for the venerated artists and critics of France's famed Academy. That Le Brun was a woman was bad enough. That she was the first woman ever to be named a Court portraitist was worse. That she was a married woman with a husband in trade was worst of all.

"It all brands you quite the loathsome creature," Tonia teased, instigating one of many fits of giggling as she posed for the talented young painter.

On the 22nd of October, two weeks before her twenty-sixth birthday, Tonia delivered in the safety and privacy she was denied before. Louis Auguste supported her insistence on the change, and came and went nervously through her seven-hour labor. He was beside her bed, holding her hand, as he made his official announcement: "Madame, you have answered my prayers and the prayers of all the people. You have given us a son."

The son looked very small when Louisa first saw him, whimpering but not crying, and quite alert.

The reaction to the Dauphin Joseph Xavier 's birth bordered on madness. Cannons boomed salutes by the hour, and the jubilation in the streets was non-stop. The excitement continued for weeks as news of the great hope realized — an heir to the throne of France! — spread to every part of the country, touching off celebration after celebration.

The doting father visited his first born son daily. He weighed less than his sister at birth, and did not gain as she had. The most the physicians and surgeons could say was that there appeared to be an unnatural agitation of his blood as it passed from the right to the left side of his heart. All they offered to "normalize the agitation," as one of them put it, were bleeding and purging.

His mother flatly refused both standard remedies. "None of them will assure me of the outcome," she insisted to Louisa, "and so none will cut into his tiny body, or fill it with their poisons."

Joseph Xavier was a good baby, curious, intelligent, and calm of temperament. But he failed to thrive. Tonia had spectacles made for her shortsighted eyes so she could more easily read the medical texts she called for. She met with virtually anyone who had a theory as to what afflicted her child and what might cure his affliction.

Month followed month, as no one and nothing alleviated the Dauphin's chronic shortness of breath, or altered his perpetual weakness. His first cold winter seemed endless, and was followed by a rainy spring. Only June brought balmy, near-perfect weather.

June also brought a reminder from Grandfather Gossip. "Your daughter is almost four, her brother nearly a year old, and you have yet to keep the promise you made before she was born."

"I've made many promises. Which one do you mean?"

"The one about celebrating the beauties of midsummer's full moon."

"Glowing white, against a field of black velvet, spangled with stars." Tonia's voice was dreamy, her thoughts gone forward already.

The 25th day of June, in the year of our Lord 1782

Dearest Papa,

I know I promised you a letter on the morning after her Majesty's marvelous fete, but so much required my attention it has taken two days to find these few minutes at the beautiful desk you gifted me with, and offer the 'every detail' you asked for.

Her Majesty approved the design and wording of the coveted invitations to her long-awaited "white party" five hundred guests received. ...

Louisa's pen paused. Papa Time's daughter and son-in-law weren't among the recipients. Since that long-ago sharing of his assault, Tonia had taken pains to keep her blood sister from any but the most inescapable meetings. Household Secretary Catherine Hyde was invited. She attended, wearing a white gown of Louisa's, hem shortened and side panels added, to accommodate the young woman's height and measurements. Without being asked, Catherine kept the Princess from having to encounter the Countess Jules of Polignac.

> *... Her Majesty attended to every detail, as she does with all her projects. It was her idea to request each guest wear white. And her idea to present them with a white domino mask to carry on their arrival in the Gallery of Mirrors, ablaze with a full five thousand candles.*
>
> *When all were assembled, her Majesty made a brief appearance in a white silk organza gown, embroidered with roses outlined in moonstones and pearls. More pearls, perfectly matched, circled her slender throat.*
>
> *The guests were then conveyed to Trianon in gilded carts drawn by footmen in white livery, through the gardens lying between the Great Chateau and her petite retreat. Each garden was in flower, and every flower was white.*
>
> *Trianon, already a fairyland, was also transformed. Globes of soft white light glowed from the shrubbery and hung from the branches of the trees. Sweet strewing herbs covered the paths. Maypoles fluttered ribbons in every meadow. All the waters were perfumed. Musician played from the shadows as the first full moon of the summer rose.*
>
> *The guests were seated at small round tables, set beneath lattice arches of moon-vines, so they*

could watch the white spiral buds shudder open, releasing fragrance while they dined on bisques of blanched fish. They cleansed their palates with coconut sorbets and enjoyed soufflés of the potatoes Her Majesty has popularized as a fit food. Dessert was disks of vanilla ice cream glazed with white chocolate. The guests were a diverse group, many with political affiliations, none chosen for them …

At eleven o'clock on the night of Marie Antoinette's "White Party," Irish essayist Edmund Burke, former member of Britain's Parliament, sat with Horace Walpole, youngest son of Britain's Prime Minister, famous for his groundbreaking Gothic novel *The Castle of Otranto.* Sauternes in hand, they watched Tonia lead a group of couples in a waltz, at the center of her own irresistible orbit.

"A dream of beauty," Walpole murmured.

"We will never see her like again," Burke agreed.

"The Greeks have the word for it, "Walpole said." "charisma."

"The Greek, and not the French?" Baron Besenval limped up, leaning on an elegantly carved white cane that was doing a poor job of support.

"Charisma. Greek for 'divine gift' or 'grace'," Walpole went on. "Charismatics can be beautiful or handsome, but their real power lies in the way they enchant us with the sheer force of personality."

"Indeed she enchants us," Besenval said, as his aide lowered him into a chair. "Such innate grace, despite the thorn she carries in her heart. The child fails to thrive." His gnarled hands reached toward them. "You both travel so extensively. Surely you must have been made aware of some new remedy she might try?"

~ Chapter Twenty Seven ~

The Dauphin Joseph Xavier's first birthday was celebrated quietly in October of 1782, as news of the Gibraltar barge disaster reached Versailles. For some time, France had been besieging an English-owned fortress on Gibraltar. The King attempted to resolve the situation by approving a War Department scheme involving floating gunpowder-loaded barges up to the fortress's walls. Something went terribly wrong; the barges blew up in the harbor. All hands were lost.

Catherine Hyde brought the sensational gazettes to Louisa first. After seeing their contents, she decided to withhold them for now. *She has enough to concern her,* she thought, oddly grateful, for once, that Tonia liked to ignore criticism.

Through that fall, though, the cartoons and lampoons and print attacks began turning on her husband the King as well. The chorus of complaints rose: His Majesty funds fatally risky business in the face of the Crown's mounting deficits; his Majesty ignores the plight of this country he rules; his Majesty fails to control his wife's wretched excesses. Arrogance! Ignorance! Weakness!

It was impossible to shield Tonia from everything, but she managed to laugh off what she heard.

"So they call me 'Madame Deficit'," she chuckled to Louisa, as they shared a chocolate in the children's suite on a bleak February afternoon. "Is it any more obnoxious than Madame Lesbian? Madame Cuckolder? Madame Harlot?"

His Majesty also succeeded in paying little attention to the insults aimed at him. Immersed in the idea of manned flight, he underwrote physicist Jacques Charles' experiments with an oil-coated silk taffeta balloon that used "inflammable air," or hydrogen, for lifting power.

Just after dawn on the morning of August 27th, 1783, Charles's trial balloon went up from the *Place des Victoires* on the west side of

Paris. Deflating, it drifted to earth miles into the countryside. The unlucky peasants who witnessed its descent screamed "monster!" at the thing appearing from the same sky as the year's hailstorms and fogs. When it finally bobbed to a halt along tilled field furrows, they were waiting, with pitchforks.

Louis Auguste's fascination with Charles led him to the Montgolfier brothers. It was their balloon he ordered launched from Versailles, at daybreak on September 18th.

The Montgolfiers had hoped to go up with their balloon, but agreed to the Royal condition that, in the interests of safety, a sheep, a rooster, and a duck would be the first passengers. The King himself witnessed the animals' crates being fitted into the wicker basket. The rest of the Royal party looked on from the balcony outside the King's bedchamber, where big telescopes had been set up.

"I won't look! I won't!" The Dauphiness Marie Therese Charlotte pouted and stamped. "I want to go close, where Papa is, and see everything there!"

It had long been clear to Tonia that her first-born shared her father's mechanical interests. Her first serious steps were in the direction of the gates he'd wrought. "Madame Royale" also shared his solid build, brown hair, and brown eyes.

"You can go close the next time," Tonia promised.

"And may I have a gown of Montgolfier silk?"

"Yes, Charlotte, painted with scenes from today, if you like."

The Dauphin Louis Xavier, not quite two, was not carried from his rocking cradle to the telescopes. He napped fitfully and coughed frequently, responding to no one but the mother who never left his side.

The Countess Jules of Polignac was also present. *With her husband, of all people*, Louisa thought, feeling an immediate, familiar guilt at her lack of charity. She wished she could give her blood sister the gift of unquestioning acceptance of this woman she'd tried and failed to see as anything but grasping and self-centered.

At exactly 12:45, His Majesty Louis the Sixteenth gave the signal to inflate the sphere of brilliant blue silk, painted with golden suns and eagles and the zodiac signs. At his second signal, the restraining ropes were cut, and the balloon rose up with indescribable majesty.

Tonia turned to Louisa. "Wouldn't it be wonderful to escape from the earth? See Trianon below, small and perfect as its model? Suspended in air, the only sound a bird calling, or ropes creaking, sailing through an ocean of sky." Her face filled with a child's wonder. "Like going to heaven without having to die first."

At year's end, another of Tonia's commoner protégés, the portrait artist Madame Vigee Le Brun, exhibited at the prestigious Academy, over the bitter protests of its all-male membership. The grateful Le Brun honored her patroness by including her recent portrait of the Royal children. In the painting, Madame Royale looked serious in her gossamer gown. The Dauphin Joseph Xavier wore a sad expression and a blue silk suit. Its lace ruff exposed the hollows at his breastbones.

How frail he looks, Louisa thought at the unveiling reception, but said only, "The tree is beautifully rendered."

"Forever tactful," Tonia's smile was rueful.

The weather was too cold to be out-of-doors at Trianon. Marie Therese Charlotte had lost interest in the cowshed and the disappearing dining table, but she liked tagging along with her mother and her friends to the newly completed theater. Despite her outspokenness, Madame Royale was shy of acting a part; she preferred applauding enthusiastically while she called for encores from her front row seat.

Marie Antoinette was a good actress. She liked to say it was the result of the summer palace playacting of her childhood, but her adult concentration and focus produced praiseworthy results.

Private performances at Trianon were one thing; Her widely publicized enthusiasm for bringing a production of Beaumarchais' sensationally popular comedy *The Marriage of Figaro* to France was quite another.

"My brother the Emperor absolutely disagrees, but it is a comedy, meant to be enjoyed for its humor," Tonia told an audience of friends at Trianon, after taking her bows as "Katherine" to Count Fersen's "Petruchio" in scenes from Shakespeare's *The Taming of the Shrew.*

"I had a letter from the Emperor." her voice mimicked his perfectly: "*I am appalled you permit this play to open. I have banned it here because it is anti-Royalist in the extreme. Seditious. Treasonous."*

"I've seen it," Grandfather Gossip called from his back row. "Quite witty. And the same aristocrats he mocks gave it a standing ovation."

Count Axel Fersen spoke from his place onstage. "I am newly returned to France, and attended a performance with the Baron. I thought it humorous, not treasonous."

"I also failed to see sedition of any sort," the Baron cackled. "But Beaumarchais did make quite the case for the uselessness of the nobility. It's rumored the play's the basis for the comic opera Mozart is composing."

"I met him once," Tonia said. "I was five, he was six, perhaps. My father was so impressed by the little prodigy he arranged for a visit to Schonbrunn. I loved his playing, and told him so. He kissed my cheek and declared he would marry me one day."

Louisa was the only one close enough to hear Fersen's whisper: "If only …"

~ Chapter Twenty Eight ~

The *Marriage of Figaro* was playing to packed theaters when Marie Antoinette was delivered of a second son, born howlingly healthy on March 17th 1785, to increasingly vocal speculation as to real identity of his father.

"I have done more than my duty to these contrary people," Her Majesty was overheard confiding to the Superintendent of her Household an hour after giving birth, as she spooned up cream of rice with biscuit: "I gave them an heir four years ago. I've given them a spare now, but there's no satisfying them. They claim he's a bastard." She licked the bowl of her spoon. "I have done more than my duty and I am done with them. I intend to enjoy life with my children from now on."

From his first lusty bawls, the Dauphin Louis-Charles proved to be blessedly robust, so much so his mother was heard to joke her sole concern for his health was the blood vessel he might burst with his bawling.

In August of that year, with her five-month-old son finally down for an afternoon's nap, Tonia and Louisa were passing through the *oeil de beouf* when the jeweler Boehmer approached. His wig slipped sideways as he made an awkward bow, proffering an envelope "with my most profuse apologies."

What is this, Monsieur?" Her Majesty made no effort to take it from him.

"A promissory note your Majesty has signed," Boehmer bobbed up, "which, begging a thousand pardons, is now seven months in arrears." Beads of sweat popped out on his forehead.

"A promissory note for *what*?"

"For the diamond necklace."

"*What* diamond necklace?"

Boehmer straightened his wig. "The one I created, featuring

seventeen large brilliants, three festoons, four pendants, double *riviere*, and four tassels."

"I *do* recall that diamond necklace, Monsieur Boehmer. You asked four million francs. I refused to purchase it."

"You refused it at that price, yes, that is correct, your Majesty." A sweat drop trickled down one side of Boehmer's bulbous nose. "But you did agree to half that amount." He licked the drop from the corner of his mouth. "You signed this promissory note." He held the envelope close enough for Tonia to take it, open it, and scan its few lines.

"A pathetic forgery, Monsieur." Red spots bloomed along her cheekbones. "I sign 'Marie Antoinette of Lorraine and Austria'. *Never* 'Marie Antoinette of France'. Who gave you this?" Her voice shook with rage.

The regrowth of Boehmer's beard began to show through the flesh tones of his makeup. "Your Majesty, I had no idea you never signed the note. Neither did His Eminence."

"Eminence? *Which* eminence?"

"Cardinal Rohan, your Majesty."

"The same Cardinal Rohan who blessed my marriage?"

"I believe so, yes."

"The same Cardinal Rohan whose reputation for sexual excess is considered excessive — even at *this* Court?"

"He assured me you made him welcome."

"I assure you he lied. His over-familiarity was so revolting I banished him from Court. Years ago."

"Your Majesty, with every respect, your directness is sometimes mistaken for a license to feel — familiar."

"I felt repugnance. How *dare* he?"

"With your indulgence, your Majesty," Boehmer was bowing again, "His Eminence conveyed the note from you when he requested the necklace."

"And you *agreed*?" Tonia's voice escalated.

"His reasons were plausible."

"What?"

Boehmer found a handkerchief, finally, and began blotting. "His

Eminence sent an emissary, Madame Jeanne de la Motte, prior to our meeting. She told me of the secret correspondence between yourself and His Eminence, and the plans you made to meet with him to receive your prize. I believed her. I gave him the necklace."

"I have not laid eyes on him since his banishment."

"He thought it *was* you, Your Majesty, at the meeting place."

"Preposterous!" She crumpled the note and threw it at him.

Boehmer cringed away. "What am I to do?"

"You are to get from my sight," the Queen of France thundered. "You are banished." She turned to the Superintendent of her Household. "Have the Cardinal come here to explain himself, as soon as that can be arranged."

It took only three days for His Eminence Cardinal Rohan to present himself to his Queen and his King as they stood side-by-side in his inner chamber. Louis Auguste remembered nothing about the necklace beyond its exorbitant price, but he agreed to witness the meeting, as did Louisa, in her official capacity.

It was easy to see how handsome Cardinal Rohan had once been as he stood, resplendent and arrogant, in a red silk moiré chasuble over his white lace cassock.

Tonia wasted no time with niceties. "I haven't laid eyes on you in more than eight years, yet you claim you took a necklace from Monsieur Boehmer with the intent of delivering it to me?"

"I did deliver it — "

"Not to me."

"In the grotto of Venus. Surely you recall?"

"How can I when I was never anywhere near the grotto?"

"Your Majesty, I know now Madame de la Motte's assertions of Royal favor and her claim you yourself wished to accept the necklace were outrageous lies. How was I to know the heavily veiled woman was not you?" He spoke with maddening calm.

Marie Antoinette displayed equal calm as she turned to her husband: "Arrest Monsieur the Cardinal as an accomplice in such crimes as are connected to the theft of Monsieur Boehmer's necklace."

The mere idea of an arrest was condemned; the uproar escalated after Louise Auguste himself summoned Cardinal Rohan to the

Oeil de Beouf crossroads, to announce the it publicly.

Grandfather Gossip, unwavering believer in the rightness of all things Tonia, was seen wringing his gnarled hands, as separate trials of the powerful clergyman and the penniless commoner Madame LaMotte were set for the following spring.

~ Chapter Twenty Nine ~

"He must *also* be found guilty." Tonia crumpled the copy of the morning's *Almanach de Versailles* Louisa had brought before handing it back. Sun streamed through the windows in the children's suite, making what looked to Louisa like a halo around the tangled curls of Joseph Xavier, asleep at Tonia's side. His brother and sister were out of doors, enjoying the mild May weather.

"Please don't pollute this space with the droppings of these scribbling vermin anymore. The slanders they print spread like disease. Claiming we carried on a secret correspondence! Insisting I *schemed* with him to acquire a necklace I coveted! Saying I took it from him in a secret *tryst!*"

"Disgusting lies," Louisa commented.

"Tell that to a country gorging on them. Tell it to all Europe, for that matter."

"Tell me you're not ordering me to make travel plans." Louisa said it with a smile; Tonia's anger evaporated.

"Truth be told, I must admit that little sharpie LaMotte laid a good plan. Hire a look-alike actress to play me. Have the Cardinal meet her in secret. Have the actress carry it to the sharpie and her henchman before she's paid to go on her way with her mouth shut. In other circumstances, I'd applaud the actress."

"I applaud you. And still wish you would change your mind about giving testimony against him in open court."

"The Cardinal must be punished. He must be brought to public account. The only way for the truth to be told is for me to tell it. The whole story *must* come out."

Louisa shook her head. "Once the pieces of the story are in full view, you cannot control how people fit them together."

"Please!" Tonia was angry again, "don't add *yourself* to the chorus insisting I hold my tongue. I cannot allow this lying hypocrite to defame me."

"The Cardinal was easy to dupe."

"So is anyone, once you've discovered their dupe-ing point." A trace of Tonia's wild old smile appeared. "His was simple. Lechery." She tucked the sleeping boy closer to her. "I was never party to it, not with him, not with anyone. But flirting with a platonic champion? Enjoying foolishness and folly and silly games?" The smile widened. "Remember the single session card party that lasted through the night and into the next day? So many distractions, filling those years before my *real* life began." She smoothed the boy's damp ringlets. "I am mother to this heir to the throne. My duty is singular. Sacred, even. He must inherit that throne."

"He will, dear sister." Louisa felt her eyes fill. "He will."

The smile evaporated. "And I will have my revenge on the Cardinal for his sins."

"Revenge is risky business." A frisson of fear shivered along Louisa's shoulders. "Cardinal Rohan is a powerful churchman. Perhaps the most powerful."

"I don't care. The Cardinal will go to trial, and he will be found guilty. I'll have that supreme pea-cock's head on a platter." Her free hand pointed to the crumpled gazette on Louisa's lap. "And I'll use those sensation-seeking scribblers to serve the whole sorry mess up to the people of France."

"I understand your feelings, but testifying? In open court? How can you be certain it serves your best interests?"

"Not mine, perhaps, but — " Tonia broke off to hug Joseph Xavier, so fiercely he woke, sobbing for breath. She took his pinched little face between both hands and kissed the top of his head. Blue veins bulged at his temples; the skin beneath his eyes looked bruised.

The sound of his little brother Louis-Charles could be heard from the anteroom, suddenly, shouting "*no*" louder and louder as he came closer and closer.

"I know he's on his way to being spoiled to the point of rottenness," Tonia nodded toward the sounds, "but when I see, or even hear, him being so — so — *alive!* I can't refuse him anything!"

"Not even if it might be for his own good?" Louisa had to ask.

"Not even then." She shook her head. "Did you hear my husband told the latest Finance Minister he would like to *resign* the monarchy?

"I hadn't heard."

"Just imagine, Louisa, the great, gawky, iron-and-wood-working former monarch living life outside this miserable fishbowl."

"And you?"

"If it weren't for my sons' divine right to the throne I would be eager to resign. Retreat. Retire. Raise all my children in peace. At Trianon, preferably. Elsewhere, if need be."

"Perhaps that can be accomplished — "

"And perhaps the Seine will dry up this afternoon. No, Louisa, my course is set."

"You'll testify? In open court?"

"I will."

"Unprecedented in French history, Tonia."

"So I'll make history. Or cause a sensation."

"Or both."

Louisa startled at a sudden cold chill at the base of her neck.

Appearing in open court almost a year later, in the seventh month of an unexpected and difficult pregnancy, Marie Antoinette did make history and cause a sensation. Without the actual necklace, testimony was all that could be examined. Unable to attend in person, Louisa dispatched her Household Secretary, the increasingly trustworthy Catherine Hyde, to hear the testimony and report on it.

All 647 stones of the infamous necklace — 2800 carats in total weight — had long since been sold off by Madame LaMotte's co-conspirators. Not one had been found. The actress who'd impersonated the Queen didn't appear in Court. No charges were pressed once she convinced the investigators she knew nothing beyond the amount of her fee for the performance she'd given.

~ Chapter Thirty ~

On June 18, 1786, with Tonia heavily into her eighth month, Cardinal Rohan was acquitted of all charges and allegations against him. Days later, Madame LaMotte was found guilty of theft and not guilty of conspiracy. She was sentenced to a three-year prison term.

The outcomes seemed to snap some last thread of civility in Tonia, who became as angry as Louisa had ever seen her.

"Rohan goes free, and that conniver likely won't even serve her sentence. *Swine!*"

Louisa was relieved she'd sent the room-servant from her salon, so it was only the two of them.

"The envy of all liars and cheats, that hypocrite of all hypocrites in his red silk robes! Prince of the Church — pah!" Tonia actually spit on the floor. "And they've made a heroine of that woman. That common thief and swindler. *She* is the one who broke the laws, not me! *Pah.*" She spit again, saw Louisa's expression, and burst into laughter. "Oh, la. When I was my daughter's age, I — expectorated was their polite term for it. I was encouraged, requested — never ordered — to refrain from such unbecoming behavior." Her shoulders shrugged. "Never mind all my brothers spit — when I tell you Joseph was the worst, I know you'll believe me."

Louisa had to laugh.

"I spit, I climbed trees, I mud-walked in bare feet — and fought having my hair washed, let alone dressed. Nobody mistook me for an arbiter of fashion."

"Not then," Louisa smiled, "but you've more than made up for it."

"True." Tonia smoothed a hand over the silk charmeuse of the Bertin designed dressing gown that made no attempt to conceal her pregnancy. "What will this one love? She must be a girl, she moves so little."

Sophie Helene Beatrice was born on July 9th, 1786, so unresponsive days passed before she was even shown to her weeping mother. Many more days passed before Tonia chose the infant's name. Through the stifling heat of August, Tonia remained periodically irrational and alarmingly withdrawn from reality, including the obvious failure of Sophie Helene Beatrice to adjust to life outside the womb. The infant's death a month before her first birthday seemed, in some macabre way, to rouse Tonia from her depressed stupor.

She only emerged to sit for the year's official portrait. When she insisted it include the Royal cradle, empty of the baby it had held, Madame Vigee LeBrun tried to reason with her.

"Do you really wish to immortalize such a sad reminder, Your Majesty?"

"Yes." Tonia's smile was grim. "And what is more, I wish you to focus the portrait on it. Drive home the fact of my loss. Let them see what they did to me."

The first-born son and heir Joseph Xavier was so often exhausted the artist had difficulty working for more than a quarter hour at a time.

The constant interruptions annoyed Marie Therese Charlotte. At nearly seven, she was adamant about having outgrown her "Madame Royale" nickname. She clearly resented the constant attention paid to the brother who'd brought an end to her only-child status, and to the brother who was now the baby of the family.

"Mama, can I *go?*" Marie Therese Charlotte pouted.

"*Yes*, go," Tonia handed two-year-old Louis-Charles to his nurses. She kept Joseph Xavier on her lap. "*Failure to thrive* was officially announced today, sister, as the official cause of death."

"Failure to thrive," Louisa whispered.

"My daughter passed her entire time in my womb being attacked on all sides. They killed her, you know, every miserable, misbegotten, evil one of them. Every tongue that wagged against me. Every hand raised in a fist. Every throat that shouted 'yes' to the lies, lies, and more lies."

"Tonia, please, try to calm yourself. For the sake of the children you have."

"I *had* four children. Now I have *three*."

Vigee Le Brun approached with the day's preliminary sketch. It showed Joseph Xavier parting the curtains of the empty cradle Louis Auguste himself had made.

"Excellent, yes, proceed. You have captured his expression perfectly." Tonia paused to blink back tears. "It's as if he's saying '*This is where my second sister, sweet Sophie, slept for the little while she was here on earth.*'"

The death came just before His Majesty King Louis the Sixteenth was scheduled to depart on his first Royal progress through the French countryside since his Coronation journey to Rheims. He offered to delay the trip until his wife was "more herself." She refused the offer, seeing him off on his historic journey before she retreated to her inner apartments, cursing the "vermin" who'd hounded her in print and in the halls of Versailles, until the strain took her daughter's life.

The King returned from his journey with an optimism his Queen's Consort's bitterness couldn't quell.

"I saw no scorn for the monarchy. None at all!" They were alone in the smallest of Tonia's antechambers. "The morning I went to the harbor at Cherbourg to see the defenses I was cheered. '*Long live the King*', they cried out, again and again. 'Long live my people!' I cheered them back."

In months and years past, this private time would have signaled a night on which they shared a bed. Before her husband left, however, his wife had made it clear there would be no more shared beds. Seeing her agony over Sophie Helene Beatrice, he'd agreed. He would never say as much, but he'd thought her age — thirty, last November — might have played a part in the infant's death.

Just now, he was eager to share the details of the most wonderful trip of his life: "I read my speeches from my own notes, and often knew what to say without even having to even look at them!"

"It must have given you such pleasure, to see for yourself so many places you'd only read about." Tonia was peering at the maps he'd marked and put in her lap.

"All those reports of public lack of confidence in government are false."

She pushed the maps off her aproned lap. "And 'Madame Deficit' was not condemned for the Crown's outgo exceeding its income?"

"Not at all," he assured her, bending to pick them up. "My subjects are so kind, so welcoming! We required no military guard." He began folding them. "Huge, the crowds were, but orderly. Honesty showing on every face, and I was close enough to see them. Simple people, and so free of all that infects the very air here." He threw up his arms, waved the maps. "Their air is free of it."

"It sounds very inviting."

"Little girls sang and strewed flowers before their good King in every town we entered. Gratitude knew no bounds when I granted a pardon or a dowry. We stopped at road-side inns. I ate sitting right beside the other patrons. Fresh eggs! And black bread, spread thick with new butter. And the sea —" his jowls quivered — "Thirty-three years I have walked this earth without laying eyes on the sea. I shall never forget it."

"I'm happy for you," Tonia reached to stroke his grey serge sleeve.

His eyes glazed with tears. "I have felt the true joy of being King just twice. Once on the day I was crowned at Rheims. And again, last week, at Cherbourg."

~ Chapter Thirty One ~

Louis Auguste's good feelings figured strongly in a decision he made swiftly, on hearing the only options for resolving the Crown's hundred million *livre* debt his gaggle of finance ministers had agreed on.

"Bankruptcy or reform," he repeated, looking past them as he spoke. "Bankruptcy is odious because my subjects would oppose it. They worry, you know. With good cause." His ponderous head swung back in their direction. "There are places in this country where they must mix bran with ferns, to make bread. Places where the taxes levied are unfair." He glared at them. "I have trusted too many to rule in my place. It is I who am the Crown and I decree reform." He stood. They bowed. "There must be bread."

Before nightfall, news of His Majesty's support for financial reform had spread far beyond Versailles. Within its confines, Her Majesty agreed so completely she called on her Household Superintendent to arrange for the sale of the Royal flatware, with the proceeds funding shipments of proper bread-making ingredients to the areas most affected by the shortages.

Louisa agreed wholeheartedly with Tonia's charitable act, but failed to get her to set aside the anonymity she continued to insist on.

"Please make an exception. Allow this act of compassionate generosity to be made public."

"And have my haters find some way to twist it?"

Louis Auguste was no more successful than Louisa had been at persuading her to let the public know.

What the public heard, and, for the most part applauded, was the announcement their King made.

"Men of good will, an Assembly of Notables, will come together here at Versailles to assist us in reform."

By the spring of 1787, the Assembly of Notables had long since been dubbed the "Assembly of Not-Ables." One cartoon posted everywhere showed a monkey at the Assembly's main podium, wearing the Royal crown, asking its audience of barnyard animals what sauce they wished to be eaten with. Through that year and into the next, criticism of his Majesty's reform edicts grew louder, along with complaints about the ever-changing parade of Ministers.

More and more often an unthinkable question began to be asked: should there be a King at all? The American Republic was doing very well without a King, wasn't it? And hadn't the Crown gone deeper into debt to help finance the American War of Revolution?

The questions continued, as did louder and more pointed debate, until His Majesty agreed to call together France's three Estates: nobles, clergy, and commoners.

His Majesty even took the unprecedented step of instructing the representatives chosen to attend the "Estates-General" to bring their lists of grievances with them.

Autumn of 1788 brought the worst hailstorms in memory. They pounded the countryside, leaving vast areas in shambles. Winter came on even more brutally. Snow and ice wreaked havoc. Ancient trees froze to death; famine piled its victims under canvas shrouds until spring thaws softened them, along with the ground they would be buried in. By New Year's Eve, all France had reason to bid 1788 an un-fond farewell, with the fervent hope that 1789 would bring better things.

Versailles bristled with flags and pennants rippling in the light warm breeze on the May morning the Estates-General convened. Women's skirts swayed gracefully, stirred by the same breeze. The sky's blue perfectly matched Tonia's eyes, and white clouds that looked ordered for the occasion sailed majestically overhead as their Majesties, and members of their party, waited to take their place in the great procession.

Louisa breathed in and out, slowly, steadily, savoring the sweetly fragrant clouds of incense rising in dancing streams from golden censers, as choirs chanted blessings on the historic gathering. If only

Papa Time could be here, to see and hear and smell, but he no longer traveled — not even past the doors of his bedroom at Rambouillet.

"I wish I'd been born in May instead of November," Tonia sighed. "It's by far a better month."

"It is," Louisa agreed, wishing everything could be as ideal as the weather. Little Joseph Xavier's struggles for breath last night had led to Tonia's desperate agreement to leeches. He'd shrieked when the physicians arrived. Shrieked all through the repeated applications of eight slimy, sucking creatures, laid in pairs along his twisted spine.

Tonia held him close through the horrible procedure, laying him in his bed when it was over, hovering until his blue veined eyelids closed.

"I want to watch tomorrow, *Maman*," he'd croaked. "I want to watch, too."

"My little monarch! Of course you will."

The sick boy did join his brother and sister and their retinues on the South Balcony. His cot was placed closest to the parapets, for the best view of the representatives of his country's three Estates massing below.

~ Chapter Thirty Two ~

The historic march began with row after orderly row of the Noble Estate, periwigged heads held high, puffed chests sashed with the wide ribbons of their ranks and honors. Brilliant sun glinted from ceremonial swords and spurs, and blazed from the jewels of the wives marching beside them. The Estate of the Clergy came next, thousands of them, from Princes of the Church, resplendent in scarlet robes overlaid with cloth-of-gold-surplices, to humble parish priests in worn black cassocks.

The Commoners Estate was the largest by far. Everyone from the wealthiest merchants and landowners to the lowliest laborers and peasants marched proudly and boisterously. Those who could afford it, and there were many, outshone even the Noble Estate in their finery. Many more, however, marched in dark, somber clothing, to protest the country's sorry state. All were cheered at every step by hordes of their fellow commoners.

Close to a million people had massed in the King's Courtyard, where the Royal party was to make its progress. At noon, the crowd parted like the Red Sea to allow their passage. Voices were heard as they appeared, howling in unison: *"Down with the King and Queen!"* Cheering overtook the chanting even before the Royal Guards penetrated the crowd in search of the perpetrators.

There was no visible Royal reaction as the ceremonies concluded, with prayers for the success of the Estates General in bringing about needed reforms.

Tonia kept her composure until the pointed tip of her red satin high-heeled slipper touched the polished floor of her inner rooms. She shook then, so convulsively the clasp of her necklace snapped. Its pearls, falling like hailstones, were the only sound for a shocking minute before she allowed herself to be helped from her Court dress. Accepting a water, she motioned to Louisa to follow her to her inner rooms.

"Those shouts," Louisa shuddered.

"Came from that warren of malcontents inhabiting the *Palais Royale*."

"Paris home of — " Louisa had trouble saying it " — my brother-in-law."

"None other. The viper who lusted for you."

"Who took his revenge when he couldn't take me."

"His lust is different now," Tonia said. "He lusts to take control of France."

The pressure on Louis Auguste came early on, to allow every man in the Estates-General one vote. An equal vote. He resisted, and went on resisting, even when the news of his first-born son's death was brought to him, as he sat in emergency conference with his Ministers in a small chamber off the Gallery of Mirrors.

His Ministers tried to detain him as he heaved himself from his chair. Halfway through the opened doors he turned to face them, pointing a quivering finger at each in turn. "Are none of you fathers?" is all he said before the doors closed behind him.

The face his wife turned to him was a ghastly mask of grief. Only the Princess was with her, at the draped table where the child's naked body lay immobile as carved marble.

She wouldn't leave her boy. Wouldn't allow him to be dressed or even covered up. Compulsively, she dipped a cloth into the bowl of water at his head, laying it over some part of his pitiful corpse, smoothing it with her fingertips, crooning fragments of lullaby tunes and nursery rhymes.

"The water is cold," Louisa touched her elbow, finally, gently.

Tonia dropped the cloth, lifted the bowl, and began flinging handfuls of water at the dead boy. "He laughs so when you do that, remember?"

"I remember."

Louis Auguste took his leave soon after. Hours passed before Tonia began to dress Joseph Xavier in his favorite sailor suit. When she finished, she pressed a few silken strands of its fringed sash between her finger and thumb: "I suppose this will put an end to the fashion for them." The face she turned to Louisa wore a ghost of a smile.

> *The 11th day of June in the year of Our Lord 1789*
>
> *My dearest Papa-Time,*
>
> *Her Majesty did not attend the protocol-encrusted ceremonies surrounding the burial. Her official statement was brief: "I have made my farewells."*
>
> *In her grief, she is all but unaware of the Estates-General vote, to transform themselves into a National Assembly.*
>
> *His Majesty was less disturbed by this turn of events than his Ministers, who retaliated swiftly.*
>
> *The first arrivals at Salle de Menus Plaisirs for the morning's session found a padlocked chain wrapped around the massive doors. The sign nailed to it informed the members of the newly-voted National Assembly the hall was being readied for the King's visit …*

The reaction to the lockout was immediate and unanimous outrage. No one seemed certain, afterwards, whose idea it was to hold the National Assembly's first session in a covered tennis court nearby, one that hasn't been used since the reign of Louis the Fourteenth.

"*In the stultifying heat of the early afternoon,*" Catherine Hyde read from the broadside she'd brought from Paris, "*the famous astronomer and mayor of Paris, Monsieur Bailly, announced the new oath taken by our National Assembly: 'We will not separate, until the Constitution of the Kingdom is established and consolidated on firm foundations'.*"

"Watch now," Tonia nearly smiled. "There'll be so much batting back and forth, you'll think those courts are being used for tennis again."

The broadside and the Household Secretary had both come from Paris, by the carriage Louisa had arranged, along with stabling the mare Perdita at Versailles. Catherine Hyde had declined an invitation to leave her Paris apartment.

"She is young enough to savor the excitement in those streets," Tonia told Louisa. "So long as we provide her transportation, and see to her mount's safety, I'm confident she can see to her own."

At the end of June, Louis the Sixteenth accompanied a Finance Minister to the tennis courts, to deliver a promise of equal taxation. His Majesty then ordered the Assembly to separate into its three Estates as they completed the work they had begun.

The Nobles and the Clergy followed the Royal party from the tennis court. The Third Estate remained seated, as their activist spokesman Mirabeau rose to his feet: "We are here by the will of the people," he began. "We will only go if we are driven out by bayonets." They cheered themselves hoarse before passing a resolution exonerating themselves from any blame.

The Duke of Orleans led a contingent of sympathizers to the tennis courts the next day, where he announced his wish to be known henceforth as "*Phillipe Egalite*."

"'*Philip Equality*' — pah!" Tonia rattled the gazette containing the account of the name change. "It should be '*Philip Traitor*'. Smirking, skulking traitor."

Louisa didn't hear. She was gone — lost in the sick, greenish light of a grape arbor in the gardens of Rambouillet. She was seeing his lecherous lips, curling with his obscene suggestions. She was feeling hers purse, gathering the saliva she spit in his face. And then it was her husband's face, sunk into his death-bed linens, spittle oozing from the corner of his mouth. She heard his hoarse, death-rattled whisper again, revealing his brother-in-law's fatal gift.

Tonia snapped her fingers gently in front of Louisa's pale face. "What is it? Are you all right?"

"Yes."

"Are you certain?"

"Yes."

"Well, then, what do you think of this?" Tonia tapped the gazette. "My husband's Ministers wish to padlock the tennis court while the whole pack of them are inside. Says so right here."

Louisa roused herself, a little. "His Majesty would never agree to that, would he? And neither would you."

"The *one* time I tried to influence an outcome, I lost." Tonia looked across the room, where the empty-cradle portrait hung. "At great cost."

"I heard Madame Vigee Le Brun has left for an extended visit to England." Louisa turned the subject.

"You heard correctly."

"You could also make an extended visit — to so many places."

"I could," Tonia stared at the portrait, "but only without the heir to the throne. I will *never* be parted from any of my children. Living or dead."

The weather grew hotter and more humid. Evenings brought enough coolness to stroll the terraces, but they sat on Tonia's balcony instead, looking down on the lanterns of the Guards. There were more every night, flashing into the darkness like huge fireflies, in rhythm with the drummers' beats.

When Louisa first entered Tonia's dressing-room, she thought Mme. Bertin was supervising two of the Palace's tire-women at work on a quilt. Coming closer, she saw it was a large, bulky vest.

"For His Majesty," Bertin sounded almost cheerful, "in the event he appears in public anywhere at Versailles he can be easily approached."

"It's a cuirasse," Tonia explained, "made of so many thicknesses of felt it turns aside any weapon. We can take no chances with his safety. An extra measure of — insurance, if you like, to maintain his safety."

In early July, Louis Auguste agreed to hire troops to provide a calming presence in Paris. It had the opposite effect; what was seen as the threat of mercenary occupation provoked the formation of a citizens' militia, a National Guard. At its head was none other than the hero of the War of American Independence. The war that had so depleted the French treasury.

The Marquis de Lafayette was quick to accept his new honor.

~ *Chapter Thirty Three* ~

At the end of the second week of July, the Baron Besenval wasted no time in paying a visit, on his return from an extended journey to "several other countries, in addition to this one."

"You delight in reminding me Versailles is a country of its own," Tonia shook her closed fan at him.

"And so it is." The scant wisps of his eyebrows arched higher. "In this country, precious few treatments for my rheumatism are new, let alone effective. I went in search. And found Axel Fersen in France, completing the last of several foreign postings. I persuaded him to join me here." He shot his lace cuffs. "He should arrive shortly."

Tonia's expression gave her away.

"I bring best wishes," the old man went on, "from Edmund Burke, my most recent host. I can see why he's one of your favorite foreigners." He shifted his spindly, linen-wrapped legs on the ottoman before his chair. "Oh, and kindest regards from Madame Vigee Le Brun. She is enjoying her sojourn in England so much."

"Her last letter came from Horace Walpole's 'Strawberry Hill'," Louisa said. "Is she still there?"

"She is," Besenval replied, "but I'm sorry to say his printing press won't be — not for long, at any rate. Claims he's growing too old to see to a business, and he has no heirs to carry on for him. I actually read his novel while I was there. Gothic as the castle on his estate."

A footman knocked and entered carrying a silver salver with Count Fersen's calling card.

"Bring him here. At once. No, no, convey him to the salon where we're taking a light lunch."

Tonia was more animated than she'd been in weeks as they went along to the salon. Despite the time and distances that had separated them, it was immediately clear that the tall, dark, handsome Swede remained her "platonic champion."

"We passed the Tuileries Palace this morning," the Baron remarked, picking at his soufflé, "just as Camille Desmoulins was haranguing the crowd."

"For a journalist, he's quite an orator," Fersen put in. "Piercing gaze, incredible voice — "

Tonia put her fork down. "And his theme?"

Besenval scowled. "Equal representation and damn what the King might wish."

"Desmoulins accused his Majesty," Fersen's smile vanished, "of ignoring his subjects' demand to disperse the foreign troops he has imposed on them."

"He looked like a conductor," Besenval added, "raising and damping their roars, bawling things like 'Will we let Louis Auguste break the spine of our strong new body of national pride?' 'No more mercenaries!' they howled back. Had to hold my ears, didn't I?""

"Indeed," Fersen replied, adding, "I much resented his earlier pronouncement that there were two dolphins on the Royal coat-of-arms, to match the two sides of the King's face."

"Yes, yes, that too. So insulting," the Baron huffed. "Shouting his questions: '*Who pays for the wretched excesses of his Court? Who fights and dies in the wars he instigates?*'"

"*We do*, they roared," Fersen shook his handsome head. "The Third Estate. I fear they are the force the Crown will soon face."

Louisa rarely slept through the night anymore, but she could sometimes manage to nap in late afternoon. She was more asleep than awake when she thought she heard calls in the hall. Something about the Bastille.

When she was admitted to Tonia's rooms, just before seven that night of July 14th, 1789, Louisa was surprised to find the Countess Yolande of Polignac there. *She's been in Paris since before Joseph Xavier died,* she thought, surprising herself with the realization the death happened only five weeks ago.

Tonia sensed her surprise.

"The Countess was a witness to the furor in Paris. I've summoned her here to tell of it."

"Then I shall leave you," Louisa bowed.

"Probably for the best," the Countess said. "Grim and gory can't be anything you'd fancy hearing about."

"My secretary will share the details," Louisa kept her tone carefully civil.

"Mademoiselle Hyde lives in Paris," Tonia explained, "but is with us almost daily." She tried to catch Louisa's eye. "She's become something of a treasure."

Louisa bowed again and took her leave. Despite every effort to rise above it, the Countess' presence unfailingly provoked jealousy, followed by guilt.

"It all started with a mob in search of arms to take up against the foreign troops," dear Julie began. "Peeking through the curtains, I was amazed at how many of them there were. They filled the street below, carrying torches, most of them, all of them shouting. You can imagine how curious we were."

"You followed them?" Tonia leaned forward.

"Not me personally." Dear Julie rearranged herself on the divan. "It was my darling Vaudreil and his wild boys who went and came back. Safe, thanks be!"

"Yes, thanks be. Now tell me what happened?"

"The crowd found twenty-eight hundred muskets at the *Invalides*, but no ammunition. A rumor spread that the Crown had hidden enormous quantities of it within the old fortress of the Bastille."

"The state prison on the other side of Paris?" Tonia asked.

"Yes. A medieval dungeon, that's what one of the wild boys called it." Dear Julie paused for effect. "The Bastille didn't hold a single bullet. Nothing but a few pitiful prisoners, debtors or feeble-minded. The mob freed them, after they killed the commandant who tried to keep them from crossing the moat."

"How awful."

"When it was over, when Vaudreil and his wild boys returned safe and sound, we all went to celebrate at the *Parnassess.* It's a café on the Right Bank where the most radical radicals gather." Julie paused for effect. "I saw the Bastille for myself. And before I even saw it, I could smell it."

"Smell what?"

"Fresh blood. Like when you pass a slaughterhouse. And smoke, from fires people had set. Dancing, some of them were, on cobbles so soaked with blood urchins were sliding on it like ice patches."

Tonia took her hand from her mouth. "It sounds like a scene from hell."

"Maybe so, if the citizens of hell are wearing leather boots with yellow tops this season, or frock coats the color of chocolate, or gowns of emerald green and bright pink, with matching bustles caught up behind." Julie fell silent.

"So this wasn't a case of the rabble going out of control?"

"One of the worst things about Versailles," Dear Julie fanned herself, "is how far you keep yourselves from reality. It wasn't rabble. It was the fine upstanding *bourgeoisie*. Would you like to hear what we heard, in the café afterward?"

Tonia took her time answering "Yes."

"They were lifting their glasses '*to my brother,*'" Julie mimicked the voice, " '*perished off Gibraltar, when the ammunition barges the cursed Crown sent exploded.*' '*To the sweet soul of my sister, crushed under the carriage wheels of an aristocrat who never stopped.*' '*To my uncle, exiled to the West Indies, died of fever with all his family, for some imagined slight against the stinking House of Bourbon.*' " She made a mock bow. "That was what we heard from your so-called rabble."

"I can't believe you went there," Tonia said. "What a foolish, dangerous thing to do."

"You would have done the same," Julie retorted, "when you still had the sense of adventure you seem to have misplaced. Before you became so boringly maternal. Before I realized how you turned my head."

"What?"

"I was so dazzled by your attention," dear Julie pouted, "but who wouldn't be? Be honest for once. You've looked down on me since the start, haven't you?"

"Where do you stay, in Paris?" Tonia's subject change was abrupt.

"At the *Palais Royale*. Why?"

"You haven't severed relations with that traitor *Egalite*, have you?"

"I haven't." Julie's fan snapped shut. "What's more, I don't intend to."

Tonia sighed. "You know how I loathed the Duke of Chartres, before he became Duke of Orleans. You even know why. It's beyond belief you support him, after all I've done for you."

Dear Julie shot up from her divan, taking two steps toward Tonia before regaining control. "You dare throw your gifts in my face?" she hissed through clenched teeth. "I *knew* you would accuse me so, sooner or later." She took another step. "You never really liked me for myself, did you?" And another. "You just wanted another *toy* — another plaything to amuse yourself with."

"Not so. I welcomed you, you were a breath of fresh air — "

"Breath of fresh air, my — my — pink and green *bustle.* What about your sneaky games of give and take away?"

"The Crown is bankrupted, in case you were unaware."

"I don't care if the Crown is begging at the doors of the Cathedral of Notre Dame — you have no right to lead people on, and then let them down. Just because they love you."

"My no longer dear Julie," Tonia spoke slowly at first, "what you and your family really loved is the fortune I lavished on you."

"And *you* loved the fun we had," the Countess' lips drew back from her pearly little teeth, "Oh, but once you had your husband's *spunk* in you, making you a mother, I wasn't fun anymore, was I? You didn't need *me* anymore, did you? Your celibate widow was enough for you."

"That celibate widow," Tonia repeated, "is the one person who cares for me, *as me.*" Her cheeks flushed scarlet. "Go."

Dear Julie obeyed, omitting the required curtsy.

A messenger appeared before the King as the sun was setting on July 14th, confirming the loss of life at one hundred twenty-eight, though the figure wasn't final as yet.

"The Commander of the Bastille," Louis Auguste murmured. "He was one of my promotions in rank on my journey to Cherbourg. Is he among the casualties?"

The messenger looked down at the list he carried. "De Launay. Yes, a casualty."

"We met and talked. He was keen on metalwork. Such a good man." Louis Auguste's ponderous head shook slowly, side to side. "He only did his duty. Followed orders to keep the peace at all costs.

He and his family, if he has one, paid the highest price for it. Tell your superiors to see they are looked after."

"Yes, Sire." The messenger was hardly more than a boy, although he was clearly trying to grow a dashing mustache. His fine new uniform was dirt-encrusted, its gold braid ripped and tarnished.

"Surely the good people of Paris were incited to this riot."

"Yes, Sire."

"And the disorders are growing, still, throughout the city?"

"Yes, Sire."

"Is it fair to call this a revolt?"

"No, Sire," the boy raised his head and looked his monarch squarely in the eye. "It is a revolution."

~ Chapter Thirty Four ~

"I'm not going to sue to regain anything I've given her," Tonia told Louisa the following morning. "You may disapprove, but I'm not even going to banish her. I'm going to sit here instead, reflecting on what makes me think I'm a good judge of character. For a minute, anyway."

The next night, July 15th, Tonia and the children stood with her husband and their father on the South Balcony, overlooking the tumult of the crowd below. She nodded, waved, and even smiled. He did his best to follow her lead, but soon gave up the pretense of normalcy. "I don't know how you do it," he whispered.

"Do what?" She whispered back.

"Remain so nonchalant. You know better than anyone I have no stomach for confrontation."

"True." Tonia leaned toward him, ever so slightly.

"But you," he went on, "you grasp life in both hands. You shake it, hard, until the outcome you desire falls free."

"That isn't always the case," she murmured.

Her smile and her wave never faltered, but as soon as they came inside, she broke all precedent by kneeling before her husband in the presence of ranks of witnesses.

"The revolt is contained by the National Guard," her voice carried loud and clear, "but for how long? You *must* crush it." Rising, she reached for his hand. "An army of your brave subjects wait to follow you into battle. I will be proud to ride by your side."

His Majesty made no move to disengage himself, but he made no response either. They stood silently, hands clasped, until it became clear his silence was his statement.

It took the hired troops three days to depart Paris. The Mayor met the King at the gates of Paris on the morning of the fourth. His Majesty said nothing as the Mayor presented him with the key to the city. But when Lafayette, head of the National Guard, offered him a new national cockade, fashioned of red, white, and blue ribbon, he pulled his three-cornered hat from his be-wigged head. Waving away any help he fastened it to the brim, as cockaded tri-corners rose like flags above the raucous crowd.

"This love-feast will not last," was all Tonia had to say of what was widely touted as a triumphant step toward *"Liberte, Egalite, Fraternite"* for every French citizen, regardless of Estate.

In early August, Monsieur Mirabeau rose again, to declare his wish to renounce each and all of his traditional privileges. One after another, the nobles followed suit, as the thrilling ideal of equal rights for all gripped them. In a matter of hours, centuries of aristocratic privileges were eliminated by those who held them.

The "Night of Sacrifices" touched off a kind of hysteria in the nobles at the tennis court, followed by days of feverish efforts by the National Assembly to make equal rights a reality. Their *Declaration of the Rights of Man* came six weeks later, at the end of August.

"I like the part about men being born and remaining free and equal," Tonia remarked to Catherine Hyde, after she and Louisa finished reading the contents of the reproduction she'd brought to Versailles. "I don't like the part that puts the authority of the nation before that of its monarch."

"You have put your finger on the very thing that divides its authors," Catherine commented.

"What was the definition of 'liberty' they give?" Louisa asked.

Catherine found the passage: *"Liberty consists in the power to do anything that does not injure others."*

"And the definition of 'law', Mademoiselle?" Tonia asked.

"The law is the expression of the general will."

Tonia shook her head. "What happens when the law is reduced to what the general will decides it wants?"

What the people of France wanted remained unclear, as September saw the goodwill of the "Night of Sacrifices" evaporate like water from a shallow pan in the sun.

The Royalists supported a government modeled on England's

Parliament, with a figurehead King who would wield no real power.

The Patriots, or Revolutionists, leaned to the model of England's former colonies, who had no King at all.

Louis Auguste took no stand one way or the other. And he took no action, except to stay as far from the National Assembly as he could.

The air was still at Trianon, but far from quiet on a late September afternoon. Cicadas droned in rising and falling chorus, as the blood sisters watched the light play among the massive oaks through half-closed eyes. The turf glowed brilliant green where the sun struck it, and bluish silver in the dappled shade. Sheep grazed in the meadow beyond their grove, where weeping willow tips brushed a pond's silky surface, and gliding pairs of black and white swans whistled their occasional annoyance.

"Who's that?" Tonia sat upright, shading her eyes and squinting. "I can tell the Major-Domo by the red and silver of his livery but who's that with him?"

A few bees, their energy autumn-sapped, bumbled in and out of the aster flowers blooming beneath their slippers, as they rose from the bench they shared.

Covered to his shoes by a heavy woolen greatcoat, the little man held a handkerchief before a face further hidden beneath a black felt slouch hat. The Major-Domo who'd accompanied him cleared his throat: "The Count Dumorier is a longtime admirer of Her Majesty. He is come to warn her of a plot." Bowing deeply, he removed himself a discrete distance.

The little man lowered his handkerchief: "The whole of the *Palais Royale* is abuzz with it — "

"You came from the *Palais Royale*?" Tonia interrupted him.

"Yes, Madame."

"Then you came from — what does that traitor call himself these days?"

"Please, Madame, I beg you to listen — "

"To some comrade of Chartres?" Tonia cut him off again. "No, make that Orleans. Or, no, wait, silly me! It's *'Egalite'* now, isn't it?"

"They have purchased all the corn and wheat on its way to Paris, to create a shortage they blame on the Crown." The Count's gloved hands shook. "Any day now, the mob they have infiltrated and encouraged will march here to protest the lack of bread — " his voice dropped to a whisper. " — but they really mean to take you all to Paris."

"Your imagination is amazingly vivid, Count Dumorier," was all Tonia said.

"Please," the little man turned to Louisa, "Please, gracious Princess, be her guardian angel now. You are her truest friend. I beg you to use your influence to convince Madame the threat is real. And imminent."

"I have trouble," Tonia interrupted, "believing the word of any associate of that vile '*Egalite*'."

"Oh Madame," the little man sank to both knees. "I beseech you! The fatal moment is near, and he is deeply, *criminally,* involved."

"Rise, sir," Tonia turned away. "Go and serve your country better than you have served your King."

"Even if I *did* believe Dumorier," Tonia said, as soon as the Major-Domo had escorted the Count out of earshot. "I can't do anything to prevent whatever he says is underway."

"He seemed so sincere. So concerned for your welfare."

"If I acted on the advice of everyone who *seems* sincere, or concerned, I'd be dancing to different tunes all day, every day. You know how little I like that. Taking advice, not dancing." Tonia hugged herself. "I left a happy childhood home behind at fourteen. *That,*" she gestured in the direction of the Great Chateau, "has *never* been my home. Every happiness I know is here, at Trianon. It is the world as I want my children to know it. The only place I can live as I choose." Her shoulders shrugged. "I won't owe that life to some slouch-hatted fool who keeps company with a nest of conspirators bent on eliminating Europe's most ancient monarchy." Her hands curled into fists. "If they really mean to bring the Crown down around our heads, they'll have to bury me in the ruins."

"Surely you don't mean that."

"I *do* mean that."

A note was waiting when they went in, from the officers of the newly arrived Flanders Regiment, requesting the honor of an audience at the dinner being given in their Majesties' honor.

Louis Auguste agreed with his wife there was nothing the Dauphin Louis-Charles loved more than soldiers. "But I am wary of any public appearance," he added. "Tell him there will be another time."

"Our other son lies four months cold in his grave," Tonia told him. "How many times did we promise him 'another time'? One that never came."

He sighed. "Let us accept the invitation."

The Flanders Regiment roared their greetings as the small Royal party entered. Pandemonium ensued when the Dauphin Louis-Charles, hoisted to stand on the head table, snapped to attention and saluted. Emptied goblets were hurled to the floor amid shouts of acclaim, along with chunks of the bread Count Dumorier had warned couldn't be found in Paris, all of it trampled beneath their booted feet.

A messenger from Lafayette's National Guard, arrived the following afternoon.

"His Majesty and his Ministers have seen this, Madame," the messenger unfolded the parchment sheet. "He wished you to hear for yourself."

"*Your Majesties,*" he began reading, "*I am on the march from Paris, accompanied by the National Guard, and a number of subjects who intend to present grievances concerning the scarcity of bread. I beg you to rest assured, and vouch that no disorder will take place.*"

He turned the sheet around, so Tonia and Louisa could see Lafayette's signature, written large across the bottom, beneath the date: *3 October 1789.*

Tonia turned to Louisa. "It appears the little man was right."

~ Chapter Thirty Five ~

The bank of lightning-shot clouds rolled closer, swallowing dusk into darkness before an intense shower subsided to a steady drizzle that cooled the night air and laid the dust of the road. Lacking the telltale dust column, the approaching mob was almost within sight of the Great Chateau's park before the pickets posted at its entrance detected their presence.

The picket was gasping for breath when he was shown to Her Majesty's reception rooms, accompanied by the Commandant of Versailles' troops, who confirmed the reports that the mob appeared to be made up of women.

Marie Antoinette shook her head. "My husband will never give his permission to fire on women, will he?"

"No, Madame."

"So *clever* of that traitor. Tell me please, will a select group of these bread-begging women be given the opportunity to voice their grievances face-to-face?"

The Commandant couldn't hide his surprise at the swiftness with which his Queen went straight to the heart of the matter. "How very astute, Madame. Yes, I am certain that is the plan."

"Then we must prepare for it."

The Commandant's King readily accepted what he proposed. He summoned his Ministers and the Court to assemble in the Gallery of Mirrors, where he stood with his Queen to receive the chosen delegates. As each woman came face to face with the despised "Madame Deficit" she listened intently, giving each question, concern and demand a sincere, thoughtful, courteous reply.

As soon the last of them left the Gallery, Tonia sought Louisa out. "They'll be shouted down the instant they tell the truth about how they were received with open arms and heard by open ears."

"How can you be so calm?" Louisa held out her shaking hands.

Ignoring protocol, Tonia grasped them until the trembling stopped. "If I allowed myself to give in to my fears, they'd fill me so full there'd be no room left for anything else. Why should I let them feast on my fright?"

There it was, her irrepressible grin.

The Court erupted in criticism of their Majesties' decision to meet with the protestors. None believed it was the King's idea. It was surely the Queen's. She should have been stopped.

Tonia, as always, laughed it all off. "They couldn't get me to wear a corset, could they?" The sisters had snatched half an hour after the children were safely in bed, to sit with laps full of needle-work neither was really busy with.

"And they've never managed to learn which charities I support."

"Anonymity," Louisa agreed.

"They haven't kept me from bringing up my children as I see fit — " she re-threaded her needle " — or prevented Mademoiselle Rose Bertin from becoming my Minister of Fashion."

"Or Madame Vigee Lebrun from becoming your Court painter," Louisa put in.

"Or Monsieur Leonard from mounting those idiotic stairs, to top off those coiffures back in the day, could they?"

The sun set without further incident, but the crowd outside swelled through the night, building great roaring bonfires, dancing and drinking around them.

"Save the Queen! — "

It was after three the next morning when the scream of the Guard at Tonia's door was cut off, along with his head, by one of the four men who'd reached her private bedroom through the maze of the Great Chateau.

Tonia startled from sleep, immediately aware that the double thuds — one light, one heavier — were no dream fragments, but the sound of real broadswords.

The additional scuffle, with the second Guard, gave Tonia the few moments she needed to activate the door-panel hiding the long-disused secret passage she'd created for Louis Auguste's marital visits.

Without waiting to cover her nudity, she plunged barefoot through the pitch-dark tunnel, oblivious to everything except a terrorizing need to know if Charlotte, Louis-Charles, and Louis Auguste were safe.

Spiders' webs caught in her out-flung hands and floated back against her sweating face. The dust swirling through the musty air choked her, but the thinness of the walls separating her from the suddenly murderous world outside kept her from coughing it out.

Sobbing for breath, she bolted when she reached the wide places and walked as fast as she dared in narrower spots, mind's eye focused on the blueprint she'd proudly initialed with her entwined "*MA*", just below the architect's name.

Tonia reached her husband's door panel in record time, dumbfounding the trio of his guards as she materialized from the wall beside his bed. They barely registered the incredible sight before she snatched Louis Auguste's dressing gown from his stupefied valet's grip. Thrusting her arms into it, she covered her nakedness.

"They are trying to assassinate me!" Her words were amazingly matter-of-fact, her hands steady as she tightened the gown's sash. "All thanks to God you are unharmed. I must see to the children. *Now.*"

Before the Guards moved, Tonia whirled around, flung open the doors herself, and charged past the Guards posted outside. They pounded after her as she sped on, to the children's wing.

Doors popped open all along the corridors, revealing bug-eyed jack-in-the-box faces. Dodging servants and trinket-sellers and lackeys, all jolting to their feet in total confusion, Tonia flew up the final steps of the last wide marble stairway leading to her children's suites.

For precious minutes, she held her sleeping son in her lap, watching and waiting for her daughter to come awake.

"I was sleeping, *Maman*," she complained as she did.

Tonia reached to smooth her hair, but Charlotte, nearly eleven, pulled away from the touch, her lower jaw pushing out in a way so familiar her mother had to smile.

"Some of your father's subjects have come all the way to Versailles just to see us," Tonia told her.

"Do we *know* these people who woke us in the middle of the night?"

"I'm afraid not. But they are subjects, poor ones, who have come here wanting to meet us, and they cannot wait any longer."

"Are their manners bad, then? Is that what's the matter?" Charlotte's snub nose wrinkled in disdain.

"That might be it. But they are subjects who don't wish to wait, so we won't make them."

"Can't we meet them in the morning?"

"We can't."

Charlotte's lip jutted further while she thought. "Well, I suppose they can look at me, but I *won't* speak to any of them."

"You needn't say a single word. Just stand quietly where I tell you to."

"Like a *tableaux* in the theater at Trianon?" The girl's face lit up.

"Exactly! And even if someone says something hurtful, or does something frightening, you'll stand firm, I know. And you won't cry."

"I'm too big for that."

New shouts rose from below as Tonia woke her sleeping son. The Commander of Versailles' troops was panting for breath when he arrived.

"Your Majesty, we have caught the men who murdered your Guards! A small band, four only, hardened criminals, killers for hire." He bowed. " They have been dealt with."

Tonia didn't ask him to elaborate. "What of the larger band?"

Audible words could be heard, horrible words, rising from the shouting outside: *"Death to the whore!" "Butcher Madame Deficit!" "We'll take her head back to Paris!"*

Tonia smoothed the folds of her husband's robe as she surveyed the room. "While I call for a shawl, and robes for my children, I wish you to round up the ringleaders." Her voice was suddenly, unnaturally calm. "When you return and we are ready, I will signal you to allow them entrance. You and your men will keep close watch, but when you open the doors, remain outside them."

"Do you command this?" The man was dumbfounded.

"I do."

The mob numbered more than a dozen; they froze at the opened doors, stunned to silence by the sight of the Her Majesty Marie

Antoinette, Queen Consort of France, standing between two unmade beds, holding the ends of a rough wool shawl across a coarse cotton night-robe, and smiling.

"Since you threaten to make orphans of two innocent children, will you do me the kindness of explaining your reasons to them?" She put the question as courteously as if she addressed courtiers. Gliding a few steps to one side, she gave the mob a clear sight of her daughter and son, standing perfectly still behind her. Neither child spoke as she took their hands and walked them through the opened doors, moving past the troops and through the throng as calmly and surely as if they were on their way to hear Mass in the morning. The fists upraised in fury went loose and slack. Only one voice howled out "*No! No!*" The rest stood mute.

The Royal family was reunited, soon after, in the safety of his Majesty's chambers. In whispers, so Charlotte and Louis-Charles wouldn't hear, Tonia tried to convince Louis Auguste to give the order to fire on the crowd massed outside: "It grows larger and more threatening with every passing hour."

"I mourn your Guards' deaths," he said, after a long pause, "but I fear more loss of life. Fear it too much to set anything in motion that might cause it."

"Your humanity outweighs your royalty," Tonia said finally. "I should hold you in contempt for that, but I can't."

"And your courage, as always, outweighed your common sense," he told her. Word of her incredible gamble had reached him before she did.

"The children were shaken, but they will be fine. They performed brilliantly. We should be very proud of them."

"I am. So how could I possibly give an order that might jeopardize their well-being?"

"We stand together on that."

"Do we also stand together on seeing no alternative but to go to Paris until the situation can be resolved?"

"*Situation*," Tonia muttered. "How quickly we find sweet words for stinking things! How long will it be, I wonder, before the attempt on my life becomes an *unfortunate incident*?"

At high noon after the horrors of the night before, their Majesties appeared together on the balcony overlooking the Royal Courtyard.

"My friends," the King announced, in a voice as strong and steady as any listener could recall, "I have decided that I will go to Paris, with my wife and children. I give all that I hold most dear to the love of my good subjects."

General Lafayette bent low over Marie Antoinette's hand, to the full-throated approval of the massed onlookers.

~ Chapter Thirty Six ~

It was almost midnight before the blood sisters were able to arrange a few much-needed minutes of intimate conversation.

"My husband swallowed it whole." Tonia set her chocolate cup down. "Lafayette's absurd claim he had no prior knowledge of the — he called it 'the despicable plan hatched by crazed terrorists to penetrate our inner rooms'."

Louisa frothed her chocolate. "Just what you'd expect a 'statue in search of a pedestal' to say."

Tonia laughed. "Remember when we first heard that? When my huge-hearted husband was emptying the Treasury to finance a war being fought to end a monarchy?" She wasn't laughing anymore.

"I do recall you pointing that out."

"And I remember there was no point to it." Tonia shifted in her chair. "And no point arguing the relocation to Paris. Temporary, of course, until adequate security measures are in place."

"Well, the palace there is surrounded by the Tuileries gardens. You know how fond Mademoiselle Hyde is of them."

"The Inglesina will have less distance to travel, won't she?"

"She will. And Mademoiselle Bertin will welcome your presence."

That brought Tonia's smile back. "She won't have to carry her creations — and her creativity — back and forth." She looked around the room, one of so many her unerring eye had transformed. "And I will tell you, truly, my sister, I have never been so frightened in my life."

"And never as brave."

"Or as foolish, perhaps," Tonia shrugged.

"The one most certain thing is — Paris will be safer. For now."

"I've already been told it's rather dilapidated, for a palace."

Scratching at the door signaled their time together was up.

Louisa stood first. "Then there will be plenty to take our minds off things."

"Plenty," Tonia repeated.

The October weather held fair enough to ready almost a thousand carriages in just two days, for a journey Tonia had convinced her children would be an exciting new adventure.

Count Axel Fersen appeared outside Louisa's carriage just as it began to move forward. He cut the same dashing figure he always did, even in the midst of the hectic confusion.

"May I join you, your Highness?" He bowed. "My groom is wild to ride my horse from here to Paris, and I am happy to allow him."

Louisa readily agreed to let him share her carriage, and was soon glad of it. He proved an attentive and amusing distraction. The combination made him an ideal companion through the unsettling journey, from Versailles' world unto itself to the unpredictable world of a great city. "I am far less familiar with Paris than you, Count," she spoke, finally, into one of several polite silences.

"It will hardly matter, your Highness. The Palace of the Tuileries has long been well protected. The gardens lack the grandeur of Versailles', but they are a substantial buffer against the" he hesitated "the clamor of Paris. And it will be a far simpler matter for Lafayette and the National Guard to ensure your absolute safety."

"They tried to kill her!" burst from Louisa.

"Please, your Highness, try to put yourself at ease." The muscles of Fersen's face contracted, but his tone remained light. "An intensive investigation has already been conducted, with the conclusion the plot was to terrorize, not take life."

"But they had knives! They butchered her Guards!"

As if on some ghastly cue, the rumble of the crowd outside swelled to a roar. Fersen leaned past her suddenly, almost roughly, to drop the blind slats and fasten the window curtains on either side.

"What are you doing?" The roars were laced with howls.

"There's no need to see, your Highness. It's enough that you must hear."

Suddenly bold, Louisa pressed apart the blind slats for an instant, no more, before she sank back into her cushions, both fists pressed against her mouth, as the image of the severed heads of Tonia's murdered guards seared itself forever: swollen masses of ghastly gray-white flesh atop thick wooden pikes, each still topped with its distinctive plumed helmet. They bobbed along, in hideous parody of fairground stilt-walkers, just out of reach of the upraised fists of the mob.

The shrieks and curses and obscene ballads were nothing in comparison to that single glimpse. The noise in her head drowned out the chant begun by the prostitutes riding astride the National Guard cannons. The marchers took it up: "*We have the baker, the baker's wife, and the baker's little boy! Now we will have bread.*"

"You don't have to be here," she told him as they waited their turn to pass through Paris' city gates.

"Oh but I do," he answered, simply. "I am her champion." His head bowed. "Her platonic champion."

Louisa hesitated before she asked "What is your idea of platonic love?"

His grin was equal parts sheepish and endearing. "You are well enough aware of my other loves, Princess" He shook his handsome head. "A husband's love for my wife, filial love for my children, carnal love for my mistress." The grin faded. "Platonic love is — more profound. It owes nothing to those affections. And everything to courtly love." His voice dropped to a whisper. "I am her courtly knight."

Her smile communicated she understood. *And I am her blood sister.*

At the Palace of the Tuileries, the Count saw her to her rooms, leaving two gold coins in the gaping chambermaid's hand, before he bowed over Louisa's and took his leave.

Despite the great efforts at preparation, the years of shut-up air in unused rooms remained dank and musty, and a film of greasy dust covered the surfaces that hadn't been under cloth wraps. The only light in Louisa's assigned room came from a tallow candle anchored in a common china teacup. It barely illuminated Tonia's hasty scrawl, on the note pinned to her pillow:

We will see each other in the morning. I remembered to have our bed-pillows packed as necessities. All else might be strange in this new place, but at least we'll have our pillows.

Louisa's was tear-sodden before sleep finally claimed her.

The next morning's sun rose, as it always did. The Superintendent of Her Majesty's Household re-established the routines of Versailles, as they had always been followed.

Tonia arrived at Louisa's suite after Mass. "A different chapel. A priest so elderly he required an altar boy beneath each arm, coming and going. Different cooks in charge of the kitchens." A timid maid-servant, clearly unused to Royal service, brought their breakfast.

"Feh!" Tonia's nose wrinkled like her daughter's. "What have these eggs been whipped with? New household indeed."

"Same old Superintendent," Louisa joked.

"Old? Since when is thirty-nine old?"

"Since September of last year."

They were relaxed, if not well-fed, when the Household Secretary was shown into a hastily appointed reception room.

"Inglesina, welcome!" Tonia greeted her. "What a fortunate thing, your having such facility in so many languages." She leveled an appraising look. "More than equal to the increase in your tasks."

"Your compensation is also increased," Louisa added, "for the task of keeping your eyes — and your ears — more open than ever."

"Although we know you already do so," Tonia assured her. "You witness what transpires outside these walls to an extent we cannot match. We know you will be truthful."

"I will, Madame." Catherine Hyde flushed to the roots of her unruly red curls. "And Princess."

Louisa motioned to the accumulation of portfolios heaped on a sideboard. "We'll speak no more of it. I hope you will indulge yourself in some way with the increase in income."

"Thank you," Catherine curtsied.

"We are removed from so much else in the way of protocols," Louisa told her, "there is no need for this one."

Catherine set about organizing as Tonia left to complete her *toilette* and check in on the children.

"Your mare, Perdita, was brought to Paris as one of the necessaries we were allowed," Louisa said. "She is stabled on the Palace grounds here. Have you seen them?"

"I haven't," Catherine answered. "They are within what has always been a secured area."

"To which you will have access, provided you can display the Royal tricolor." Louisa reached into a pocket and withdrew one of the red, white and blue grosgrain ribbon badges the National Guard checked at all entries and exits. "And be honest, please. Do you think it safe enough to make your way to Rambouillet? I wish to continue correspondence with my father-in-law, with less frequency and more discretion. Do you understand?"

"Yes, Princess. I have always enjoyed riding to Rambouillet. By routes other than the high road."

She is so sincere, Louisa thought. *And so matured.* "And when we have worked our way through some of this, if you have no further commitments for the balance of this afternoon, it would give me so much pleasure to hear you sing."

Catherine did, performing several of the *a capella* rondeaus that were Louisa's favorites.

~ *Chapter Thirty Seven* ~

The rest of that October saw no more blood, no more murder, no more rioting. Some said it was the sight of the Royal Family, escorted by drunken prostitutes and pike-carrying rioters, parading their trophy heads, that awed the people of Paris into silence.

"I told you all would be well if we came and lived among them." Louis Auguste insisted, as he, Tonia and Louisa were finishing a first intimate dinner. "My loyal subjects. My good people!"

"Like the ones who shared their bread and cheese with you on the road to Cherbourg?"

"Yes, yes."

"I wish I had been at your side, to meet those loyal subjects."

"These pears are perfectly ripe, aren't they?" Louisa changed the subject.

"How quickly he forgets," Tonia whispered minutes later, as the dining salon doors were closed behind him. "Forgets the loyal subjects who penetrated the Great Chateau in the dead of night, intent on murdering me in my bed."

"Don't speak of that, please."

"So, sister. Are you becoming as much an ostrich as my husband?"

"No, but — it might bring bad luck."

"Bad luck might be a change for the better."

The sun rose and set. Days became weeks, then a month. Wagons loaded with goods continued to arrive at the Palace of the Tuileries, rolling proof that the stay was no longer brief. Daily life divided "this country of Versailles" from "this city of Paris". New servants were brought on, to replace those maintaining order in that "other country."

The reduced space also brought the unexpected and much welcomed benefit of adjoining private suites. For the first time in years the blood sisters could hold hands and embrace free of observant eyes, however downcast.

They immersed themselves in the work of making their surroundings more habitable. Needed repairs were made and thorough cleaning carried out. Carpets were laid, tapestries hung, furniture arranged, kitchens set up, linens distributed.

The National Assembly also moved from Versailles to Paris, taking up where they'd left off in pursuit of "liberty, equality, and fraternity" under a Constitutional monarchy.

Tonia's "Minister of Fashion" hadn't shuttered her shop on the Rue de Colombe. Mademoiselle Rose Bertin came to the Tuileries most mornings, brisk and bustling, bringing her seamstresses, samples, and blessed air of normalcy.

Bertin and her troop observed all protocol until the newly-installed room-servants withdrew from the blood sisters' adjoining suites. She would smooth her crisp white country apron then, patting at the hair escaping from the gray-streaked bun that was the only untidy thing about her. Lifting her signature egret-neck scissors on their gold neckchain, she would make the eagerly awaited announcement: "Madame, Princess, give us this day!" At the scissors' drop, her seamstresses and hatmakers opened the boxes they all could escape into, for the duration.

At month's end, Monsieur Leonard, Tonia's "Knight of the Comb", wrote from Belgium that his "crise de nerfs" at the goings-on appeared to be over.

"Crisis of nerves is his chronic state," Tonia remarked, as she finished reading his letter. "Still, he writes he hopes to be back in France before my birthday. If anyone can do something with my souvenir," she patted at her simple coiffure, "it will be Monsieur Leonard."

The very day of their arrival in Paris, Tonia's silky, ash-blonde hair had begun to fade, becoming stark white in a matter of weeks. Others laughed when she dubbed it her *"souvenir"*; Louisa couldn't bring herself to think of the shocking change as anything anyone would wish to keep as a reminder. And she couldn't keep from crying out the night she opened a small white satin box.

"I wove it myself," Tonia told her. She held out her right hand. "And this one too." A matching ring of her white hair circled her forefinger, above the fire opal she always wore.

"I felt like a salmon swimming against the tide," Leonard was paying his first visit since his return to Paris. He didn't need to add he referred to the emigres departing France. Their numbers swelled daily. The Countess Yolande of Polignac was long gone, to a warm welcome in Russia. Hers was the one name neither Tonia nor Louisa ever mentioned.

Madame Vigee Le Brun, the artist Tonia had so controversially made her Royal portraitist, was also in Russia. She'd left with Tonia's blessing, and any number of commissions. Ambassador Mercy had returned to Austria, where Tonia's brother Joseph still ruled, despite being reported ill. The Pope offered France's Royal family refuge, but the National Assembly, clergy included, refused to allow the heir to depart the country.

November arrived, and with it Tonia's thirty-fifth birthday. Rose Bertin visited the day before. "The samples are superb," Tonia told her, fingering the pieces of *peau-de-soie* in her lap. "I can't wait to see the finished gown."

"It will be ready for the celebration," Bertin assured her, "even if my women have to sit to it all day and all night and into tomorrow morning. We are so pleased you've agreed to the blue, instead of black."

It was a lovely party, complete with her favorite lobster souffles, but Tonia lost her composure at the sight of the cake. It was pretty enough, though plain in comparison with the incredible confections of years past. The central decoration, nestled in a wreath of candied violets, was the alabaster miniature of the Temple of Love. Tonia's shoulders shook as she touched the one remaining relic of her fairytale Trianon model. The rest, like so much else, had been ruined in transit.

In December, the National Assembly issued 400 million francs' worth of Treasury bills, or *assignats*, with the result that many more tables saw a bit of meat, even a Christmas goose, in honor of the holiday season. *Phillipe Egalite's* role in creating the shortages that led to the "Bread March" remained unproved.

At the New Year, 1790, a deputation from the National Assembly came to Palace of the Tuileries to meet with the Queen. They expressed sympathy for the horrible fright she'd suffered, gave reassurances that those involved were misguided madmen, and requested the honor of her presence at the theater that evening.

"Is it possible, my dear Princess," Tonia said to Louisa, in a voice clearly audible to all, "that I can enjoy any public amusement while I am still chilled with horror at the blood that was spilled, the blood of the faithful defenders of our lives?" Her steely blue stare found every pair of eyes in the room. "I can forgive," she said, finally, "but I cannot so easily forget."

Louisa sat at the portable writing desk she'd had made. Designing it, and choosing its fittings, were welcome distractions from her growing unease at the reasons given that blocked a return to Versailles.

"It isn't about *our* security at all," Tonia had complained just yesterday, as she took the chair beside the one Mademoiselle Hyde occupied. "It's about *their* politics."

The Household Secretary visited weekly, less often astride the faithful Perdita, more often in the company of Rose Bertin because it was less conspicuous. Between them, the two women came with the news and left with the things they could be trusted to keep private.

A letter to Louisa's aging father-in-law would be included today. She still wrote regularly, despite the mental state that likely kept him from grasping what she wrote. His replies no longer sounded like his own voice, but it was a link. *A Papa Time, and a blood sister,* she thought. *No relation by birth, but family. My family.* She dipped her pen.

> *The 7th day of August in the year of our Lord 1790*
>
> *My dear Papa,*
>
> *The 'Fete de la Federation' celebrating the first anniversary of Bastille Day's insurrection went on all last month. The citizens of Paris danced in the streets wearing red felt "liberty caps" pinned with the red, white and blue cockades we all wear, regardless of rank or position.*

Sunday last marked the fete's final parade, in honor of the first anniversary of the Declaration of the Rights of Man. Her Majesty was magnificent in a cloth-of-silver gown, a cockade the only adornment in her white hair. She sat, and made certain her children sat, silent and respectful through what truly seemed endless speeches about one hope for a better world ...

The summer wore on, along with the Constitutional process. Tonia agreed with her husband — publicly, at any rate — that this was the best way forward. It did not keep her from bringing up the fact that the document declared loyalty to the nation, to the law, and to the King — in that order. His Majesty missed the hunting that had become far too complicated to arrange. His Queen Consort did not request a visit to the Trianon retreat she sorely missed.

The chestnut trees hung green and glorious over the *Champs Elysee* through early autumn. Swallows and seabirds dipped between Paris' bristle of chimneys; the river Seine sparkled where sun struck water through its coating of refuse. With the great river machinery shut off, the fountains it fed were dry.

Hastily boarded windows and entryways disfigured one great building after another, as they were stripped to the walls and left to the care of the fewest possible servants.

Those who remained couldn't get enough of the historic happenings, which seemed to be taking place without any of the "excesses" condemned by Sir Edmund Burke in his *Reflections on the Revolution in France.* The book of essays was still selling briskly at year's end.

The 11th day of February in the year of our Lord 1791

With the Civil Constitution a reality, the cumbersome numbers of the National Assembly have been reduced to a 745-member Legislative Assembly. I was diligent in obtaining correct numbers for you. Their newly established Legislative Hall can accommodate them all, as they take on the task of carrying out the momentous changes in our government.

Some two hundred are led by well-known conservative Mirabeau. They sit on the right side of the Hall, so they are called "the Right". They all support a figurehead monarchy similar to England's.

About a hundred fifty are determined to abolish the monarchy altogether. They sit on the left side of the Hall, so they are "the Left." They are led by Monsieurs Danton, Marat and Robespierre — all of whom, I am sorry to report, with ties to your son-in-law ..."

Louisa shook a drop of ink over the last words, blotting, before she wrote *Phillipe Egalite* in the grayish space. She felt relief her Papa Time wouldn't recognize the new identity her nemesis claimed. And his caretakers would be glad to get word they knew to be accurate.

... Some three hundred as yet unaffiliated members separate Left from Right. No clear leader has emerged from their voting majority ...

On May Day, Monsieur Mirabeau, the leader of the Right, was granted a secret audience with his Queen. His message was clear: "The Center will not hold, Madame. When they do move, I fear it will be to the Left."

He paused for effect, bowing a head so large it interfered with his otherwise fashionable appearance. "Madame, I have come to implore you to consider what can happen when the Leftists sworn to dissolve our monarchy prevail."

She sat silent.

"I implore you to recall the dissension that provoked your presence here."

She still said nothing.

"Your situation even now, Madame," his voice dropped to a dramatic whisper, "*is no better than house arrest.*"

"I thank you for your concerns, Monsieur," she spoke, finally, "and for the kindness you have showed in coming to express them. You have my word I will give all you have told me serious consideration."

"And you have my word, Madame, that I will assist you, in any way I possibly can."

~ *Chapter Thirty Eight* ~

In other times and circumstances, the celebration of the French monarchs' twentieth wedding anniversary would call for lavish preparations to be well underway. May 15, 1790 passed unmarked by any public display.

Louisa offered only spoken congratulations to them both. "I have donated to our Guardsmen's families, in both your names." Her grin was rueful. "Apologies, Madame, for not maintaining your anonymity." The Royal couple dined in private before retiring to their separate suites.

Ten days later, Mirabeau was found dead, amid chilling rumors his end had been hastened by poison. Baron Besenval brought Tonia the frightening details, along with his heart-felt farewells, as he prepared to leave for England.

The man Tonia dubbed "Grandfather Gossip" two decades ago needed two canes to stand upright, and a servant at each elbow to move forward. Once settled into the softest chair in the reception room, he dismissed his servants and she dismissed hers.

"How can I bid you farewell," he began, "and sail for England knowing you remain in harm's way?" He thumped one cane on the uncarpeted floor. You *must* take Monsieur Mirabeau's death as a sign, sweet one, that the time has *well and truly come*, for you to secure safe passage from France." He slumped back against his chair-cushion.

"My dear Grandfather," Tonia smiled. "Will it relieve you to hear it's already planned?"

"Oh yes," the old man breathed. "Yes *indeed*."

Tonia leaned closer. "I will travel as a Swedish national, a 'Madame Korff', who happens to be a friend of Count Fersen's — "

"Fersen!" Besenval's lantern jaw dropped. "That sly *devil*, he never let on to me, though, to be truthful, our paths haven't been crossing all that often. Your champion to the rescue! But of course — exactly as it should be."

Tonia eagerly shared the details. "He's been to Monsieur Louis, the carriage maker, who has nearly finished our *berline*. It seats six inside, four outside, up on the box and at the rear."

"Surely you're decorating the interior?" The old man teased.

"Suggestions, yes, a few. The cushions are white taffeta, with matching double curtains. And there are several ingenious storage compartments, designed to hold the things that will make 'Madame Korff's' journey comfortable."

"Ah, yes, the Swedish matron. And who else?"

"She — no, I — will be accompanied by her — my — two children and a pair of domestics — their governess, Madame Tourzel, and my husband," she giggled. "You can't imagine how I tease him about being my obedient servant!"

"I *can* imagine!" The Baron's tone was light, but his bright-brown eyes shimmered with unshed tears. "Trust you to find the fun even in the grimmest reality. What amazing spirit! What incredible bravery!"

"What a load of flattery!" Tonia giggled again. "Which of course will get you anywhere."

"Will it get me more of the juicy details?"

"Absolutely. 'Madame Korff' and her party have passports allowing entry to Belgium. That's our first destination. We'll have the King's Swiss Guards as our outriders, and escort troops as well, once that's safe. My hairdresser, Monsieur Leonard, will carry messages between them; he will also carry the jewels to finance our future once we reach Belgium. That's the first step."

"And such a step! I am so relieved! Tell me, though," the Baron frowned. "What of the Princess?"

"She has already left for Rambouillet, where she waits for a signal of our successful passage. My *couturier*, Mademoiselle Bertin, is taking care of that."

"Your departure is imminent, then?"

"Imminent. No later than June 25 — earlier, if possible."

On the twentieth of June, 1791, Tonia finished supper early.

Dismissing her ladies-in-waiting and room-servants, she sat alone in her salon, wanting Louisa with her, wishing they'd put off their furtive good-byes. When the delicate chime of the gold ormolu mantel-clock struck ten, she stood, shook herself, and went upstairs.

Her daughter Charlotte was pouting at the things she would have to wear on the journey. At almost thirteen, she'd long been free to choose.

"The color's so dull, *Maman,* the cut so *drab*. Not a single feather on the bonnet! And cotton stockings! If I have to dress like this in Belgium, I won't go there. I *won't.*" She stamped her foot. "If the people outside of France want us to live with them, why can't they just come *fetch* us?"

"I wish they could," Tonia soothed her, able to smile now. "They aren't allowed, so it's up to us to leave France for another country. I left Austria for here, when I was only a year older than you are." Her father's voice echoed in her mind's ear: *"Lorrainers love to live ..."*

Living on. That was the business at hand.

"Charlotte, dear, you'll love this grand adventure once we're settled — elsewhere. You won't have to dress like this, and neither will I. So. What do you think of *my* disguise?" Tonia twirled around in her gray poplin dress and black wool shawl. Her plain brown felt hat was draped in a face-covering veil. "Peek-a-boo," she cooed, pulling it up and down.

Charlotte laughed and applauded. Tonia reached out with the reassuring hug her daughter didn't always allow.

Louis-Charles wouldn't budge from his nest of covers, not until she said, "There'll be lots of soldiers where we're going." That brought him out of his bed, where he flew into a rage at the sight of his disguise.

"Not a dress, *Maman*!"

"Yes, a dress." At five, too young to fully understand the need for disguise, the little boy nodded "yes" to her questions: "Remember before we came here to Paris? When all those rude people came in the middle of the night to look at us?"

"I do, *Maman.*" His pout weakened.

"Well, some people on our way, who are just as rude, might peek inside our *berline,* looking for a little boy. When they see a little girl, they'll just go on."

"And if they don't, the soldiers will get them!" His pout vanished. "Can I have my uniform on underneath, *Maman*? And can I take the dress off as soon as no one's peeking at me?"

"Yes! And yes!"

When she was satisfied her children were as readied as possible, she sent for Madame Tourzel, the discrete governess she'd found for them when they first reached Paris. Putting a finger to her lips to remind them to stay silent, Tonia opened the door to the hallway, where a sentinel paced back and forth

"Quickly now, and quietly," Tonia whispered, as the sentinel paused at his far turn.

"Like hide and seek?" Louis-Charles whispered back.

"Only we *stay* hidden," Charlotte hissed at him.

"I knew that!" He was indignant. "I'm not *stupid.*"

"*Mon petites,*" Madame Tourzel's voice quavered from her place behind them, "Silence, I implore you."

They went quietly then, down the stairs and out into the King's Courtyard, where a common hackney cab, with Count Fersen its driver-for-hire, waited with the dozens of carriages, there for His Majesty's retiring ceremony, the *coucher.* Indoors, once his bed-curtains were closed, His Majesty would don his own disguise and make his way, separately and on foot, to the prearranged meeting place.

Holding her children's hands, with Madame Tourzel a step behind, Tonia eased into the Courtyard, keeping in the substantial shadows of the carriage rows as she shepherded them to the cab.

"You'll be going to the *Place du Petit Carousel*, a short walk from here. I'll follow you there soon, and so will Papa. Meantime, you will have Count Fersen and Madame Tourzel with you. You must mind her, now, both of you."

The plan of staggered departure was firm, and Tonia had consented, but it was awful now. She shrank back into the shadows as the *coucher* came to its end, straining her shortsighted eyes to pick out the hackney's roof from the others lurching through the gates.

The directions to the *Place du Petit Carousel* had been clear; the distance was mercifully short before she made out the dark bulk of Fersen's cab with the blue kerchief tied to its rear steprail. Her husband's head poked through the curtain as she rapped at the door.

"*Where have you been?*" he hissed.

"*At a garden party!*" she hissed back, her retort softened by his great guffaw and the children's giggles.

"It nears midnight," Fersen kept his voice low. "Inside, quickly please." The *berline* they would use, with its trio of Guard driver-grooms, was hidden some five miles away, by the Metz Road. Fersen drove as fast as he dared; they reached it in under an hour, boarded and settled themselves. The thinnest sliver of a midnight moon gave no illumination as Fersen maneuvered the hackney cab to the road's deep ditch-edge. Unharnessing the skittish horse, he overturned the vehicle and leaped up onto the *berline*'s driver- box.

He whipped the horses to a gallop, keeping their pace fast until they reached the first posthouse, at the town of Bondy, where six fresh horses waited, harnessed and ready.

Fersen played his role to the end: "Farewell, Madame Korff," he bowed as he opened the *berline* door. "Godspeed to you and to yours."

"We thank you, sir," Louis Auguste was solemn.

"From the bottom of our hearts," Tonia added, thinking what a strange *tableaux* they made: *the dashing Count they think my lover; the naïve husband, who never wished to be King; the good wife, who has never cuckolded him.*"

They slept as best they could through the night. At six the next morning, the *berline* left Meaux, the second posthouse. The sun rose on an otherwise untraveled country road. Tonia helped her sleepy son remove his frilly skirt. Bird calls, the occasional low of cattle, and the steady rhythm of hooves on packed earth were the only sounds.

Tonia removed her plain brown hat and stretched both arms toward the ceiling. "The air smells so fresh. We must let more of it in."

Madame Tourzel rolled up the leather curtains, followed by the double taffetas. The new day's brightness filled the cushioned space as Tonia opened the food hampers, introducing the contents as "*monsieur boeuf la mode*" and "*mademoiselles oeufs en gelee*", to laughter and applause. "There are cheeses too, one, two, three, four, five kinds

— one for each of us, and enough to share — and these rolls!" Leaning close, she slipped her fingers into the napkin-lined basket. "La la! Still warm!" They ate them with sweet butter from a glazed pottery crock and plum preserve from a porcelain pot.

"Is anything better than a picnic?" Louis-Charles demanded, through a mouth crammed full. No one even mentioned his manners.

~ Chapter Thirty Nine ~

The road ran straight east, to the forest of Argonne. The occasional farm wagon that appeared took no notice of yet another *émigré* carriage. On they went into Champagne, with its sloping hillsides full of grapevines, vivid green and brown against the chalky-white earth.

They reached the next relay station at ten that morning.

"I prefer to relieve myself outside instead of using the chamber pot." Louis Auguste made the unexpected announcement as he opened the carriage door, stepping down not fifty feet away from a few onlooking peasants.

"Madame Korff's" domestic servant was completing his call of nature when they motioned him over. He stood with them, nodding at their harvest talk, oblivious, until the lead horse grew so impatient the groom holding its bridle bawled "We depart, we depart."

"*These* are the people of France." Louis Auguste shifted his bulk on the *berline's* seat. "Good people. Not the murderous *provocateurs* choking the life from our cities." The face he turned to Tonia held a wistful eagerness. "Let us remain here! Right here!"

"You know we cannot," she spoke gently, "much as we might wish to. Not at this time."

"Well then, is there still a need to travel *incognito*?" He waved out the window as the *berline's* driver started the team. The onlookers waved back. "We are out of danger now."

Through the rest of that day, it seemed they were, as "Madame Korff" and her party put Chaintrix, Sainte-Meinhold, and Clermont behind them at three-hour intervals. Only one more town, Varennes, remained before the last way-station, at Montmedy. The escort troops waiting there could fall in behind them, openly, as they covered the final fifty miles to the Belgian border.

"Varennes — Montmedy — safety." Tonia sang the names like a

nursery rhyme with the children.

All was quiet when they stopped to light the carriage-lamps just outside Varennes. Tonia turned her cheek to the coolness of the taffeta cushions and drifted to sleep, waking as the *berline* halted at the appointed place in the upper town.

No one was there. No relay horses. No waiting innkeeper.

Five endless-seeming minutes ticked by, ten, before the driver set the brake and started down the steep hill leading to the lower town, where, hopefully, some simple explanation awaited.

The instant Tonia heard the cries, "*Stop! Stop!*" she needed no explanation.

The troops were politeness itself as they escorted the Royal Family to the second floor of the town grocer's house. At five o'clock the following morning, an *aide-de-camp* to General Lafayette climbed the stairs. Standing at sharp attention beside the hastily-made up bed where the Royal children sprawled, sound asleep, he read out the Legislative Assembly's official decree:

"*We hereby give an order to all functionaries to arrest all members of the Royal Family, to give them safe escort to Paris, and to secure their safety in that city.*" Finishing, he set the paper down on the foot of the bed.

Tonia lunged for it, ripped it to pieces, dropped them to the floor and twisted her heel on them before she spoke: "I would have burned it, but for the absence of a fire in the hearth." She stared down the *aide-de-camp*: "I cannot keep you from carrying out your order, but I refuse to let you contaminate my children with it."

Like the fountains of Paris, Rambouillet's no longer played. Unlike Paris, the inhabitants of the great estate had long since adjusted to cycles of good years and bad. People in the surrounding villages and countryside were reluctant to blame the aristocratic lord of their manor for plunging the country into its state of crisis. He'd always seen to it they were looked after; they returned the favor now, shielding him from hard truth, as rivers of resentful countrymen flowed by, on their way to larger towns and great cities, eager to add peasant and commoner anger to the Third Estate stew already simmering there.

Louisa found Papa Time less in touch with reality than ever, lost in territory familiar only to him. He had no idea who she was, or where he was, but he was serenely happy there. His condition was familiar to the blessed minimum of servants and others who saw to his care. Louisa made arrangements to ensure they were all well provided for now and into the future. It helped pass the time there, which hung heavy on her hands, heart, and soul as she waited to hear news of her blood sister and her family.

The days went by; no word arrived from General Boulle, who was providing courier relays as well as escort troops from his position in Belgium. No courier carried the coveted report, that "Madame Korff", her daughters, and domestic servants, were safe in Belgium.

Louisa's wait ended three weeks into June, when she took the smaller replica of Bertin's scissors from the desk she'd designed for travel, fitted with items she wouldn't have to send for. She snipped the blue satin ribbon around the folded letter; a small lace packet fell into her lap.

She opened the letter first. *Dictated,* she thought. And worded with care, in the event it was intercepted:

"Treasure did not pass. At Paris location under further guard. L. sent word to B. who sent enclosed via C.

Her hands shook as she fumbled the packet open. *Leonard and Bertin and Catherine.* Her breath stopped at the sight of the ring braided from pure white hair. The ring that matched the one on the little finger of Louisa's left hand. She rubbed it like a talisman, lost in utter recall of that imp's face, as Tonia pricked their fingers with an embroidery needle, in the middle of the magical night that made them blood sisters.

Papa Time didn't comprehend what Louisa told him the following morning, about her return to Paris. He asked no questions and raised no objections, contenting himself with tuneless crooning as he unpinned a gaudy brass-backed pocket-watch from his bedgown, holding it out to her with a flourish that stung her to tears.

His caregivers voiced their worry at her departure, but the Princess had a ready response: "I took a vow," — she was gracious, matter-of-fact — "to serve Madame with every energy at my command, to the greater glory of my God and my Queen. I cannot make light of such an obligation." They understood, and saw to it she was readied to depart in a matter of hours.

Louisa reached the Palace of the Tuileries by one in the afternoon. June's full moon was high before a four-man contingent of the King's Swiss Guards and Lafayette's National Guard presented arms at the salon she'd been shown to.

Tonia had never looked more regal, sitting upright, her back not quite touching the pale peach damask of her chair back. She wore a *crepe de chine* dressing-gown in the shade of blue she loved. The *Alencon* lace wrapped around her shoulders was fragile as cobwebs, with a pattern as minute. Her hair was freshly washed, and the air in the room smelled faintly of the same *'eau de vie'* cologne Louisa had helped Tonia send to her mother the Empress, once upon another time. Their allotted time was limited to twenty minutes, so their embrace was wordless and brief. Their hands, their arms, and their lips sent sufficient messages.

Tonia stepped back first, turning to the side table holding her chocolate makings. "There's no milk, only sugar and water. Until they locate a cow who'll swear to uphold the Civil Constitution."

Louisa had to laugh as she settled herself in the matching chair. Neither spoke as Tonia carried the tray to the table between them. The only sound was the jingle of their frothing sticks as they sipped in a silence Tonia finally broke.

"They threw rotting vegetables." She stared at the far wall. "Pelted them, against the taffeta curtains, until our thin line of guards fastened the leathers. It was so beastly hot, huddled there in the dark." Her voice seemed to come from a distance. "And worse when we were made to leave the carriage. For refreshments, they said, but really it was so they could parade us through a forest of those horrible wooden pikes, held aloft in murderous hands, surging forward, barely being held back."

"Sister," Louisa reached for her, but Tonia was lost in the horror of the actual experience.

"They shouted unspeakable things. We tried to cover the children's ears — " she didn't realize she was demonstrating " — but it was useless."

Louisa tried to bring her back. "How did they know where to go in search of you?" She set her cup down. "Northwest to Belgium was the last route anyone was supposed to think about."

"Pillow talk, is what I've already overheard, I'm sure I was meant to. Someone in my husband's service told his mistress, who told her lover, who went to Lafayette's National Guard." She poured the last of the cooled chocolate. "The pursuing hounds knew where to follow the scent." She sipped. "I did the stupidest thing when I first heard the call to *Halt*! Pulled my veil down over my face."

"Not stupid. Wise instinct, to try to hide yourself."

"Instinct, yes, but wise?" She reached across the table.

"I'm here," Louisa reached back, rubbing a finger over the ring she'd returned.

"It was placed on the dressing table," Tonia whispered, "where I couldn't miss it. On your instructions?"

"On my instructions."

"I have seen everything." Her luminous blue gaze riveted itself on Louisa's face. "Heard everything. And forgotten nothing."

The doors swung open, admitting the Guards, who presented arms as the two women stood. Ignoring all public protocol, they held each other close, wordless, for a minute, perhaps more.

With the Royal escape attempt successfully foiled, Lafayette handpicked the National Guardsmen who would, "stand between the Royal Family and any further harm or embarrassment," his proclamation read, closing with his personal pledge to make them, "safe and comfortable, indoors and out."

The hollow drumming of a summer cloudburst startled both sisters awake, in their separate suites, at what should have been sunrise. It subsided to muttering thunder as suddenly as it began; and the Superintendent of her Majesty's Household was already dressed when she was summoned to a meeting.

Louisa watched the Guardsmen arrive and mobilize for the outdoor excursion. Watched Tonia's genuine interest work its customary magic. "Citizen companions," she called them, graciously, even cheerfully. Observing how the younger ones jostled for Tonia's attention made her smile.

They stepped across the threshold of the final doorway, into a glorious morning. The rain had washed everything clean, from the brick paths underfoot to the trees overhead. The leaves looked like they'd been cut from silk and hung along the branches. The sun shone through them in sparkling bits and pieces, making diamonds of the clinging drops of water.

"There is nothing else like it — not in this life." Tonia breathed deeply.

And there is no one like you, Louisa thought, saying only, "You are the life that tempts me."

"The life you could lose if you stay." Nothing in Tonia's manner or expression altered, but Louisa sensed the flinch, the tremor.

"That may be so, my sister, but it is my choice to make. And I have made it."

"Why?"

"The impossible question."

"There *is* an answer," Tonia insisted. "There has to be."

They were well out along the path before Louisa spoke, slowly and thoughtfully. "All my life I have feared change — more than anything else, perhaps. Now *everything* has changed, and I'm surprised at how little fear I feel, because we are together. Come what may."

"Indeed," was all Tonia said, but tears stood in her eyes, and Louisa's.

"What is it that made us friends?" Louisa asked. "Made us blood sisters?"

"As well ask what brings the sun out, after a rain," Tonia answered. "A natural order that defies explanation, but you can be certain will always be there."

"Come what may," Louisa said again, as they turned for the Palace. Together.

~ Chapter Forty ~

Three weeks later, in an atmosphere thick with resentment, Paris marked the second anniversary of the storming of the Bastille. Tensions escalated three days after that, when a huge crowd gathered at the *Champs de Mars* for an "End the Monarchy" rally. Violence broke out; the National Guard was brought in; nearly fifty lives were lost in the open firing.

The Massacre at the *Champs de Mars* became an instant rallying point for growing opposition to Lafayette. The people in the streets — and there were more of them every hour — were quick to express their hatred of their former hero. He favored the Royals too much, always had, always would. He'd made martyrs of his own countrymen, and for what? Putting down opposition to damned Bourbon rule.

By month's end, Lafayette's popularity was a thing of the past. Without power or influence, the "statue in search of a pedestal" was all but excluded from August's Constitutional Day celebrations. There was less bloodshed than Bastille Day, but those who owned homes, shops, businesses, or property watched unemployed workers and the extremely poor riot in the streets; watched what looked and sounded like anarchy; felt the first stirrings of the fear prey feel, in the presence of predators.

In September of 1791, Louis Auguste was made to swear to uphold the finalized Civil Constitution. It kept the monarchy in place, but decreed the King could only be addressed as the "representative of the people."

His only remaining power — if it could be called that — was to veto any law the Legislative Assembly passed. No veto could take effect for five years, so in reality there was no stopping anything they chose to start.

Louis Auguste appeared before them and swore his oath, before collapsing in tears afterwards, in private.

“The humiliation,” he sobbed against Tonia’s shoulder, as she held him silently.

In October, Count Axel Fersen began going from one European court to the next, and to England as well, to see if some way might yet to be found to take the entire Royal family from France. He approached Austria’s Emperor, Sweden’s King, and England’s Prime Minister. All expressed sincerest sympathies, but avoided commitment to action.

Fersen communicated in coded letters, ingeniously smuggled by trusted Household Secretary Catherine Hyde. The intrepid young woman Tonia had dubbed “Inglesina” showed surprising aptitude and patience in deciphering them and composing replies, along with enviable cleverness in conveying them to their recipients.

In November, Tonia’s thirty-sixth birthday came and went, unmarked by any celebration. There wasn’t even a cake, not since a young National Guardsman reported a pastry cook’s comment about the notorious Marie Antoinette’s days being better off shortened.

By year’s end the Legislative Assembly had decreed that no “citizen companion” of Louis Auguste needed to stand in his presence. He seemed not to know or care about the disrespect, unless it was shown in the presence of his son or daughter. Even then, he simply stopped whatever he was doing or saying, and left the room.

On the afternoon of the eve of the New Year, the same National Guardsman who’d warned of the pastry-cook’s possibly poisonous intentions escorted a nervous young country girl to Tonia’s suite, where she and Louisa were having afternoon chocolate, still without milk. The Guardsman looked the other way while the plump blonde girl performed an outlawed curtsy.

“Y-y-your Majesty,” she stammered, standing upright. “Y-y-your Highness,” she held a woven willow basket out to Louisa. “I b-b-bring you white chocolate t-t-truffles, and almond-c-c-croissant for her Majesty, and g-g-greetings from my m-m-mother.”

“Babette!” Louisa cried out, realizing the former lady-in-waiting was the girl’s mother.

“That is m-m-my mother’s name, your Highness, and m-m-mine too.” Louisa motioned for her to set the basket beside the chocolate pot. The girl took her careful time lifting out the napkin-wrapped desserts: opening them; smoothing the napkins; making a living wall of her wide body; ensuring the Guardsman couldn't see the message, written large and dark enough on Louisa's napkin for Tonia to read without her spectacles:

> *Warmest greetings for the new Year of Our Lord 1792*
>
> *Word of your plight has reached me here in the country. I know you are watched closely, and trust my Babette has succeeded in showing you this, my most urgent message to you:*
>
> *In the state of Pennsylvania, in the United States of America, true friends of the Crown have found and purchased a sizeable tract of land. Upon this land they plan to build a colony called Azilium, where the Royal family and their dear ones can taste the fruits of true liberty in unassailable safety.*
>
> *If you agree to come to Azilium, I humbly beg you to say to Babette 'White chocolate is my favorite.' If you do not agree, I beg you to say 'dark chocolate'."*

"Allow me to call for my husband," Tonia looked up. "He will so enjoy these."

When he arrived, she served him herself, arranging the napkin so he would be certain to see its message.

No one spoke as he read, while savoring every crumb. Finishing, finally, he nodded to the nervous girl: "So delicious." He rolled the napkin, and, sighting the distance, tossed it in a perfect arc. The white cloth fluttered into the basket hanging from Babette's arm. The landing brought a small, sad grin to his fleshy lips.

"Dark chocolate," he broke the silence. "The dark chocolate is my favorite."

Babette's apple-dumpling cheeks flamed scarlet; an explosive "*No!*" escaped before she clapped her hand over her mouth. Backing away, she forgot to curtsy. The Guardsman who'd brought her called for his companions, and they were off, with Babette hugging the bakery basket, and its contents, tight to her side.

"We'll all be fine," Louis Auguste told the two women when they were alone again. "We know counter-revolution is underway, but we cannot know how and when it will succeed. We also know these United States, the very union I supported, boasts many places that would surely enchant us, and people who would surely embrace us."

Tonia and Louisa exchanged a look, but no words, waiting for what he would say next.

"I cannot abandon my country. Not now. With the outcome of our very government, and its monarchy, at stake. I must do my duty. As King."

"As King," Tonia whispered, "your duty bids you remain."

His round face broke into a genuine smile. "I must. And so we will put our minds to what we *can* do. There is so much." His smile widened. "Did you know I dug turnips in the gardens here yesterday with Louis-Charles's help? For the first minute or so, at any rate." It brought the laughter he clearly hoped for. "We had them in our soup last night. Gave it a nice flavor. Creamy."

"To creaminess." Tonia raised her chocolate cup; Louisa followed suit, touching the delicate rim of her unmatched cup to the King of France and his Queen Consort.

~ Chapter Forty One ~

By the third anniversary of the storming of the Bastille, the red liberty caps that made their first appearance atop its ruins were the only headgear a French citizen could safely wear in public; the red, white and blue ribbon cockades were no longer enough to prove solidarity with the cause of *Liberte, Egalite, Fraternite.* Wigs had all but disappeared, in favor of hair cropped short and left unpowdered. Loose cotton trousers held up by suspenders replaced men's breeches and silk stockings. They wore them with collarless waist-length jackets. Women also adopted this "*sans-culotte*" style of dressing.

Three months earlier, in April, 1792, the well-known doctor Joseph Guillotin's invention was first tested. A fervent supporter of the Revolution, Guillotin was a true believer in the ideal of *egalite* being extended to the execution of its enemies. Historically, only the Noble estate were sentenced to swift and merciful death by beheading. Since even the most experienced ax-man sometimes botched his grisly work, Guillotin designed a portable beheading machine swift enough, and error-proof enough, to be considered humane. The result was named for him: *guillotine.* Enemies of the Revolution could now take comfort, however cold, in executions that happened before victims realized they were happening.

May brought factions within factions to the Legislative Assembly, and food rioters to the streets, along with the ever-present political protesters. The Assembly continued to support the *assignat* as the nation's currency, though it lost value daily. Basics of life such as having enough food became an issue for citizens who had never experienced hunger. Because the people wanted something *done,* much energy was expended pushing the same tired horses faster — what does a carousel horse care whether it gets anywhere, so long as it *moves*?

In the confines of the Tuileries, the blood sisters spent hours dividing the daily rations into fair shares for all those looking after the Royal family. On a morning in mid-May, when told there was no bread, Tonia lost her temper: "Is there no baker in this so-called Legislative Assembly? Is there not an edict in place concerning what bakers must do if they have no loaves left at end of day?" She held up the sheaf of requests for bread they'd reviewed. "They must remove and distribute what has been left on their baking marbles. Give the people *that* 'cake', at least."

The broadsides got it immediately and horribly wrong: *"Let them eat cake!"* they shrieked. Overnight, they became the most infamous words *Madame Deficit* never uttered.

New flames fanned old hatreds, as Prussia added its military might to what Austrians and others were openly, even boastfully, calling a "counter revolution." The carousel spun faster as May's days passed. When the Austrians were reported advancing, the Legislative Assembly called the people of France to arms, to defend the revolution against counter-attack. Orators could be heard on street corners, haranguing irritable, uneasy crowds that never thinned out. The most frequent subject of the harangues was the Royal family. Nothing could be proven, but the certainty grew that *L'Autrichenne*, the despised Marie Antoinette, was involved in treason.

By the end of May, French generals were urging the Assembly to make peace; French officers were emigrating instead of fighting for the cause; and French soldiers, seeing no way to victory, were deserting in huge numbers. Many found their way to Paris.

On June 20th, a year to the day after the Royal escape attempt was foiled, a rumor flashed through the overload of red-capped Guardsmen and the pulsating mobs of hungry, angry citizens: foreign troops were about to invade Paris! The official written descriptions avoided using the word "riot" to describe what happened when the crowds in the Tuileries' gardens broke into the Palace itself. The two-hour time frame of the "disturbance" was stressed instead.

To the blood sisters, days could have passed while they huddled with the children in a small ground-floor storage room, while utter chaos roared overhead.

“The wood flooring is inlaid.” Tonia’s whisper was soft but harsh in Louisa’s ear. “It wasn’t built to carry such weight!” At that very instant, the wheel of a cannon sliced down; choking dust swallowed the stale air, illuminated by shafts of light from the widening hole. Charlotte and Louis-Charles clung to their mother in mute terror as broken lathing and chunks of plaster cascaded down, and the cursing maniacs above struggled to free the stuck weapon. Tonia folded her arms over her children, pressing them close to muffle their cries. Her lips found Louisa’s ear again: “Now I know how a rabbit feels when a fox finds its burrow.”

Louisa could only nod, and try her best not to scream.

Hours passed before the mob noise faded and movement felt safe. The storage room door was blocked by fallen debris, and no amount of pushing or pulling succeeded in opening it far enough to let even Louis-Charles through.

“It’s the only way out.” Tonia pointed up at the ruined ceiling. “You are taller, but I weigh less. So! Help me climb on your shoulders.” She turned to her children, huddling close to the faithful Madame Tourzel. “And you, my dears, “stand over there, so nothing we dislodge hits you on the head.” She hit her own, giggling.

How she takes charge, Louisa thought, as her hands trembled and her shoulders shook with the effort to keep her sister upright.

“We’re here!” The crown of Her Majesty’s white head barely reached through the gaping hole the cannon wheel had torn in the ceiling. Guards and more Guards materialized, to lift them up and out of their hideaway.

Reassured that her husband was safe in another part of the palace, Tonia led the way to the nearest reception room. Guards there were building a furniture barricade at the splintered doorway.

“Just until they can take us to our rooms,” Tonia soothed the children as she set them on a pair of crude but intact wooden stools the guards had found. She smoothed and straightened their clothes. “No telling what’s likely to happen next.” Her tone was matter-of-fact, bordering on cheerful, “but no matter how rude anyone is, no matter what horrid things they shout, or how nasty they might look, you mustn’t be frightened of them. We’re here, we’re together, and we'll soon be with Papa. Imagine it's a play — wouldn't all this be an exciting scene in a play?"

Charlotte and Louis-Charles agreed it would. "And you won't be afraid then, will you?" They agreed they wouldn't.

"Are *you* afraid?" Louisa whispered when Tonia came to stand beside her.

Tonia cocked an ear to the growing swell of shouts and curses. "If the *chaise* over there wasn't upturned to keep them at bay," she said, "I'd faint onto it."

Louisa raised an eyebrow. "I'm the one who faints, remember?"

"Humor?" Tonia's head came up. "At a time like this?"

"What *better* time?"

~ Chapter Forty Two ~

The uneasy Guards faced raised fists and snarling faces, seen and heard through every gap in the furniture, come to see the slut! Whore! Bitch! With her hand in their pockets and her foot on their backs. What they saw, as the guards held the barricade, was a pale, exhausted woman, looking far older than her thirty-six years.

The first rioter to speak had no sympathy, "We will hang you!" she screamed, as the man just behind her brandished his spear-tipped wooden pike. A disheveled doll hung from it, noosed around its broken neck.

Their target took several steps towards the barricade. "Will you tell me, please?" she spoke directly to the woman, "what harm I myself have done you?"

The woman gaped at her.

"My fellow citizeness," Tonia continued, her voice calm, her gaze steady, "If I have committed a crime that carries hanging as its punishment, can you name it, please?"

The woman hung her head.

"Was my marriage to the King of France, in accordance with solemn and binding contracts, such a crime?"

The woman's shoulders hunched.

"Was it a crime to give the people of France an heir — " she faltered, for the first time " — a surviving heir? To the throne?"

The woman ducked from sight.

From where she stood, Louisa watched a Guard manage to halt the progress of a man carrying a calf's heart impaled on an iron skewer, above a sign scrawled with *'Heart of an Aristocrat'*.

The woman Tonia had confronted stood upright, looking first at her, and then at her children, sitting quietly, side by side, on their stools. "So a cat *may* look at a Queen," she said, smiling at her jest.

Tonia smiled back.

"I also have a boy and a girl," the woman added, pointing, "close to them in age."

"And have you a child in heaven as well?" Tonia inquired, gently.

"Two. Why do you ask?"

"I also have two in heaven."

"Your Majesty." The woman's rags barely covered her, but her curtsy was the equal of the most accomplished courtier's.

The lout with the pike who stood behind her lost his patience. Snatching his filthy red liberty cap from his grease-matted hair, he thrust it at Tonia, snarling, "If you love the nation, let's see that heir you gave us wear *this*."

"Of course I love the nation," Tonia replied, taking the stinking cone of felt from him as graciously as if it were a bouquet of flowers. "I love the nation," she repeated, placing the cap on her boy's bright blonde head, where it immediately fell to his shoulders.

"*Maman*," he cried out from under it, "I can't breathe!"

"It's a game, dear, just a game." She whisked the cap off. "Peekaboo," she crowed, clapping her hands until he giggled. "Peekaboo!" She dropped it back. He giggled again.

Hours passed after the barricade was dismantled, as a grotesque parade was ushered through the room. Few hurled insults now; most left their signs and props on the far side of the splintered doorway. Some bowed, or curtsied. Others attempted to catch and kiss Her Majesty's hands. The sheer force of her presence, and her personality, transformed the threatening mob scene into something very close to a Royal audience, conducted amidst smashed furniture.

When the last body was gone from the room that reeked of them, Tonia saw the children safely to bed and closely guarded before asking to be taken to the King.

Louis Auguste's state of agitation kept him from speaking coherently, or even comprehending what his trusted Swiss Guards reported. He interrupted his pacing back and forth across his bedside carpet to greet his wife. Once he grasped that the children were fine his *cris de nerfs* returned full force, and he was lost to it.

"There's nothing to be gained from staying here," Tonia remarked a few minutes later, quietly enough so only Louisa caught her words. They set off, then, through debris so deep it was difficult to keep their balance.

"How did you manage to think we'd need to put on our outdoor shoes?" Louisa asked.

"You heard the glass breaking," Tonia answered. "With the very air we breathe poisoned by the great sweet wind of *liberte, egalite , fraternite*, I don't need more poison from an infected cut."

Evidence of the frenzy was everywhere as they picked their way in sturdy shoes, past heaps of knife-slashed curtains and upholstery, through blizzards of feathers, and coils of horsehair. Shredded canvas clung to corners of gilt frames; faces and limbs were hacked from marble statues; broken glass and porcelain shards covered the ruined floors and carpets.

Tonia's self-control never left her. Not even when she picked the splintered arms out of the heap of what had once been a favorite boudoir chair and held them to her like broken bones: "I worked the needlepoint on these pads when I carried Joseph Xavier." She turned a bright, blank face to Louisa. "I see him in my dreams you know, so many nights. He waves to me from the basket of a hot air balloon. Like the one that went up from the gardens …" her voice trailed off. They walked on, until a ghost of a grin lifted the corners of her mouth: "Do you suppose I'll be forgiven for feeling the need to redecorate?"

Those who heard their peals of laughter echoing along the marble halls were certain they'd gone mad.

In the wake of the "disturbances" at the Tuileries, the Legislative Assembly declared a state of clear danger existed. They approved any measures to defend against foreign invasion. After heated discussion, the Assembly agreed that the Royal family should remain at the Tuileries. More discussion was needed before the Princess of Lamballe and the children's governess, Madame Tourzel, were also "accepted for residence", as the official *communiqué* put it, before they approved the smaller, unused rooms on the palace's two topmost floors; inner rooms, judged "least likely to permit mischief or harm."

In the early morning of of July 12th, 1792, a motley assortment of guards gathered on the palace steps, ready to obey the Assembly's command to show "all due courtesy" in moving the Royal party to their new quarters, with such furnishings and belongings as were needed. The remaining retainers were unceremoniously escorted from the palace, with instructions to send for their things when they knew where they would be staying.

Within an hour of reaching the new rooms, Tonia had placed the children in Madame Tourzel's charge. She and Louisa then proceeded to exhaust themselves arranging familiar basics in cramped, unfamiliar spaces. Despite the severity of their circumstances, they worked efficiently and companionably, side by side, stopping only when a pleasant young serving-girl appeared in the opened doorway to remind them they had missed the mid-day meal, and ask what she could bring for supper.

"Omelets, if that can be arranged," Tonia replied. The chocolate service had yet to be unpacked, but they welcomed the food when the girl returned to the anteroom they'd fixed as Tonia's personal reception chamber. Tonia thanked her, adding "and we will also be needing soft cloths and warmed water." The girl knew what she meant. "Of course," she replied, closing the newly hung door behind her. They waited, in the same limp calico gowns and dirt-streaked muslin aprons they'd worn all day, for the things they would use to accommodate "General Krottendorf."

"Remember how upset it made my mother when I'd ride in the middle of the 'General's' march?" Tonia's question ended the shared silence.

"Astride, no less." Louisa felt the corners of her mouth turn up.

"The general barely creeps for me, these days."

"I haven't heard his footstep in months," Louisa said, smiling a little more. "I'm certain it it has something to do with the strain we're under."

"But when he marches, we've come to march together, haven't we?"

"We have."

"Another level of blood sisterhood, yes?" Tonia lifted her face, framed in gossamer white strands. The peachy bloom of her cheeks had faded, the flesh was sunken, but nothing — not the deaths, not the destruction, not the danger they lived and breathed — had dimmed the fire of those amazing blue eyes. There were gray-green hollows beneath them, but they shone, still, like fires perfectly banked, so clear Louisa could look through them to the truth of — there was nothing else to call it — the love there.

The sound of carpenters and plasterers could be heard first thing after a night that brought little sleep. The howl of human voices swelled as the day wore on, building to the crescendo of Bastille Day itself. The Royal party made no public appearance. They remained in their rooms, doing their best to ignore the snatches of overheard rumor, of invading armies, summary arrests, bloody murders.

~ Chapter Forty Three ~

On July 25, the Duke of Brunswick signed a manifesto stating the goals of the Austrian and Prussian forces he commanded. The document was blunt: eliminate anarchy and restore King Louis the Sixteenth to his throne. The last lines were a direct threat: summary execution by firing squad awaited anyone apprehended attempting to harm any member of the Royal family.

Riots broke out in the hundreds of locations where the Manifesto was posted. The Assembly was behind some of them, hoping to raise the troops Paris would need to hold off an Austrian-Prussian invasion, if that was to happen. The rumor that England was coming in on the side of the counter-revolution added fuel to the flames.

Fierce *sans-culottes* from the rough seaport of Marseilles responded by the hundreds to the call for volunteers. They brought a horrifying new anthem with them. The King's loyal Swiss Guards filled the courtyard of the Tuileries, keeping the crowds at bay. They still surged close enough for the shouted strains of the *"La Marseilles"* to reach the inner rooms:

"Allons enfants de la patrie!" — "Arise children of your country!
To arms citizens!
Form your battalions!
March on, march on!
Let our fields be soaked in their impure blood!"
Let our fields be soaked in their impure blood!"

Madame Tourzel stopped at Tonia's anteroom as the sun was setting on shouting crowds and roaring bonfires, before she went to ready the children for bed.

"I hear it was written in less than twenty-four hours," she told the Princess and the Queen, "at the request of Strasbourg's mayor."

"Strasbourg's mayor," Tonia repeated, softly.

"And I was told the anthem was composed to inspire our French troops to victory over the forces of the Duke of Brunswick."

They thanked her as she left, and their unease gathered like the darkness of the night whose stars they couldn't see. The street sounds never slackened. Worst of all came from the pikes the rioters ran along the wrought iron fences surrounding the Palace, a sound like skulls, grinding their teeth.

"What are you thinking?" Louisa's question broke the silence in the room.

"Of the day the mayor came out to greet me," Tonia sighed. "Strasbourg. Where I first set foot on French soil." Another set of pikes ground past. "I have begun to think, if we ever expect to set foot on safe ground again, someone must flee the country. Someone who comprehends what is happening here. Someone who can plead the case for our — deliverance."

Louisa shuddered, before nodding agreement. "I think the someone must be female — "

" — or a male someone, in the female attire he prefers."

Louisa had to smile. "There were a few at Court, weren't there?"

"My favorite was the Chevalier d'Éon. Those beautiful dresses he wore, with his military ribbons, both so proudly. He was a spy for my husband's grandfather, did you know?"

"As a matter of fact, I did, after I finished reading the memoir he published as 'Mademoiselle d' Eon'."

"Bless him. Her." Tonia shook her head. "He emigrated some time ago, so you can't recruit him. Her."

"I wouldn't have. But," Louisa blurted the sudden thought, "no one really does take note of the comings and goings of women. Even here. Even now."

"Dear sister!" Tonia reached a hand across the table between them.

"And if asked, a woman need only give a plausible explanation for her presence — "

" — here, or there, or anywhere!" Tonia interrupted. "But how can a woman succeed where a man did not?"

"Count Fersen's plan to remove you from danger was bold and clever," Louisa acknowledged. "But you are not removed." Her grip on Tonia's hand tightened. "What if the plan hinged on a woman from here, from inside? A woman able to — how did you put it? — plead the case for deliverance? That someone could be me," she heard herself say.

"You? Impossible."

"Perhaps, but we will never know for certain unless I attempt it, will we? I think there is an excellent chance of success."

"And I think you need to sleep on it."

~ Chapter Forty Four ~

That night's sleep was elusive. Louisa tossed and turned, between unforeseen elation at the chance of escape, and stark fear of the unknown to be faced. At what price? It was like the myth she'd learned as a little girl, of Scylla and Charybdis. They were the names of two huge boulders, guarding the gates between rough and calm seas. Even as a child they'd seemed malevolent, waiting to crush and trap anyone who dared travel between them. Now she was the one offering to set a safe course, between these days' random acts of terror, and tomorrows' unknowns.

I look — haggard. The latest tiring-maid assigned to her couldn't eliminate the puffed and reddened eyelids. S*he did her best,* Louisa thought, setting her hand mirror down and picking up the skirts of her morning-robe. *Am I ready?*

Tonia wasn't dressed for the day either. And she wasted no time picking up where they'd left off. "If you still think an attempt should be made by a woman who is not an immediate member of the Royal family, why can't Madame Tourzel go?"

"Madame is loyal, yes, but she isn't widely traveled."

"And you are? I'd hardly call Rambouillet travel."

"True. But is it wise to suddenly deprive your daughter and your son of yet another anchor in their lives?"

"You propose to deprive *me.*"

"We are adults," Louisa countered, "and the travel will only be to England."

"England?" Tonia repeated, dumbfounded.

"Strawberry Hill. Where Baron Besenval is enjoying Horace Walpole's hospitality. In the company of Edmund Burke."

"And your visit's purpose?"

"Assistance in making direct contact with the Prime Minister."

"Monsieur Pitt? Why not approach him through our French

Ambassador? He is already there at the Court of St. James."

"Has he accomplished anything on our behalf?"

"I take your point," Tonia conceded.

"It would be better if we present as private persons — I mean citizens."

"We?" Tonia's brows rose.

"You were right about my lack of travel experience. Someone who is experienced should be included."

"Aha! So it's some*ones* now."

"You didn't dub her 'Inglesina' for nothing. English was Catherine Hyde's first language, and she is so able to record details and arrange travel fearlessly."

"And what manner of private person do you propose to become?"

"I will be a Quaker matron. She will be a young woman from difficult circumstances our Quaker congregation undertook to educate. We succeeded, and so she grew into a well respected journalist, eager to interview Monsieurs Walpole, Burke, and Pitt, for a French gazette devoted to subjects of interest from abroad. A perfect cover for someone who will be seen in the act of writing things down."

"Believable characters, and a plausible reason. You surprise me."

"I surprised myself," Louisa countered.

"You know ..." Tonia gave Louisa an appraising stare. "If your appearance could be altered enough, you might pull such a subterfuge off." Her expression lit up. "Your hair! We'll cut your hair!"

"My *hair*?"

"Yes, your hair. It's the best way." Tonia went around to the back of Louisa's chair and picked up the single thick braid. "Pity Monsieur Leonard isn't here, to wield his magic scissors." She looped the braid around her hand. "About this much, I think. How many years will we be cutting away?" She wrapped another loop. "Ten?" And another. "Twenty?"

Louisa felt the absence of weight on her scalp. "Perhaps not — quite so many."

"And perhaps Mademoiselle Bertin could stand in for Monsieur?"

The no-nonsense couturier to her no-longer Majesty could and did agree, not only to stand in, but to take care of whatever else might be needed. "I believe I can identify those of your — keepers — trustworthy enough to convey you to my shop." She glared around the stuffy space allotted for storage of the dressmaker's tools and materials. "All must be done there."

Louisa spoke for the first time. "Have you any ideas for disguising my hair without the need to cut it?"

Bertin bustled behind her.

"I do, your Highness. As good fortune would have it, a young freedwoman in my employ came from a sugar island in the Caribbean. She brought a fascinating braiding method with her, one that would preserve most of your hair."

Tonia clapped her hands. "I knew you would come through."

"It will be my pleasure, and the girl who wears those braids so fetchingly will be honored to create them. And another excellent aspect of the hairdo? If they are not bombarded with pomades or perfumes, they need not be undone until — "

" — until such time as it's safe," Tonia finished for her. "When do we begin?"

"Plan for two days, at most, for readying the garments, and all else you will need. On the appointed day, it would be best to arrive early." Bertin came around to face them, snipping her golden egret scissors. "The braiding procedure is a lengthy one."

"Could what I'm feeling be hope?" Tonia asked after Bertin left.

"It could," Louisa agreed, "Provided our secretary-courier agrees to participate."

"Mere formality, I'd wager. If I still wagered, that is." Her jest brought Louisa's welcome smile. "To share chocolate?"

"And sing, perhaps?"

Princess and Queen applauded each of the vocal selections Catherine Hyde had chosen. "Remain with us for a while?" Tonia gestured the Inglesina to stand as she went to drop a final curtsy. "We're having chocolate brought," she added.

"Yes, thank you." Catherine took a chair, and a cup.

A companionable silence stretched as they sipped. Tonia was the first to break it. "Dear Inglesina. You are such a valued source of information. And of opinions we welcome for their honesty."

Louisa took a deep breath. "You have been so successful in your circumspect comings and goings I have a proposal for you to consider."

Catherine listened to the description with clearly growing excitement, speaking without hesitation when Louisa finished. "You have seen fit to praise me as your eyes and ears. Let me be your fleet feet now."

"We cannot know any outcome for certain until the attempt is made," Louisa told her, "and we wish you to make it. Will you?"

The girl flushed with pleasure. "Of course I will."

"Then we must make ready," Tonia told her.

"I *am* ready." Catherine insisted.

The single clock on the simple mantel finished chiming midnight as the blood sisters shared chamomile tea, even though neither expected it would bring the soothing sleep it once had.

"Are you sure you're *r*eady? You *could* let her go on her own, you know."

"I know," Louisa responded.

"Do you know how hard it will be for me to let *you* go? I am praying for acceptance. Begging the Virgin to help me accept you leaving me when — when — we both know there might be — no safe return."

"That could happen between morning and night here."

"You risk this for me," Tonia said. "It should be the other way around. I'm the fast-forward one, you're the hang-back. It's so not like you to be so — so — "

"-is bold the word you're wanting?" Louisa finished for her.

"Bold, yes. And out of character."

"Not for you," Louisa said. "But since you must remain here ..." she trailed off.

"Can't you stay with me? Can't the Inglesina prevail on her own?"

"She hasn't the history with the gentlemen who will be our conduit to Pitt, and beyond. As soon as there is news worth sending you, I'll send it."

"The very day?"

"If it's possible."

~ Chapter Forty Five ~

Neither of them expected Bertin's summons to come as soon as it did, but the messenger arrived as they breakfasted, confirming her readiness to attend to them, as of the following dawn. The sisters shared no chocolate that night; the next morning, Tonia wavered between staying or going as far as the Rue de Colombe, to the shop closed to the public for the day.

"No amount of disguise will keep you from being recognized," Louisa pointed out. "The risk is far too great."

Tonia acceded, finally, to Louisa's uncharacteristically stubborn insistence, and so wasn't among the passengers in the common hire-hack, taken to protect them from being seen, as they made their slow, circuitous way. Once there, the shuttered windows and stout outer walls kept them from being heard.

The hours passed there proved a welcome respite from the Palace confines, as the Princess, and the secretary-courier Bertin had come to know and admire, underwent their transformations.

The young freedwoman, clearly the offspring of one white parent, did cut Louisa's hair, from knee to near waist-length. The dozens of braids she created, between regularly spaced parts, were woven so tightly they gave the appearance of a close-fitting cap.

Once the braiding was accomplished, a trio of Bertin's most trusted tire-women were called in. They folded the papers that would ensure the Quaker women's safe passage from France into gray serge pockets stitched into their dress hems and waistbands. They went on to fill soft felt bags containing the pieces of Her Majesty's personal jewelry she wished to be held safely, outside France. Bertin herself tacked them to the undergarments spread on a trestle table. They relaxed as the work progressed, teasing among themselves, not caring if the soon-to-be Quakers heard.

"We're making such exceptions to the rule that no woman can keep a secret," one boasted.

"That's a man's rule," another countered

"What rules a man anyway?" the third wondered aloud

"His privates, his head, his heart-likely in that order," Bertin shook her thimble-topped finger at them.

As they worked, Louisa and Catherine reviewed the particulars of their journey. Quaker women unaccompanied by a man or men was no strange sight. Even now.

They would leave for the coast of France aboard a "diligence", a slow watercraft ideal for transporting those with time to spare. They had none, but the leisurely route along the loops of the Seine reduced the likelihood of pursuit.

The diligence would reach the French coast at LeHavre, where they would cross the English Channel by ferry to Brighton, hiring the fastest available carriage to take them to Horace Walpole's retreat, Strawberry Hill. Advance notice had been smuggled out to him, but there was no way to know whether it had arrived. Or would arrive, before they did.

Eight hours passed before "Sarah Small' and her protégé "Jane Green" were ready to present to the world. Louisa's braids were invisible beneath the coalscuttle bonnet of plain gray grosgrain Bertin herself had created. Catherine's coppery hair was trimmed and coiled under a similar bonnet. Their dark gray serge dresses stopped short of the floor, in practical Quaker fashion, displaying their serviceable black leather shoes.

The blood sisters saw little of each other through the three all but sleepless nights, and days made more difficult by the weight of the imminent secret they shared.

Louisa fretted about how much, when, and even why Papa Time needed to know. In the end, she summoned the Major Domo from Rambouillet to take what might be her last letter to the man's master, who clung, still, to his life and his collections, so far gone into his remote state of mind she disclosed nothing of the upcoming mission. *They will hear soon enough, out there in the countryside. If they haven't already.*

Tonia concentrated on discovering which of the Swiss guards

assigned to the Palace might be trustworthy enough to assist if the need arose.

A guard, usually Swiss, was posted outside any room they occupied. The same guards supplied any ladies-in-waiting Marie Antoinette or the Superintendent of Her Household might request. Louisa seldom made such a request, and Tonia wasn't certain enough of their loyalty to approach the few she chose. She made more than one attempt to persuade Louisa to change course, but her sister remained calm and determined, in midstream already.

Seeing a chance to try again, on the afternoon of the night before, Tonia took it. They sat close together, barely speaking above a whisper.

"I should be the one to pass as 'Sarah Small', off to England with her protégé 'Jane Green'. You know what a good actress I am."

"You are a better mother. And wife. And — I want to say Queen." Louisa's rare anger flashed. "Want to shout it, as loud as I choose, over and over, everywhere. Even if the walls do have ears."

"Don't go."

"I must."

"At whose command?"

"My own. Is there a stronger command?"

Tonia could only nod.

"All will be well. Believe that." Louisa reached for her. "Oh, my blood sister. Closer than my own blood."

"And to me, but for my children." Tonia took a deep, shuddering breath. "Go with God, dear sister."

The embraces, and kisses, were the most intense of their lives.

~ *Chapter Forty Six* ~

At a quarter past noon on the last Monday in July, Catherine Hyde slipped into an angled opening between two rows of venerable hornbeam hedges in the gardens of the Tuileries. The narrow alley was open to the sky, invisible to passersby. She was there less than a minute before the Princess materialized from the opposite hedge row, suddenly and noiselessly.

"Your Highness!" Catherine began a curtsy, but Louisa motioned her to rise.

"No need for such formality now. That is all it is, really — foolish form, empty of any meaning. The curtsy will be obsolete soon. And a Quaker lass such as yourself would hardly offer one."

The Princess wore a simple percale dress. A matching drawstring bag hung from one elbow, and her face was all but obscured by a finely-woven Livorno straw hat. "Thank you for being so prompt," she spoke in a near whisper. "Is 'Jane Green' ready for all that will commence with the coming dawn?"

"She is," Catherine replied, "I mean I am."

The Princess spoke swiftly then, without hesitation, as if she had rehearsed the words many times: "One message remains as yet undelivered. It is the reason I summoned you here." She lifted the deep hat brim, until her soft brown eyes caught Catherine's green ones. "I have reached a decision that concerns you. I am not leaving with you tomorrow."

"But your Highness!"

Louisa put a gloved hand to Catherine's lips to stop her cry of astonishment. "You are well acquainted with every aspect of the plan. The only difference is you will be carrying it out on your own, a feat I am certain you will accomplish. With distinction."

"But your Highness — "

" — Any argument you raise is futile," Louisa cut in, her voice firm and steady. "This way is best for all of us. You must not attempt to dissuade me." She bent closer. "You have demonstrated so often, in so many ways, how capable you are of making your way through, overcoming obstacles, meeting challenges."

Catherine ducked her head. "I was born in England, but I have lived here most of my life. I cannot believe you would trust me to carry out this incredible mission without you by my side!"

"You must believe it, because that is the journey you will undertake at dawn tomorrow. I have sent word of this turn of events to the Baron, and to your hosts at Strawberry Hill. You will remain while they make and carry out a successful plan."

"Can I return then?"

"Certainly. As soon as we can assure your safety."

"We?" Catherine repeated. "Her Majesty agrees to all of this?"

"She not only agreed, but she assisted with a number of details, and looks forward to welcoming you back to France."

"When? When will she welcome me?"

"You will be the first to know," Louisa's smile was rueful as she reached into the drawstring bag and withdrew a velvet box. She pressed its filigreed catch, adorned with the twined letters "*MA*," revealing a gold repeater watch, set with alternating diamonds and pearls, on a chain of braided gold. "You have seen me wear this gift from Her Majesty on many occasions. It is yours now, to keep and to wear, the better to remember your time with me. With us."

She reached back for a small wooden box. It held an exquisite miniature of her portable writing desk. "Go on, open it. Please."

Catherine slid the top panel aside. A gold key lay there, in a niche of French blue velvet.

"The watch is for you to remember time. The key is for you to remember me. I am sending the actual desk to you, in a larger crate marked as textbooks, the better to evade prying eyes. It will contain 'Sarah Small's' costume and bonnet, along with the jewels she was to carry. It will also contain — " Louisa shook her head " — what might surprise you. You have all the papers you require with you now. But you have never seen, or possibly even imagined, the ones you will find in the desk — in a secret drawer the key will open."

"Your Highness."

Louisa's gloved hand went to her lips. "There have been many public occasions and private experiences I wrote about afterward. Conversations, anecdotes, descriptions, even feelings and opinions. I won't dignify these records by calling them a journal, a diary, or memoirs. But I have come to believe them worth keeping. They hold another kind of key, to my life, and your own. You are the best person to have them."

"You honor me."

A sudden shout near their hedge struck them both mute. They bowed their heads while a substantial group passed close enough to rustle the stiff hornbeam branches.

"I am also making you a gift of the mare Perdita," Louisa continued when they were gone. "I do think it wisest if you leave her here until — until we can be more certain of the future." She pulled a last parcel from the drawstring bag. "And I also want you to have this." Wrapped in plain white butcher's paper was a gold-enameled pocketbook, with a sapphire clasp the size of a thumbnail.

"You will find money inside and a cheque drawn on a Swiss bank. There is a banker, a Monsieur Bonny, in Vatican City, who will honor it."

"I — I don't know what to say."

"There's nothing further to be said. I had planned to ask you to favor me with a *rondeau* — any of the ones you chose when last you sang for us." Tears glazed her soft brown eyes. "But every minute spent here increases the chance of our discovery. So will you sing one when you are safely away? I will not hold you to when, or where. Please sing it as you did, that night, with all the freedom of your youth and your gifts."

The Princess of Lamballe removed the glove from her right hand and extended it for Catherine to kiss. The only ring she wore was the one fashioned from Marie Antoinette's white hair. "Godspeed, 'Jane Green'," Louisa whispered, as she melted back into the hornbeam hedge.

The son of the most trusted of the Swiss Guards was waiting where Louisa had left him. Without a word spoken, the boy — *he can't be more than ten* — set off, a few careful lengths ahead of her, back to a palace much less grand than the Great Chateau at Versailles. *We called Versailles a country, once,* Louisa thought, *for good reason. There is no reasoning here.* She kept her hat brim pulled low, and her steps careful, as she made her way back to where her sister waited. *What waits for us?* The boy darted further ahead. *For him?*

The light was so dim in the narrow inside hall Tonia couldn't see who approached at first. She screamed when she saw. "Dear God! You've been delayed?"

"No. I've come back."

"With the Inglesina?"

Louisa's shoulders lifted in an almost imperceptible hug. "She will be bound for the diligence."

"What?"

"I cannot leave you behind."

"But you seemed so certain." Tonia shook her head. "So ready. So — unafraid."

"I wasn't unafraid. But yesterday — it wasn't fear, but certainty. That I belong here."

Tonia held out her arms. Louisa walked into them. "Yesterday is history," Tonia whispered. "Today is — us. Tomorrow? A future we cannot know."

"A future I will face with you."

Nothing more was said. Nothing needed to be. They held each other until a maid, sent up from the kitchens with a breakfast plate of bread, cheese, and and grapes found them blocking her passage.

The rest of the day, and the week, passed without a plausible reason presenting itself for the privacy they craved but couldn't manage.

~ Chapter Forty Seven ~

Louisa made her way to her room before the sun rose fully, but couldn't sleep. She returned to Tonia's side at dawn, where she learned word of the chaos to come had been delivered by a pair of guards Louisa hadn't recognized as they hurried past.

"The King's powers are suspended, but the monarchy itself is not abolished," Tonia told her. "He won't say 'dethroned,' but that is what has happened." Louisa could only nod agreement. "They've formed an 'Interim Executive Council' to exercise those powers. A radical named Danton is at the helm of the crazy ship." She gestured to the windows. "I've already sent for such help as can be mustered, to help us — prepare."

Louisa didn't need to ask for what. She did ask if anything was known of the whereabouts of — she forced herself to say "*Egalite*".

"Still in his self-preserving self-exile somewhere," Tonia's lip curled. "But all this should bring him from his hiding hole into the spotlight again."

The blood sisters spent the morning making such preparations as they could, for what threatened to be another popular assault.

Hour by hour, it became increasingly clear panic was setting in. Louis Auguste bellowed at the sight of a painting hanging askew, a curtain tassel unfastened. Tonia flinched visibly with every scratch at her door. Louisa kept her shaking hands hidden in her skirts. Only the children were shielded, safe in their inner rooms, guarded at their lessons and games and meals by the faithful, and unflappable, Madame Tourzel.

"There's no cause for further alarm. Sanity will surely take hold again, and soon!" Louis Auguste was immoderately, almost offensively cheerful, when he paid the sisters a noontime visit. He insisted on their accompanying him to review the Swiss Guards.

"There are nine hundred of them," he nearly shouted, "nine

hundred, I tell you, massed in the Courtyard at this very moment, together with sentries and National Guardsmen and two troops of cavalry, all at the ready!"

Since the dawn of Louisa's return, she'd watched a dark thing lurking behind the bright clearness of Tonia's blue eyes. It emerged only when she believed no one else was looking. Louisa saw it now.

"And I have been assured," Louis Auguste's eyes had begun to bulge, "assured! A band of nobles pledged to protect us gathers, even as I speak! They call themselves 'Knights of the Dagger'."

He refused the triple-padded cuirasse when it was brought.

"I don't need it," he insisted. "I need to review my Guards. I must do so. *Now*!"

The demand was met before he could grow any more agitated. He cut anything but a kingly figure in his unbuttoned coat, his wig askew and shedding powder. The sight did replace Tonia's dark thing, with a more familiar expression, of fond amusement at his ungainliness.

The Swiss Guards roared their acclaim as Louis Auguste addressed them with tears in his eyes: "Praise God for your loyalty. I give you two commands: you are to ignore the ravings of the lunatic Council. And you are to fire *only* if fired upon."

By late afternoon, there was nothing left to do but wait. As night fell, word reached them that the city of Paris was being run by a "Revolutionary Committee." There was no clear information on how the "Interim Executive Council" figured in the control shift, or if it continued to play any part.

The adults didn't undress or retire for the night. Gathered in the safest of the inner rooms, they repeated rumors: Count Fersen was at the Vatican arranging their escape; Ambassador Mercy had prevailed on Austria to spirit them away; the "Knights of the Dagger" had overthrown the "Revolutionary Committee."

Louis Auguste dozed in his chair, shuddering awake intermittently, repeating, "all will be well," or, "we must have faith," before drifting off again. Despite the presence of enormous crowds, a strange silence fell over Paris.

It was one in the morning when the eerie call-to-arms of the tocsin sounded faintly, somewhere outside the city walls, but coming closer and closer.

At sunrise on August eleventh, the body of the Commander of the National Guard was discovered floating in the Seine. He had last been seen alive on his way to appear before the "Revolutionary Committee."

The discovery shattered the ranks of the four thousand Guardsmen under his command. They deserted in droves, and hundreds signed on with the opposition. Within the hour, a minor official of the National Assembly brought news of the death to the Palace.

No mention of murder was in the message the self-important man recited from the notes he held: "Given the increasing influence of the Revolutionary Committee that has led to this unhappy state of affairs, the safety of the Royal party can be guaranteed only upon acceptance of the direct and immediate protection of the National Assembly." He interrupted himself to gesture to the invisible outside, where an ominous new sound could be heard.

"Cannon," he announced. "Soon to be firing on the Palace itself. You *must* let the Assembly preserve you as they determine the next step."

"Is it fair to say this is our worst storm yet?" Tonia whispered to Louisa.

"It is," Louisa whispered back.

"We must weather it somehow."

~ Chapter Forty Eight ~

Their departure was well and closely guarded, but the cries of *"Dissolution or death!"* and the constant obscene cursing kept their heads down and their steps swift. The small party consisted only of the dethroned King and his former Queen, the couple's two children, their governess, and the Princess Lamballe.

"We will send for the rest as soon as you are safely away from here," the official had assured them. "We cannot risk a larger party because we have only one chance to get through. An increase in your numbers would make things impossibly cumbersome."

Pandemonium broke out at the sight of the disheveled group when they reached the converted riding school on the far side of the Tuileries Gardens, where the National Assembly was headquartered, and already in session.

"Your physical safety can only be guaranteed within." The official was surrounded by his excited peers.

Louis Auguste cocked his head to the sounds none could avoid hearing. "I will enter." His voice was all but inaudible over the hissing rattle of smaller arms, the wall-shaking boom of cannon fire, the screams of human targets. "On one condition. You must take my order to the Swiss Guards. They *must* lay down their arms."

"We cannot debate in his presence!" The howls went up as the doors were opened. "The rules forbid it."

"He cannot be held elsewhere!" Other howls countered. "Overrule the rules."

"Reporter's box, reporter's box!" New shouts emerged.

The debate was short, sharp, and audible to the six held behind crossed swords. The reporter's box the Assembly agreed to was a room, tucked beneath the speaker's platform.

Ten feet square, its ceiling was so low Louisa could touch it. A small grilled opening faced the audience. They took turns looking through it, as they listened to the National Assembly debate the abolishment of the monarchy in France. And voted to do so.

While the National Assembly voted the monarchy's end, and the former monarch baked in what felt like an oven, five hundred of the Swiss Guards who obeyed his command to lay down their arms were butchered on the steps and terraces surrounding the Palace of the Tuileries.

Marie Therese Charlotte slumped silently against her mother, her sweat-darkened hair pasted to her skull. Louis-Charles' fair skin blotched red and dripped with perspiration as he whined for water. What they had was in an open jug, hot as the air, beside biscuits so stale they needed sucking before they could be bitten into.

Nightfall did little to dissipate the heat. The shouting and haranguing went on above them, and out in the Hall. Sometime after ten, a new terror was added: "Smoke!" the howl went up. "The Tuileries is burning!"

"Your custody must be made more secure." The door to the reporter's box swung open, and they were surrounded by a few National Guardsmen, and many more of the Revolutionary Committee. There wasn't a familiar face among them, but their blood-red caps were all too familiar.

They were hurried through the Hall to an obscure exit, where a carriage large enough to accommodate them all waited. It stopped only once, at the *Place de Vendome,* where the statue of Louis XIV, the Sun King, was being toppled. No one spoke. No one could, as the carriage plunged its way through a sea of heads and fists, surging with ever-greater strength against the protective shield of armed guards. The passengers kept their eyes closed, their ears covered, and the curtains fastened.

Tonia was the first to peek through them when the carriage stopped. "Dear God," she gasped. "They're taking us to the Temple Tower!"

"Where?" Louisa spoke for the first time.

"The grounds and the castle belong to the Count of Artois. We dined here, after the Opera, at least once, don't you remember?"

"I don't remember."

"You do; you must! There's a building at the back of the gardens, the 'Temple Tower.' I insisted Artois have it pulled down because the sight of it made my flesh creep. It's like a dungeon in a fairy tale — they *cannot* mean to keep us here."

"They do." Louis Auguste's voice was hollow.

The Tower's ten-foot-thick walls did ensure their safety, and the gift of silence. The eight rooms on four floors were sparsely furnished and not very clean. The six of them were cramped into the middle two. The top and bottom floors were occupied by the soldiers and municipal guards assigned to keep constant watch.

Louisa spent the first night on a pallet in a passageway outside Tonia's room, screened off from all but the most prying eyes. Three days later, the Constitutional celebrations marking the third anniversary of the *"Fete de la Federation"* proceeded, unseen and unheard inside the Tower's curving stone walls, where Louisa continued to sleep on a pallet.

Their new keepers proved kind enough. They willingly played the endless backgammon games that filled Louis Auguste's waking hours, while the women occupied themselves with needlework. Louis-Charles was wild with excitement at having so many soldiers at his beck and call, and did everything he could to avoid lessons with his father or Madame Tourzel. His sister took pains to ingratiate herself, displaying a changed attitude toward everyone but her mother. Tonia was undismayed.

"I *so* disliked my mother the Empress's efforts to make me into someone I wasn't," Tonia explained to Louisa the first time her daughter left the room rather than submit to a hug. "I haven't done that to her. I've let her choose, and she's chosen to be amenable to everyone but me. Serves me right for insisting she's free to be herself." She looked up from the handkerchief she wasn't embroidering. "At this rate, she'll be no comfort in my old age."

Louisa couldn't bring herself to laugh. Or to take more than a nibble of the stale loaf Tonia had sliced and buttered. She hardly slept on her cot in the hall outside Tonia's door; hardly woke before a deep fatigue enclosed her, like some invisible suit of armor. More and more often, she gave in to it; to sleep was to stay the mind, the soul, from the chronic fear that wanted so to sink its claws.

On the night that marked the end of their first week in the Tower, Louisa spoke of how she felt, as quietly as she could, to avoid being overheard by Madame Tourzel or the Guardswoman, all focused on their needlework.

"Does it seem bizarre that I rarely feel those claws?" Tonia responded. "I truly step from second to second, through each minute, until they become every hour, and so the days go. That's how we were at Trianon, do you remember?"

~ Chapter Forty Nine ~

The "September Massacres," as they came to be called, were five days of the devil's work. An accurate victim total was never established, of priests, primarily, and aristocrats, who were called before a self-appointed court of masked judges. Acquittals were nonexistent. Guilty verdicts carried an immediate death sentence. Between the second and the seventh of September, 1792, as many as fourteen hundred people died in or near the courtyard of the prison of *La Force.*

The night they came for Louisa was hot and still, after the blazing red sky of sunset. The last light had been strong enough to penetrate even the small, thick panes of the window cut into the Temple Tower's wall. They were finishing supper when they heard the unusual commotion on the ground floor. Before anyone at the table could begin to react, a dozen strangers crowded into the room.

One of them, Liberty-capped and minus all his teeth, made a mockery of a bow before announcing they were "emissaries from the Municipal Government of Paris. The Princess of Lamballe is wanted for questioning."

The regular guards materialized in force, but could do nothing. Louisa and Tonia clung to each other, whispering, their eyes shut tight. When the moment came, they had to be pried apart. As they all but dragged Louisa down the spiral of stone steps, Tonia stood stock still at the top, her arms embracing empty air. "*Sister!*" she heard, faintly, from somewhere below, before there was only silence.

Louisa was taken to the smaller of the two buildings comprising the prison of *La Force.* Before this, through everything, she had steadfastly refused to take anything stronger than a calming cup of chamomile or mint tea. Now she accepted the laudanum, freely offered by jailers who preferred their prisoners stupefied. She welcomed the oblivion it brought, even though it confused her waking state to the point where she lost the ability to think with any clarity of what had happened.

On the second day, word arrived from Papa Time, carried by his Major-Domo, in a fiercely-mustached disguise that under any other circumstances would have made Louisa laugh. As it was, she was hard pressed to make sense of his urgent message: *I am offering any sum for your release. You must stay strong. This will soon come to an end. "Do whatever they tell you — it will be all right."*

"What? Who said that?" Louisa struggled to identify whose voice she thought she heard. The Major-Domo's? Or Tonia's? Or one of the ruffians who came and went from the dormitory holding area, where sobs sounded continuously, alongside manic laughter?

On the second of September, Louisa was transferred to the *Grand Force* side of the prison. She was placed in a small cell that would have been uncomfortable had she not been given a dose of laudanum so strong she sank onto the pallet and lay unmoving until seven the next morning, when she taken from her cell to the tribunal area.

She counted seven judges — *isn't seven a lucky number?* — seated at the long table opposite the gated enclosure she was led to. The hoods they wore were unsettling, but not unfamiliar, since most of her guards went masked. Their initial questions seemed routine enough: "Your name?"

"Maria-Theresa-Louisa of Savoy-Carignan, Princess of Lamballe."

"Your position?"

"Citizeness. Formerly Superintendent of the Household of — Citizeness Marie Antoinette."

"Your marital status?"

"Widow of Stanislaus — Prince of Lamballe — "

"Cause of death?"

Without the sedative filter of the laudanum, Louisa was quick to notice the brief ripple of movement from judge to judge, starting at the far left of the table, ending with the questioner at its center.

"No response is required," the central figure intoned. "We will move on. Have you any knowledge of cannon being mounted and pointed from within the Royal apartments on the tenth of August last?"

"What are you speaking of," Louisa began, before the same judge cut her off.

"You are required to answer the questions, citizeness, not ask them. Let me repeat: have you any knowledge of cannon being mounted and pointed from within the Royal apartments on the tenth of August last?"

"I do not. The apartments were all interior rooms — "

"We are aware of this." He cut her off again. "Do you know the locations of the secret doors of the Tuileries?"

"I do not."

"Have you, since you have been in the Temple Tower, received and written letters, which you sought to send away secretly?"

"I have not."

"Do you deny all these charges?"

"I do."

"Then we will move to the next stage."

"We thank you for your cooperation." The judge sitting at the far right spoke, in a calm, even respectful voice. "If it continues, you will be able to take up your life as it was."

Which life is that? Louisa wondered, wildly.

"One thing, and one thing only, is required of you," the judge continued. "You must swear two oaths in the presence of this company of witnesses." He lowered his hooded head to the papers on the table before him, and began reading aloud: "I, Maria-Theresa-Louisa of Savoy-Carignan, vow I am and will remain faithful to the Constitutional government and to each tenet of its establishment. Do you so vow?"

"I can and will swear to that," Louisa replied immediately, a rush of relief flooding through her.

"Do you, Maria-Theresa-Louisa of Savoy-Carignan, vow your hatred for your former king, for the woman who was his queen consort, and for all their heirs and assigns?"

Louisa gripped the railing of the enclosure even more tightly, struggling to breathe slowly, deeply, in, out, the way Serafina had taught her oh, such a long time ago. *Serafina's dead and buried, you must answer, help me, help me please. Who do I ask? No one is here. I must answer. Answer."*

In a voice surprisingly strong for the weakness that assaulted her, she did: "You have heard me swear willingly to the first vow. To the second, how can I? There is nothing I can accuse the Royal family of. Nothing." The breath she drew was a gasp, but she let go of the railing. Standing to her full height, she shook her head. "To hate them is against my nature. They are my sovereigns. I have served them for many years, and have never found reason for the slightest complaint."

"Swear," the middle judge intoned, as she tried to draw breath from air that seemed to offer none.

"I cannot swear hatred. It is not in my heart."

Murmured discussion began among all of them. A minute passed, and another, before the judge at the table's far left spoke, for the first time.

"Set Madame at liberty," he rasped.

Is his voice disguised, like his face? That black gaze? Could it be? — Louisa couldn't even think the name. Amazingly, she could speak: "Am I acquitted?"

"You are set at liberty."

~ Chapter Fifty ~

Guards materialized. They escorted her past a woman being all but carried in, sobbing piteously. Louisa shook her head against any assistance that would have brought their touch, concentrating all her attention and all her strength on walking upright to the great doors at the far end of the hall.

The courtyard was a shocking change from the interior. Even without the sun shining, the sudden expanse of sky overhead was bright enough to bring spots up before Louisa's eyes and stop her forward motion, as a guard bawled out: "*It has been decreed that Madame is to be set at liberty*."

"*How about equality and fraternity*?" another howled.

The spots receded, and Louisa saw what appeared to be heaps of clothing piled against the walls; wet clothing, soaked in the blackish streams of water snaking along the stones. People crowded around the piles. S*crubbing the clothes? No. No smell of soap. No. It smells like —* she'd not been near an *abattoir* since she was a child in Turin, going to the great cathedral where the shroud that covered Christ's body was kept. They'd passed a slaughterhouse one day, close enough to smell the blood. This was the same stench.

Before she could cry out, strong hands grasped both her elbows from behind, lifting her, moving her toward the courtyard's wooden gates until she was close enough to see the great forged chains, the huge lock.

"Where are you taking me?" Louisa found her voice. "Where am I going?"

"To your eternal reward or damnation, darling, depending on how you've lived your life."

What? "What did you say?"

"That I have a heart. Big enough to make it easier on you."

Louisa never saw the guard take aim, or the pike descend. Never heard his last remark: "At your service, your Highness." The blow shattered the back of her skull just where it met her neck. Her hands began to come up, to feel for the place of shrieking agony — but there was no shrieking agony. There was no sound at all. There was nothing.

The force of that first blow hurled her into the front ranks of the waiting mob. Her last breaths still bubbled blood from between her lips, and her limbs jerked spastically as blow after blow ripped her flesh and smashed her bones. One eye never closed, even after her head was hacked from her body.

No one pronounced the Princess of Lamballe's death. The pulped mass of her corpse was added to the piles against the walls, along with about a dozen that hour.

One of the onlookers left for Rambouillet before noon, in the fastest *cabriolet* he could hire. The coachman had no idea for whom he was driving, and Papa Time's Major-Domo wanted to keep it that way, until he returned to the frail old man few believed had any sense left. Since his first day at Rambouillet, the Major-Domo had felt nothing but affection for its foolish, harmless master. He had no intention of telling Papa Time the truth of what had happened to her — even if he *couldn't* understand a word that would be said to him.

The driver chattered on, blissfully ignorant of his passenger's connections, oblivious to the progressive revulsion on his fare's face. He ticked off the latest list of casualties, ending with, "and that princess, the bitch's girlfriend, what's her name? Not the one who got out while the getting was good — the other one, the one who stayed? The friend to the end."

"Louisa, Princess of Lamballe," his passenger said.

"Lamballe, that's right. Well, she was finished off in the courtyard of *La Force*, just this morning — and afterward, I heard," the coachman's voice turned conspiratorial, "just before they took to the streets, they did quite a piece of butchery on her."

"Butchery?"

"Butchery. I know wild Indians and cannibals do such things, but I have to tell you it's hard to believe that Frenchmen — Frenchmen! — no matter how drunk or blood-crazed would go in for scalping."

"Scalping?"

"Not the hair of her head, no. It was the hair from her *privates* they took. The fellow who carried her head through the streets wore it as a mustache."

The coachman was quick to halt the flow of his gossip when the fellow beside him cried out and cringed away, hanging his head over the *cabriolet's* side as he retched. "It's this *miasma*, Sir, sorry. The road dust and the air's moisture can make it downright sickening. There's some lavender pastilles in a tin there if you need something on your stomach to settle it."

Tonia was in an inner room of the Temple Tower when the first servant to see what was coming staggered there, speechless with horror. One of her guards egged her on, as she got up to go and see what it was that had so terrorized the girl.

Another servant took pity: "You had better stay away," he advised, in a hoarse whisper, adding, "because it pains me to say it is the head of Lamballe out there, brought to show how the people take revenge on tyrants."

There was much discussion afterward, followed by unanimous agreement, that it was the only time in her whole ordeal that citizeness Marie Antoinette was ever seen to faint.

~ *Chapter Fifty One* ~

Neither child was told of Louisa's death, only that she had gone missing, and was going to return as soon as she could. The fiction didn't last. Nor did the hope that some miraculous change might manifest itself, to somehow set them free. "God's will" was invoked more often, inside and outside the walls of the Temple Tower.

Papa Time suffered a fatal stroke a month to the day after his daughter-in-law met her end, amid whispers he'd come to his senses just long enough to comprehend the grisly details of her butchery — long enough for it to be the death of him.

The "September Massacres" touched off what history would label a "Reign of Terror" that seemed more like a "reign of confusion" to those who lived through it. Factions formed within factions and rivals were ruthlessly eliminated. To be aristocratic — or anyone on the wrong side when sides changed — raised the odds of being arrested without warning, imprisoned without charges, and far too often executed before any sentence was passed.

Lunatic asylums filled with escapees from the madness in the streets that threatened their lives. Outside the asylums, bizarre behavior abounded. Obscene parodies of sumptuous balls were held, where women proudly sported thin red ribbons around their necks, signifying loved ones lost to Doctor Guillotin's humane killing machine.

Ecstasy and anguish galloped side by side, as the growing ranks of those condemned for treason, among other reasons, including revenge, turned to every kind of physical coupling, to escape where they were and what was about to happen to them.

Across the English Channel, at Strawberry Hill, a bedridden Baron Besenval fretted helplessly. His aging host, Horace Walpole, gave orders to make his printing presses operational again, in the futile hope that the pamphleteering pen could prove itself mightier than the murderous sword.

Count Fersen continued his fruitless efforts to rally significant support. Even the retired Ambassador Mercy, who no longer held any power, was denied permission to leave Austria, or to enter France.

In the first months of their imprisonment, a few frantic attempts were made to get Louis Auguste, Marie Antoinette, their children, and Madame Tourzel out of the country. Too many ears, however, overheard the furtive, whispered plans; too many of the wrong palms filled with coins that failed to buy their freedom. No one, it seemed, could be trusted to look after anything but his or her own survival. More prayers were said, more and more fervently, for resignation to "God's will."

On the second day of November, 1792, Tonia declined to celebrate her thirty-seventh birthday.

On the eleventh day of December, her stout, sad-eyed, 39-year-old husband was brought before the National Assembly. "Citizen Louis Capet," as he was now called, was charged with having committed various crimes, including high treason.

The "due process" dragged on for nearly a month before he was found guilty. The debate over his punishment ended in a final vote of 361 to 360 in favor of execution. The deciding vote was cast by the late Princess of Lamballe's brother-in-law, *Philippe Egalite*, formerly known as the Duke of Chartres and of Orleans.

On January 20th of the new year, the night before his execution, Citizen Capet was escorted from his Temple Tower rooms on the floor above those occupied by his wife, son, and daughter. The jailers stood just outside the doors through the hour allotted for his farewells. They could overhear only one thing the condemned man said, to his 7-year-old son: "Swear you will never attempt to avenge me." Louis-Charles's reply was unintelligible. His 14-year-old daughter wept hysterically; Marie Antoinette was not heard to weep. In the final minutes, with Marie Therese Charlotte's tears dried, and all possible prayers said, they stood in a circle, embracing.

"I am so saddened Louisa will not be with you," Louis Auguste whispered to his wife. Since the day of her death, no one had spoken her name aloud. It nearly brought Tonia to the tears she'd sworn she wouldn't cry. Not until after … .

"I will be with Louis Joseph soon," he comforted her. "Dwell on that alone."

"We began dying with his death, didn't we?" she whispered, above the heads of their surviving children.

"We did," he whispered back.

"We have done what we could."

"All else," his great head bowed, "is in God's hands."

The following morning, Citizen Capet asked but was not allowed to see his family again. He was taken from the Tower to the *Place de la Revolucion*, where the guillotine had been made to order by a German contractor, under the supervision of the French Academy of Surgeons. It stood surrounded by an enormous, largely silent crowd. The small meannesses that began with denying him a last glimpse of his family continued, to the moment a drum roll was prematurely ordered, with the intent of drowning out his final words of forgiveness.

The procedure was the same for each of the thousands sentenced to die by guillotine. At the top of the scaffold stairs, the condemned was blindfolded and placed face down on a moveable wooden platform, which was then rolled forward until the neck lay neatly in the cut-out bottom half of a two-piece wooden stockade. The top was then fixed in place, and the final command given. The blade's descent lasted less than a second; its speed and force caused the severed head to jerk upward, involuntarily, before falling forward into the wicker container placed there to receive it. The crowds called it "sneezing into the basket."

They came in full regalia for Louis-Charles the day after Louis Auguste's execution. They had finished breakfasting; Marie-Therese Charlotte had left the table for the supply closet on the floor above she called her tiring room, to have her swollen eyes and disheveled hair tended to.

Tonia turned tigress at the sight of them. "*I can't lose you too! I*

WON'T," she shrieked, grabbing for him, holding him so tight he squirmed to be free of her pinioning arms.

"You're not losing me, *Maman*," he twisted away from her. "Can't you see I'm right here? They just came to take me marching, that's all, *Maman*, please say I can!" He was practically quivering. "Say I can!"

She stared at him a long moment, eyes shining, until a slight trace of a smile forced its way across her lips. "Of — course you can. Darling." He came into the arms she reached out to him. She knew, as he did, in a place deeper than thought, stronger than feeling, she would never hold him this way again. *How can I bear it? How can I be expected to bear it?*

Tonia wanted to charge the scum in uniform who filled the doorway, grinning and stinking. Wanted to charge like a maddened bull, crushing the life from them, stamping their stupid faces into a pulp unrecognizable as human. *Do unto them what they did to* — he was slipping out from under her embrace, hurrying over to the objects of his desire.

Reinforcements materialized, surrounding the boy as he was marched from the room. The cruel indifference of their expressions sent a clear message, but all Tonia wanted was to turn tigress again, to leap at them in full, cursing glory, claws shredding any exposed flesh within reach.

Charlotte returned to the room within the hour, less puffy around eyes still twitching with the strain. On learning where her brother was, she disintegrated again. "They stole him," she screamed at her mother, "like they stole my father, and you let them! *You let them*," she howled through new tears. "How could you? 'Stand up for yourself,' you told me. Speak my mind. Never lie." Her Hapsburg chin had never thrust so far out. "What of the lies you told *me* — when was it? A week ago? About our being released to Austria in exchange for French prisoners? About going to live in Vienna? *No more!*" She collapsed into a chair, and wouldn't let Tonia near her.

"It's not lies. There *is* a plan to that effect."

"I don't believe you."

"There are negotiations," Tonia bit back how unlikely they were to succeed.

"And what about the Princess?" Charlotte erupted again. "What about *her*? You lied and lied and lied some more about her, didn't you! Saying she was a missing person when she was a dead person. *Dead!* And you didn't lift a finger to save *Papa!*" She hiccupped to a halt, still not letting her mother near her.

The pain Tonia thought intolerable worsened after that morning. She struggled to control it when her firstborn was present, as Charlotte's blame and bitterness deepened. The gap between them took its place beside the malignant growth of a dread she could no longer escape.

Marie Antoinette came as close as she ever would to begging, but Louis-Charles was never brought to her. Through the false spring that preceded the true one, the despised, disgraced former Queen Consort was never seen to give in to fits or vapors. She never showed sorrow or despair; never played the *coquette;* never demeaned her birth-right. The ever-changing roster of her keepers understood their superiors wanted them to torment her in any way that might cause her to lose her unfailingly gracious composure. Some of the keepers came closer than they ever knew to succeeding; most didn't harbor hatred deep enough to keep trying.

Dozens of individuals, murderers, arsonists, rapists among them, were assigned to her service. They charged at their new positions eager to please by besting the Austrian bitch. They came away dumbfounded, and sometimes, profoundly changed, by the calm face of courage Marie Antoinette showed.

~ Chapter Fifty Two ~

By the summer of 1793, when the "Widow Capet's" trial began, the epidemic of "sneezing into the basket", once confined to the environs of Paris, had spread throughout France, thanks in part to the guillotine's portability.

Tonia entered the Assembly Hall and took her place before her judges like the royalty she truly was, refusing with a small smile the many arms offered to support her along the way. She sat silently, listening intently, saying nothing, giving no sign of fear, or even nervousness.

Marie Antoinette displayed open emotion only once, when a signed copy of the "confession" her son had purportedly given to his "esteemed colleagues" was read out in court. In it, he stated that after his father's death his mother had often come to sleep in his bed with him.

"*Incest!*" howled an accuser, from somewhere in the crowd packed into the trial hall.

"Who *are* you?" Tonia demanded, rising from her assigned place, her back a ramrod, the Hapsburg chin of her haunted, haggard face thrust up and out, righteous fury flashing from her bloodshot blue eyes. "With apologies for my rudeness, whoever you are, I call you *coward*." She wasn't shouting, but her voice rang to the vaulted rafters and back. "Although I fully understand why you would prefer not to show your horned head."

The chief judge, his identity masked only by a thin black domino across his eyes, held up both hands, gesturing for silence. Tonia turned a full one hundred-eighty degrees to face him. Suddenly, unaccountably, she glimpsed the gaping ring of openmouthed courtiers, in the middle of the Rhine River; heard the roaring adulation at the Opera shake the floor of the Royal box.

"If I were still a wagering person," she was clearly heard to tell the judge, "I'd wager you have outfitted my beloved boy with his own uniforms, swords and pistols. Encouraged him to swagger and swear. And *coached* him to make and sign this 'confession,' knowing full well he has no idea what he confesses to." Her composure began to desert her as she turned to face the onlookers. "A mother comforts a son and you make monstrousness of it. Are none of you *mothers*?" She gathered her skirts and sat down.

A copy of the verdict was brought to her that night, in advance of its public announcement. She sat on the narrow bed where only she slept to read it. The widow Capet had been found guilty on all charges, including incest.

Turning it over, the 38-year-old woman in the black cotton night-gown and white muslin mob cap asked the startled young jailer for quill, ink and a writing board.

I was a queen, she wrote, in her round, clear script, *and you took away my crown.*

A wife and you killed my husband, she wrote on the next line.

A mother and you deprived me of my children. My blood alone remains. The quill tip quivered; an ink drop formed. *Take it, but do not make me suffer long.*

She handed it over without her signature, along with the ink, letting the quill flutter to a plank floor like the one in the upstairs room of the inn at Varennes, where their flight to safety was brought to its abrupt end, and her virtual imprisonment begun.

That night, she dreamed of the balloon ascension she'd watched from the Royal Balcony at Versailles.

On the day Marie Antoinette went up the steps to the guillotine, she put the image of that balloon before her; so blue it held its own against the intense brightness of the October sky. The sun and its rays were blazoned on the balloon, above a pair of leaping golden dolphins. She put her first-born son into the gilded basket slung beneath the great rounded swell of its silk. Had him smile to her, and wave. She put his father in his Coronation ermines beside him, one arm around his son's waist, the other around his daughter's.

Tonia felt Louisa's presence. Put her blood sister beside her. Saw them joining hands, stepping off the scaffold into air they could carve a passage through, high above the heads of a crowd already waving the white cloths they'd brought, to dip in the blood the straw wouldn't soak up.

She reached the platform utterly unaware, her face upturned, her hands held out.

The guard who heard her "Excuse me" thought — and would tell everyone who would listen, to the end of his days — that she'd apologized for stepping on his foot. In her tunnel of the brightest light, by Louisa's side again, Tonia barely felt her red-heeled slipper connect with his black leather boot. The *excuse me* was to get beyond him, to her children, her husband, her mother, her father and all the rest who beckoned.

Informed she could say last words, she nodded. "I ask," she spoke clearly enough to be heard by many in the front ranks, "forgiveness for my sins, but not my crimes. I have committed none." The crowd noise swelled, but she no longer heard.

They covered her eyes with a black kerchief, settled her slender form in its white shift on the rolling platform, closed and locked the wooden collar. Barely a second later, before the crowd had time to grow quiet, or even shudder in anticipation, the hissing blade plunged all the way through the neck of the last Queen of France.

~ FINIS ~

~ AFTER WORDS ~

Some readers might be left wondering what happened to the two surviving children of Marie Antoinette and Louis Auguste. Their daughter, Marie Therese Charlotte, was released to the Austrians in December of 1795 and taken to Vienna, in exchange for French prisoners of war. She never married or bore a child. Their son and heir Louis-Charles never left prison after the coerced testimony against his mother was added to the list of her purported crimes. He died there, in June of 1795. DNA testing on a portion of his heart, preserved at the time of his death, was done in 2000. It confirmed his identity. Online search offers much more.

The continuing interest in Marie Antoinette, her era and her end, is reflected in a wealth of biographies and novels that expanded my knowledge and insight.

Among the biographies, alphabetical, by authors, are: *Marie Antoinette,* by H. Delalex, A. Maral, N. Milavanovic; Carolly Erikson's *To the Scaffold: The Life of Marie Antoinette;* Antonia Fraser's *Marie Antoinette: The Journey;* John Hardman's *Marie Antoinette: The Making of a French Queen;* Evelyn Lever's *The Last Queen of France;* Caroline Weber's *Queen of Fashion: What Marie Antoinette Wore to the Revolution;* and Stefan Zweig's *Marie Antoinette: The Portrait of an Average Woman.*

Novels include Juliet Grey's trilogy: *Becoming Marie Antoinette; Days of Splendor, Days of Sorrow;* and *Confessions of Marie Antoinette.* There are also *The Royal Diaries: Marie Antoinette, Princess of Versailles, Austria-France, (1769)* by Kathryn Lasky; Meghan Masterson's *The Wardrobe Mistress: A Novel of Marie Antoinette;* Sara Teter Naslund's *Abundance: A Novel of Marie Antoinette;* and Elena Marie Vidal's *Marie Antoinette, Daughter of the Caesars: Her Life, Her Times, Her Legacy.*

The author welcomes, and will reply to, reader questions and comments. Contact at suttonjc.writer@gmail.com

About the Author

J.C.Sutton's writing life has included a freelance business, as well as arts reviewing, copy and ghostwriting. A bookseller by profession, her articles, essays and poems have been widely published. This is her third novel.